A Rather
Difficult
Conundrum

A RATHER DIFFICULT CONUNDRUM

GEOFFREY START

The Book Guild Ltd

First published in Great Britain in 2024 by
The Book Guild Ltd
Unit E2 Airfield Business Park,
Harrison Road, Market Harborough,
Leicestershire. LE16 7UL
Tel: 0116 2792299
www.bookguild.co.uk
Email: info@bookguild.co.uk
Twitter: @bookguild

Typeset in 11pt Adobe Jenson Pro

Printed and bound in the UK by TJ Books LTD, Padstow, Cornwall

ISBN 978 1835740 170

British Library Cataloguing in Publication Data.
A catalogue record for this book is available from the British Library.

To Kath, Connie and Jamie, with love.

CHAPTER 1
MONDAY, 7 AUGUST 1922
BLAKENEY

We heard their car pull up, and I glanced at my watch. It had just gone past ten, and I wondered whether I should be offering our guests comforting mugs of cocoa. A raised voice was coming from the hall, and then the drawing room door was flung open and in burst a rather heated Sir Chester Eastoff, followed in his wake by a somewhat flustered Mildred Bessy, our housekeeper, who in turn was followed by Lady Alberta Eastoff, imploring her husband to remain calm.

'As your new employer, I demand you get off your fat backside and you and your bloody agency work around the clock until my daughter is found and rescued.'

Well, this is going to be different. I've always been led to believe that a good client relationship is based on effective communication, positive behaviour, and above all, trust!

'Can we get a few things straight, Sir Chester? One, my derrière, I have been reliably told, is perfectly formed.' I stole a quick glance at Libby who raised her eyes to the heavens. 'Two, you are not my employer, and three, you do not demand anything. If we are to work together – and at the moment, that's a big if – we don't have to like each other, but one thing that is absolutely essential is that our working relationship must be built on mutual respect and trust.

'If you don't trust me, I can't do my job, and if I can't do my job, I can't solve your problem, and if I can't solve your problem, you will not get your daughter back. So, the equation is a simple one, Sir Chester: trust me; if not, about-turn and drive back to London!'

That should put him back in his box.

He looked totally taken aback; I don't suppose anyone had spoken to him like that in years. Whilst he was struggling to regain his equilibrium, I took the opportunity to size him up.

He was a tall, handsome man in his late fifties, with chiselled features and a pronounced chin. His hair was slightly longer than the current fashion dictated and swept back, with flecks of grey running through it. I thought it looked quite bohemian and wondered if I should try and adopt a similar style. But then again, Libby might have a say on the matter.

Lady Alberta looked aghast. 'Chester, why oh why in heaven's name do you do this? Your anger will not solve anything, it will just exacerbate a bad situation and make it worse.'

She was also tall, and elegant, with high cheekbones. Her hair was auburn, curly and long, falling over her shoulders. I thought she must be in her mid-forties.

'For goodness' sake, Sir William is right. You have to learn to trust people and more importantly, trust him. Now, shall we try again?'

'Sorry, Alberta, you are right.' He took a deep breath and cleared his throat. 'Please accept my apologies, Sir William. My anger, I'm afraid, has been the cause of far too many issues throughout my life. You are our last hope, and I can assure you we both have absolute total trust in you.'

There, I've nailed my colours to the mast. Now it's just a matter of conquering that little demon of self-doubt that my father sowed, that sits on my shoulder, whispering thoughts of negativity in my ears, that I would fail!

'Apologies accepted, thank you. Now, welcome to our home, and please allow me to introduce Libby, my wife.'

Elizabeth Alice had been my wife for the past ten years, a successful artist painting landscapes of the North Norfolk coast and portraiture. Since we'd been married, three of her works had been selected for the Royal Academy Summer Exhibition. Her studio was at the end of our garden with beautiful views over the Fresh Marshes and the North Sea beyond. But above all, she was my rock.

'We've had a guest room prepared for you as you will no doubt—'

'That won't be necessary as we are booked into the Blakeney Hotel. Now can we get on?'

'Chester!' Alberta shouted.

'Sorry, darling. Sir William, I'm finding it very difficult to rein in my emotions. Receiving that ransom note earlier today has totally rattled me and I'm not used to being rattled, I'm used to being in total control and the one that does the rattling.'

Now why doesn't that surprise me?

'I can only imagine what you are both going through. Please, take a seat. Maybe a drink might help? Lady Eastoff?'

'Thank you, Sir William, I'll have a Campari and soda.'

'Libby and Wispy, please.' Normally when I told someone my nickname it would generate some sort of a reaction; not a flicker, but I suppose in the circumstances that was hardly surprising. I was christened William Lucien Fescue, but since my first term at Gresham's I was always called Wispy, on account that on my first school report my housemaster likened my character to that of a will-o'-the-wisp, coupled with the fact that when fescue grass is blown by the wind it can be described as wispy. Hence the name Wispy was struck.

'Chester?'

'Scotch and soda.'

A please wouldn't go amiss!

'Libby, darling?'

'Do you know what, I fancy what Alberta is having.'

I mixed the drinks and made myself a pink gin in the process. I raised my glass. 'To you both.'

I sat down and opened my brand-new notebook, which was already labelled 'Miss Florence Eastoff'.

'Now, can I take you both back to the twenty-sixth of June before Florence disappeared? Please take me through the events of that evening.'

'We went to a performance of *The Marriage of Figaro* at the Royal Opera House, leaving Lennox Gardens at six o'clock. Florence was working in my study on an article which she had to submit the next day for her Wednesday column. The article was on continental cuisine.'

'Really? How fascinating.'

Chester looked daggers at me. I shrugged. 'I have a passion for gastronomy.'

He continued. 'We returned home just after eleven thirty. Strutton, our butler, let us in and informed us that Florence had retired early at ten o'clock. We had a nightcap and went to bed just after midnight.

'Next morning, Alberta and I came down for breakfast at eight. Florence was an early riser and normally beat us down, but she wasn't there. We thought nothing of it, but she still wasn't down at eight thirty, so we asked Strutton to send someone up to her room to see if she was well. He sent up our housekeeper, Elsie Carter. After a few moments we heard her pounding down the stairs shouting that Florence was not in her room.'

I imagined the uneasy creeping feeling of panic that must have started to spread through them.

'Along with Strutton and Elsie we searched the house from top to bottom, but there was no sign of her. Florence never goes out without telling us and if we are out, she always leaves a message with Strutton or Elsie.

'A sense of dread now set in, and we both felt sick to the pits of our stomachs as we knew something was terribly wrong. I called the police, and an Inspector Finkelstein arrived with his sergeant from Scotland Yard a little while later.'

I glanced at Libby and raised an eyebrow. She replied with an imperceptible nod. This was excellent news and a bit of good luck. Inspector Tony Finkelstein had played a vital role in our first major case and the arrest of the real murderer of Viscount George Thurmaston, leading to the acquittal of Miss Josephine Leighton for his murder. He had become a firm friend and ally.

Chester continued. 'Inspector Finkelstein and his sergeant checked the house for any signs of a forced entry and found none. After questioning the staff, he sat down with us.'

Alberta picked up the story. 'Elsie confirmed that a shepherd's check suit was missing from her wardrobe along with a silk shirt, a pair of low-heeled Oxfords, and a silk and cotton raincoat. Which in Inspector Finkelstein's opinion suggested she had gone out somewhere of her own volition. We strongly disagreed with this, but he suggested that there was a first time for everything and in all likelihood she would return that evening.

'He asked us about her personal life, and we gave him the details of her best friends Miriam Popkin and Sadie Lee-Hunt from her boarding school, Wycombe Abbey. They are still inseparable. Then her two great friends from Durham University, Opal Jackson-Webb and Loretta Magnus, who again are joined at the hip, and they all get along famously.'

'Did the inspector contact all of these friends?'

'Yes, he did, and each of them confirmed that they had been in touch with her recently and she was her usual exuberant self. And to a girl, said to the inspector it was totally out of character for her just to go off somewhere.'

'Boyfriend?'

'Various relationships over the years but nothing serious.'

'Is she in a relationship at the moment?'

'No.'

'How do you know?'

'Not only are we mother and daughter, but we are also best friends. We confide in each other.'

'I see. Tell me about Florence the person.'

Alberta opened her handbag and took out a small framed photograph and handed it to me. I studied the picture and handed it to Libby. She was elegant and had her mother's beauty and a smile that radiated warmth and confidence.

'Gracious, where do I begin?' She took a deep breath and exhaled slowly. 'Very well, we both likened her to the three As: adaptable, adventurous and affectionate. She is fun-loving, passionate, quick-witted and highly intelligent. However, she is hot-headed, impetuous and with a quick temper like her father, the love of my life.'

'So, she might have gone off on a whim,' I ventured.

Chester sprung to his feet, shouting, 'No, she bloody well didn't!'

Alberta tugged at Chester's jacket. 'For goodness' sake, you are not helping matters. Now sit down!' He did with a harrumph, folding his arms across his chest.

Alberta continued. 'I think from me she inherited my compassion and empathy, but that was more often than not overshadowed by her quick temper and total self-belief that she was always right.'

'I see, and has she always wanted to be a journalist?'

'Yes, she loved creative writing at school and was encouraged by her English teacher Miss Ruby Ardley, and she knew then that she wanted to be a journalist. When she left school at eighteen in July 1916, she convinced Chester that Eastoffs needed a weekly newspaper to help the morale of the workforce, who were manufacturing warships at a rate of knots to support the war effort.

'Chester allocated her an office, and her first paper was published in the first week of August and was a huge success. It highlighted achievements of the week, an idea of the week to improve manufacturing, and focused on the staff. There was an employee of the week; birthdays were announced, with individual birthday greetings. She encouraged staff to let her know of any births and marriages, and obituaries were penned for the dead.'

'Quite forward-thinking,' remarked Libby.

'Terribly. There were her thrifty recipes of the week, which were hugely popular, and she ran a monthly short-story competition, which she and Chester judged. The winner would have their story printed and their picture taken with Chester for the newsletter. She carried on until she went off to university. Chester has her first and last front pages framed on his study wall. We were both exceedingly proud of her for that achievement.'

'Gosh, I can understand her desire to go into journalism. She must be a talented writer,' I said.

'Very. She celebrated her twenty-first birthday on the twenty-second of January 1919 and she sat the entrance exam for Durham University, which she passed with flying colours. She went up to university that September to read English. She loved university life and excelled both socially and intellectually, and left with a first.

'But above all, she was our loving daughter, and we miss her so very much. All we want is to have her back.'

At this point it was obvious it was all getting too much for her as tears were welling up in her eyes. Chester put his arm around her and held her close. I waited until she had regained her composure.

'Tell me about her job.'

'She applied for a job at the *Daily Chronicle* and much to her surprise was offered work as a feature writer on the women's desk. She loved it, but equally she found it frustrating as what she really wanted to do was to be an investigative journalist. She felt she was being pigeonholed as a woman. But as she often told us, you had to be working for a paper to keep an eye on the main chance.'

'Did the inspector contact the paper?'

'Yes, he contacted her editor, Miss Eunice Wade, and she confirmed that she didn't turn up for work that morning. Eunice also confirmed to him that she had spoken on the telephone to a very excited Florence the evening before about a call she had just taken from a source about a potential scandal at a Paris fashion house.'

'What did the inspector make of the call?'

'He thought it was interesting and in all probability might be the reason Florence left the house early that morning.'

'When was the last time you heard from Inspector Finkelstein?'

Chester continued. 'About three weeks after she disappeared. He came over and told us that despite their exhausted efforts, they had found not a jot of evidence that could lead them to finding her. It was his opinion that she had made the decision, for whatever reason, to leave home on her own volition. At this point I regret to say I lost my temper and accused him and Scotland Yard of being a bunch of incompetent buffoons. To give him his due, he took it rather well, and once I had calmed down, I did apologise.'

That's the pragmatic inspector I know.

'He did concede, however, that everything he had learnt about Florence made her disappearance seem out of character.'

Out of character? From what I've learnt in the last half hour, of course it's bloody out of character, Tony!

'And that officially she was a "missing person" and the Yard were keeping an "open mind", whatever a bloody open mind is. And I can officially tell you here and now that we are far from coping; we are in a state of living hell. We are in purgatory and sick with worry. She is our beautiful child and we will do absolutely anything to find her, and I'm telling you now she didn't go off on her own volition!'

A look of utter dejection spread across their faces, so I suggested a short break whilst I recharged our glasses, giving them a chance to regain their composure. I took my time mixing our drinks and by the time I handed them refreshed glasses they had regained their equilibrium.

'May I have a look at the ransom note?'

Chester took an envelope out of his briefcase and went to pass it to me. I held up a hand to stop him and went to my study and returned with a pair of white cotton gloves, my fingerprint kit and my well-worn briefcase.

'Are you the only person to have handled this?'

'No, Strutton handled it as well.'

I put on my gloves and took the letter from him. 'I am going to need to eradicate your fingerprints from the ransom note and envelope, and to do that I need a set of your prints. Do you have any objections?'

'Not at all.'

'I will make arrangements for Strutton's prints to be taken as well.'

I examined the envelope and the ransom note. The text was constructed from cut-out letters of a typeface used in cheaper book publishing. I read the note:

'My dearest Lady Alberta and Sir Chester,

'Florence sends her love. She is missing you so very much. She is such a beautiful woman that it would be a terrible shame to have to disfigure that beauty in any way, wouldn't you agree? Do not involve the police because if you do, you will never see her again. I will be in touch again when I am ready.'

I was intrigued by the watermark on the paper used for the ransom note: Brousses.

I put the note and its envelope into a manila document wallet and placed it in my briefcase. 'I will get these checked for prints when I get to London.'

But don't hold your collective breath; the likelihood of finding prints is nil.

'Did she have any enemies?'

'How the hell do I bloody know?' snapped Chester. 'Well, not that we were aware. But I'm sure with her forthright approach she may well have upset a few people along the way. But that wouldn't have bothered her unduly. Like father, like daughter. I'm bloody proud of her!'

I checked my wristwatch, a Rolex Trench Officer's watch and a dearly treasured possession. It had just gone twenty past eleven.

'On the subject of enemies: Chester, do you have any?'

He snorted and chuckled. 'The shipbuilding business is rather ruthless, cut-throat, and highly competitive. Deals are done on fine margins just to get the contracts and then we find other ways of improving those margins. Tendering isn't always as fair as it should be. So yes, I'm sure that I'm not on a few people's Christmas card list.'

'I see. Can I suggest due to the lateness of the hour we pick this up in the morning when we are fresh? And can I ask you to think of anyone who could have a grudge against you enough to really want to hurt you? I recommend you breakfast here rather than at the Blakeney Hotel, so you can sample the delights of Thelma's cooking and we can continue our discussions. Shall we say eight?'

'Fine.'

'One last question: I assume you don't want the police involved because of the threat in the note.'

'That assumption is correct. I don't want them within a hundred miles of this.'

We went out into the hall and Mildred appeared, marginally less flustered than earlier, with the Eastoffs' chauffeur in tow. I thanked her for staying up and keeping the chauffeur company, and informed her that Sir Chester and Lady Alberta would be joining us for breakfast at eight o'clock the next morning.

*

'Well, darling, this is going to test our mettle.'

'Libby, you are so right, but do you think I can do it?'

'Wispy, I will never tire of telling you that you are the most courageous, resilient and adorable man in the world. What's in the past is gone. Your father might have doubted your abilities, but what's more important is that I believed in you the first moment I saw you. If anyone is going to find her, you are. As I have told you many times over, you started this agency for a reason: to prove that you are as good as your father. Well I've got news for you, Sir William: you are far, far better than him.'

She embraced me in a hug and my doubts melted away, and she whispered in my ear that it was time for bed.

CHAPTER 2
TUESDAY, 8 AUGUST 1922
BLAKENEY

The Eastoffs arrived just before eight and Mildred showed them into our dining room. Mildred had been with us for as long as I can remember; that is, she had been here from my first memories and was always there for me during my childhood. We live in the small North Norfolk village of Blakeney, and Fescue Hall, our home, has been in our family for generations. My grandfather was a baronet, and on my father's death I too inherited the baronetcy.

I introduced them to Strangely and his wife, Constanza, who had joined us for breakfast. They arrived at seven thirty so I could brief them on the new case. I decided that Strangely's Christian name, Marjorie, would suffice rather than having to explain the origins of his nickname.

They own Marsh Farm in the nearby village of Langham. Strangely is an integral part of my agency. I met him in the Norfolks, where we served together and became great friends. His war was worse than mine as he was injured on the first of July, the first day of the Battle of the Somme, when some shrapnel pierced his right thigh, and he was sent home on medical leave. Mind you, he returned to active service four months later, albeit with a limp, which unfortunately is a bit more pronounced these days and he uses a walking stick when it starts to bother him, which is normally in cold weather.

He is four years older than me, forty-five, and he too went to Gresham's, though our paths never crossed. When our friendship

11

blossomed in the army, he told me why his nickname was Strangely. He is of Scottish heritage and was christened Marjorie Dougal Drye. Marjorie, I have to say, is a unique name for a fellow; however, his middle name is Dougal, an anglicised form of the Gaelic name Dudhghall which means 'dark stranger'. Hence Strangely was born, and he much prefers that to Marjorie.

Constanza Clara Drye was Strangely's wife, and like Libby she was extremely creative, specialising in ceramics. She too had a studio on their grounds. Both women were heavily involved in the organisation of the annual Blakeney show that was held on the August bank holiday Monday. Libby was chairman and Constanza was the secretary, on top of which they were both the best of friends.

I made the introductions and Chester didn't bat an eyelid at Marjorie's name. We helped ourselves to breakfast and Thelma, our cook, had put on an excellent spread as usual. The Lincolnshire sausages, black pudding and back bacon hailed from our local butcher, Arthur Bollock. The Yarmouth bloaters were smoked in the next village of Cley, by Oswald Tungate in his smokehouse. The eggs came from Strangely's Maran hens, the grilled tomatoes from our greenhouse, accompanied by Thelma's home-made baked beans, fried bread and toast. On the table was her home-made strawberry jam and thick-cut marmalade. Mildred served tea and coffee, then after straightening a painting of Blakeney quay by Libby, which hung over the fireplace, left us.

Chester appeared to be in a calmer place than yesterday, so I decided to wade back in with further questions. 'Well, Chester, have you made a list of any enemies that would go so far as to not send you a Christmas card and, more importantly, want to hurt you in some way?'

'Three readily spring to mind that fit into that category.'

Three! Bloody hell. One I can understand, two at a push, but three? Then again...

'A year ago, I won a contract to build two extremely large cargo ships for the British India Steam Navigation Company. I was bloody exasperated as we had been tendering for their business for a while and had not won a bean, and I'll tell you for one, Sir William, I don't like losing!'

'Really, that doesn't surprise me, Chester. But what did you do?'

'Do? What did you think I did? I took control, which maybe I should have done earlier. I personally oversaw the tendering process and delivered the tender, signed by me, into the hands of their chairman, and we won the damn thing. Game, set and bloody match to me.

'They normally used MacCabe Shipbuilders on the Clyde, and Edle Schiffbaugesellschaft on the River Weser. They took great exception to the fact that I won the tender, and MacCabe accused me of underhand tactics in securing the deal. I took them both to court and won substantial damages for libel. Outside the court, Mungan MacCabe threatened to destroy my business and Count von Delmenhorst threw down a glove and challenged me to a duel.'

'Good Lord, a duel, how quaint. But on a serious note, you certainly know how to pick your enemies; along with yourself, these two are giants of the shipbuilding world.'

'Yes, they are, although not so much Delmenhorst as he was struggling after the war, but he seems to be on his way back.'

'And did they carry out these threats?'

'No, they were mere bluster, full of hot air and piffle. The only way they could hurt me was by undercutting me on future tenders, and if they wanted to do that, they could keep the business because Chester Eastoff doesn't work for nothing!'

'Seems a fairly logical approach to me.'

'Of course it is, it's bloody common sense. Having said that, I was still concerned that our tender system was not robust enough, and after we won that contract I launched an internal inquiry into the whole process, on the twenty-eighth of February. The inquiry drew a bloody blank. I'm still not convinced by the inquiry's findings, and my gut tells me there was something untoward going on in our tendering processes, which is reinforced by the fact that we've since won another contract to build a cargo ship for British India, overseen again by yours truly. So once you've found Florence and returned her safe and sound, it's my intention to rip the procurement department apart piece by piece, limb from limb, and if I find one jot of complacency, or worse still, corruption, I swear to God there's going to be a crucifixion!'

Well that might be worth watching. 'How did MacCabe react to you winning another contract?'

'It prompted yet another tirade from the man, threatening to hurt the very existence of my business.'

'And how did you react to that?'

'I told him to grow up and put his toys back into the nursery where he belonged.'

I smiled at him. 'And how did he react to that?'

'Not well. He swore revenge.'

'When were these latest threats made?'

'Late May.'

'And the duel?'

'As I don't know one end of a bloody épée from the other, I told the count that the only duel I was prepared to have would be over future business, in a court of law.'

'So, they might have plotted the kidnapping of Florence?'

'They might, but highly unlikely. Why would they risk throwing away everything they had worked for? They may not like me, they may even hate me, but they are not bloody daft.'

'I take your point, but they both have pretty strong motives for revenge all the same. And your third enemy?'

'Ah, the architect Mr Walderne Smithers. In early 1911, I commissioned a new wing to be built at Eastoff House, our country estate, in keeping with the original design and architecture. Mr Smithers' firm won the bid and managed the contract from start to finish. Alberta and I were happy with the new wing up until the fifteenth of January 1919, when the whole blasted wing collapsed. Luckily no one was in there at the time.'

'Crikey, it must have made one hell of a mess,' Strangely said.

'It bloody well did and I wasn't happy. I contacted a specialist surveying company who confirmed that substandard building materials were used throughout. So, I sued Smithers and won, and his company was liable for the total cost of rebuilding the wing. And that sent his company into liquidation.'

My, he does seem a tad fond of litigation.

'And he threatened you?'

'I suppose in a way he did. He was a weak and ineffectual man, and directly after the case he wrote a grovelling letter imploring me to be lenient and to not seek the total amount of damages, so that he could salvage his reputation. He said if I couldn't show him that kindness, he would take his own life.'

'Did he?'

'How the hell do I know? Good riddance to bad rubbish.'

'Where does he live?'

'I haven't a clue, but I suppose it could be in Chichester, where he had his practice.'

'And you have heard nothing of him since his company went into liquidation?'

'Not a peep.'

Mildred reappeared and replenished our teas and coffees and then busied herself clearing away the sideboard of our dishes. Once she had finally finished, I continued.

'Has anyone ever threatened Florence?'

'No, of course they haven't. What a bloody stupid suggestion!'

Seems a pretty logical question to me.

'Wait, Chester, there was that incident with a gardener,' Alberta interjected.

'You're right, but I doubt very much that insignificant piece of human detritus would have the intelligence to kidnap a cat, let alone Florence.'

'That may be so, but you should tell Wispy what happened.'

'Very well.' He sighed. 'At Eastoff House an assistant gardener became infatuated with Florence and made a foolish pass at her, pinning her against a wall and trying to kiss her. Florence fought him off, and in the fracas our head gardener, Thomas Postlethwaite, heard the commotion and sprinted to the scene and hauled him away. Our butler, Groves, and Postlethwaite dismissed him instantly without references and frogmarched him off the estate. In hindsight I should have had him arrested for assault and now he would have been banged up in prison and left to rot.'

'And when did this incident happen?'

'It was when Florence was in her first term at Durham. She came home for a weekend with us, I think from memory either the second or third weekend in October 1919.'

'And what was his name?'

'I haven't got a clue, you'll have to have a word with Groves and Thomas. I enjoy the gardens but don't actually get my hands dirty.'

Really, why doesn't that surprise me?

'Can you contact Groves and tell him to expect a call from us? Now, is there anything else we need to know?'

'No, we've told you everything, and if anything further occurs to us I'll contact you immediately. But what I need from you and your agency is one hundred and ten per cent commitment in finding our daughter, starting from now!'

What does he envisage we're going to do? Swan around and have a seance to locate Florence?

'Chester, I said to you yesterday *if* we are going to work together, and as of yesterday that was a big if. I have removed that *if*, and once I've decided to take on a case we all give it our total commitment.'

'That is the correct answer, Wispy, well done. Now, darling, we must get back to London, and I trust you won't be far behind.'

God, the man is insufferable.

I consulted my watch; it had just gone ten fifteen. 'I have to set a few things in motion here first, but we will aim to be on the four o'clock from Norwich.'

We saw them out to their car and waved them off.

*

'There's absolutely nothing subtle whatsoever about him,' said Strangely.

'No, there isn't, he's about as subtle as a brick, but on the plus side I suppose you know what you're going to get. Now to action. How's your German?'

'Non-existent.'

'Good, then that qualifies you to visit Count von Delmenhorst. I'm sure his English is impeccable; if not, you'll just have to speak loudly, slowly and gesticulate a lot. You'll need to call Ernest to locate Edle Schiffbaugesellschaft, and get him to send a telegram to the count to alert him of your impending visit.'

'Can I use your study and I'll call him now?'

'Of course.'

Once Strangely had made his call, Libby and I saw them off and we agreed to meet at Holt station just before two to catch the train to Norwich.

*

I went into my study and called the office. It was answered by Ernest White, our office assistant and a fairly new boy; a local lad, having lived in the area all his life. He'd left school at fourteen and had been working as a porter at Fulham Potteries for four years when he applied to an advertisement we placed in the *Evening Standard* for an office assistant. What he lacked in formal education he made up for with his sharp wit, great memory and natural intelligence. So, I took him on.

'Morning, Ernest. Is Wanda in?'

'Morning, Sir William. I'll pass you over.'

Miss Wanda Rosie Cushway is truly a wonder – superbly intelligent, attractive, with an effervescent personality but also slightly eccentric. Her passion is entomology and she never travels anywhere without her sketchbook, magnifying glass and a few specimen bottles. She is even a member of the Royal Entomological Society.

Two years ago, she'd answered an advertisement I'd placed in *Country Life*, for a private investigator with managerial skills. From a shortlist of five – four of whom were men – she was the outstanding candidate. I'd offered her the job on the spot.

She came to us straight from university, having just graduated with a BA in Classics and English from Lady Margaret Hall, Oxford. Her insightfulness, vision and attention to detail were the glue that kept our agency together.

Her attractiveness and intelligence, on the other hand, were a double-edged sword. She wanted to find love and men were attracted to her, but they were often cowed by her intelligence.

I brought her up to date on all that we had learnt since she travelled back to London late yesterday afternoon. She'd been staying with us for the bank holiday weekend as we were entertaining Lord and Lady Alfreton and their daughter, Miss Josephine Leighton, after successfully proving her innocent of the murder of her fiancé, Viscount George Thurmaston. Her case was our first major success and they were guests of honour at our Blakeney show.

Up until then we had had limited success. I started Fescue's Detective Agency in April 1920 and Lord Watlington had been our very first client. His prize herd of one hundred and twenty pedigree Jersey cows were raided from his estate in Oxfordshire. We eventually tracked them down to a farm in the village of Coniston Cold in North Yorkshire, some two hundred miles away.

This was followed by two more unlikely successes. We tracked a missing Rembrandt to a pawnbroker's in Shoreditch High Street, and a stolen bronze statue of Medusa by Thomas Thornycroft to a scrapyard in Bognor. An interesting résumé, but more importantly Sir Chester heard about our success in the Leighton case and that's why he had tracked me down via his barrister.

'Can you tackle Miss Eunice Wade at the *Daily Chronicle*, and track down our erstwhile architect Mr Walderne Smithers who thought he could build on sand?'

'Of course. I'll arrange to meet her as soon as possible and try to find Smithers.'

'Excellent. We can catch up at some point tomorrow. Can you pass me back to Ernest?'

'Sir William.'

I briefed him quickly on our new case.

'Blimey, I've never done a kidnapping.'

'Good to hear that, Ernest, as you might not be with us now if you had. Now can you send a telegram to Mr Mungan MacCabe, of MacCabe Shipbuilders, requesting an urgent meeting this Thursday in connection with the disappearance of Miss Florence Eastoff? Refusal is not an option. If this reasonable request is acceptable, can you book me on tomorrow evening's Caledonian sleeper service to Glasgow?'

'Right away, Sir William.'

'Good man. I also want you to pop over to Lennox Gardens and take the fingerprints of Strutton, the Eastoffs' butler. I'll see you tomorrow.'

Next, a meeting with Inspector Tony Finkelstein of the Yard. I was told he was in, but he was not answering his telephone. I left my number with the desk sergeant, and he promised to track him down. I went off to find Wilbur Goodrum.

Wilbur was mowing the lawn with his new Atco motorised mower, and I had to shout at the top of my voice to be heard. 'Morning, RSM.'

Wilbur Goodrum, our gardener, handyman and chauffeur, had seen action in the Second Boer War. He was in the Norfolks and their regimental sergeant major, hence my addressing him as RSM.

'Morning, Captain,' he shouted back. I too had volunteered at the outbreak of the Great War and joined the Norfolk Regiment, serving in the Seventh Service Battalion. When I went in I was a second lieutenant and rose to the rank of Captain. I'd had a relatively good war, evinced by the fact that I was still in one piece. I managed to signal to him to cut the motor.

'How's the new mower going?'

'It's fantastic, and doesn't the lawn look a picture. Look at those lovely lines. I'm so pleased you bought it on my recommendation.'

'From memory, Wilbur, you couldn't be doing with any newfangled mowing machine. You said it was unnatural.'

'Did I? I can't remember saying that.'

I made a mental note to see what other labour-saving devices I could find for him. I had heard somewhere recently that a motorised rotavator was being developed. That should test his sensitivities as to what was unnatural.

'Never mind, the time now is twelve and we need to be on the two o'clock train to Norwich, so we will have to be on the road at half past one.'

'Yes, Captain, I'll have the motor car out front at twenty-five past.'

'Good man, see you then.'

*

I turned to head back up to the house and was met by Mildred striding towards me.

'Inspector Finkelstein is on the telephone for you, Sir William.'

'Thank you, Mildred.'

I shut the study door and picked up the receiver.

'Tony, thanks for getting back.'

'Shalom, Wispy. It was only a day ago I left your delightful house, and can I say that the lovely Mrs Finkelstein was enchanted by your village and ventured on the subject of holidaying there.'

'You and Mrs Finkelstein would be most welcome at Fescue Hall any time.'

'Thank you, but Mrs Finkelstein has an inclination to rent a cottage. Now I assume you are not calling me for her fabled chicken soup recipe?'

'As much as I would love to learn to cook Mrs Finkelstein's celebrated chicken soup, that wasn't the reason for my call.' I relayed the events of the last day and a half.

'Mazel tov, Wispy. So Florence didn't decide to leave home on her own volition. I owe the Eastoffs an apology. A kidnapping: now that is serious. I'll alert the commissioner straight away.'

'Whoa, stop there, Tony.' I read him the ransom note.

'I see, and Sir Chester agrees with this?'

'He doesn't want you within one hundred miles of the investigation. I'm coming up to London later today. Can we meet for lunch tomorrow?'

'Of course. Do you know Regency Street?'

'Off Horseferry Road?'

'That's the one. I'll meet you in the Regency Café at one o'clock.'

'Sounds rather grand. I trust I'm in for a gastronomic surprise.'

'Wait and see!'

*

I joined Libby in the drawing room and consulted her on our lunch requirements, and pulled the bell pull. Mildred appeared moments later, and I ordered some rounds of Thelma's dry cured ham with tomatoes and English mustard, with some of my pickled marsh samphire and onions, accompanied by her delicious home-made lemonade.

It was one thirty and time to be off. We went out to meet Wilbur, and Mildred and Thelma were there to see us off. 'Right, RSM, to Holt station.'

'Captain.' And he held the door open for Libby.

'Darling? Aren't you forgetting something?'

'No, I don't think so.'

'Briefcase?'

'Gosh, and my notebook. You clever old thing.'

'Less of the old, and I'm not a thing.'

'Sorry, darling.'

I sprinted back into the house and into my study. I grabbed my briefcase and quickly looked around to check that I wasn't missing anything else, and my gaze fell on the portrait of my father. There he was, staring straight at me in his colonel's uniform of the Royal Military Police.

Who would believe it – well, maybe not you, Father – my second major case in as many months. Some people have faith in me and my abilities. Now, Wispy, old boy, it's time to turn your inner demons of self-doubt into self-belief. Onwards and upwards!

I stood to attention and saluted him, then ran back to the car and we were off to Holt to meet Constanza and Strangely. On the journey

I told them about my arrangements to meet Tony Finkelstein and my thought process so far, and they were both in total agreement with my decision.

I also agreed that Constanza should accompany Strangely to Germany. They had made a formidable team in Boulogne in April, and they needed a repeat of their success in Bremen.

*

The four o'clock train from Norwich to London was on time, and we arrived back at Sloane Square shortly after seven fifteen. It was a pleasant evening, so we decided to walk. Constanza and Strangely had been keeping an eye out for a house near us and in late June had purchased a property in Glede Place, just around the corner. They named it Cley Mill.

We walked around the corner into Cheyne Walk towards our house, Salthouse, named after a village near our home in Blakeney. It was an arts and crafts house, built and designed by the architect Charles Robert Ashbee. I went up the steps and tugged on the bell pull. A few moments later, Eleanor Larcher, our housekeeper, answered the door.

'Good evening, Lady Elizabeth, Sir William. Lovely to see you.'

'Thank you, Eleanor,' replied Libby.

'And how exciting, a kidnapping!'

'How on earth do you know that?' I exclaimed.

'Mildred phoned to let me know of your arrival and she just happened to mention it.'

'Did she indeed.'

'Yes, she did. And a high-profile kidnapping come to that. Who would have thought it; a very rare occurrence indeed, if not unique here in Great Britain. My, your second real case. It beats rounding up Jersey cows in some remote Yorkshire village.'

God, we've only been here for five seconds and she's putting her oar in.

'Thank you, Eleanor, for your insightfulness.'

'My pleasure. Alice will have dinner ready for eight thirty.'

'Excellent. Now Libby and I need to freshen up.'

Alice's food was up to its usual high standard and dinner was a gazpacho followed by chicken galantine with shaved truffles, Jersey royals and a green salad with fines herbes and a sharp French vinaigrette, accompanied by a chilled bottle of Viognier, which had apricot and peach notes. Wonderful. For dessert we had strawberries and cream, then a simple cheeseboard of my two favourite cheeses: Montgomery Cheddar and Colston Bassett Stilton. Absolute heaven.

CHAPTER 3
WEDNESDAY, 9 AUGUST 1922
CHELSEA

Our office was located just around the corner on Lawrence Street, in a small townhouse opposite the Peabody Estate, where Ernest lived with his parents, and a few doors down from our local, the Cross Keys. So, all in all very conveniently situated near our house. As I shut the front door behind me, I was greeted by a beautiful sunny morning, and literally a minute later I pressed the office doorbell and was greeted by Ernest.

It was as welcoming as usual, light and airy, and it put me at ease. It had a curious atmosphere with the smell of beeswaxed furniture and the slightly earthy scent of the hundreds of reference books that lined our floor-to-ceiling bookcase. Wanda and Strangely were already at their desks; he was on a telephone call and by the sound of it was struggling to make himself understood.

'Good to see you, Wanda. Have you come down from your success at the Blakeney show?'

'I have and I'm planning on broadening my repertoire of pickles.'

'I see I am going to have to up my game somewhat.'

I won the Blakeney Piccalilli Cup for taking the most golds, but Wanda had beaten me in the chutney class, taking gold for her spiced plum chutney, which was no mean feat.

'Did you manage to contact Miss Eunice Wade?'

'I did and I'm meeting her at eleven o'clock this morning. She sounds rather interesting.'

'Excellent, and—'

'Count von Delmenhorst, thank you for agreeing to speak to me.'

Strangely had to my amazement actually got through to the count, and Wanda, Ernest and I sat and listened to his side of the conversation. He wasn't having to enunciate every word or speak loudly. He replaced the receiver and a smile broke out across his face.

'Well that went well. I'm going to meet him on Thursday evening once I've sorted out travelling to Bremen. He says there's a nine o'clock train from Paris tomorrow morning which takes over ten hours to get there, and he has insisted that we are his guests at his castle, Schloss Delmenhorst.'

'How very civil of the chap. And how did he react when you said you wanted to discuss the disappearance of Florence?'

'I would go so far as to say he was looking forward to my arrival.'

'Gosh!'

'Now I had better go and book our ferry and train tickets.'

'Fine. When you get back I will have left for my meeting with Tony, so please leave a copy of your itinerary and contact me once you've met the count. Bon voyage, or should I say, *Gute Reise!*'

'Do you know, I'm rather looking forward to the trip.' And off he went.

'Now, Wanda, before we were interrupted by the count I was about to let you know I've arranged to meet Tony Finkelstein at one o'clock.' I outlined my thought process, and she was in total agreement.

'And I was about to say I've drawn a complete blank on our architect Mr Walderne Smithers. From the research that I have done there is no trace of him in Chichester, he appears to have disappeared into thin air. But I will track him down.'

'Of that I have no doubt.'

'Thank you.' Wanda checked her watch. 'Cripes, I must be off to the *Daily Chronicle*.'

*

'Now, Ernest, I have some research I want you—'

The telephone rang and Ernest answered. 'Fescue's Detective Agency.' I heard a booming voice from the other side of the room, and Ernest had to hold the receiver away from his ear for fear of being deafened. 'Hold on one moment, I'll see if Sir William is in.' He put his hand over the mouthpiece.

'Sir William, it's a Mr Mungan MacCabe, and I think you might have gathered he's not very happy.'

'Oh dear, that's a shame, let me see if I can placate him.' I took the telephone from Ernest. 'Mr MacCabe, many thanks for responding so quickly to my telegram, much appreciated.'

'Sod your bloody telegram. I have nothing whatsoever to do with Eastoff's daughter's disappearance, I'm not a bloody pagan, and I'm far too busy to see a private investigator, even if you are a knight of the sodding realm.'

'Mr MacCabe, we can either do this the easy way or the hard way. The easy way, if you have nothing to hide, is to meet me; or the hard way, for you at least, is that I will get my Scotland Yard colleague to have a word with his friends in the Glasgow constabulary and bring you in for questioning. The choice is yours.'

The line went quiet and I wasn't going to break the silence. I had counted to fourteen in my head when he spoke.

'Very well, you'd better come up.'

'If I may say, a very wise and intelligent decision, Mungan. I will travel up overnight tonight on the Caledonian sleeper. Can you arrange for me to be met tomorrow morning at Glasgow Central station?'

'No, I can't. Tomorrow morning I'm chairing a board meeting.'

'Well you'll just have to un-chair it, or else I shall revert to plan B.'

'You're a pain in the arse, Sir William bloody Fescue. Very well, I will have someone meet you tomorrow morning.' With that, the line went dead.

What an absolutely charming man. It must be a general trait of the shipbuilding fraternity to be as rude and as obnoxious as possible!

'Now where was I, Ernest? Ah yes, can you find out as much as you can about the watermark, Brousses? It was on the stationery that the ransom note was written on.'

'I'm onto it.'

'Good, and can you confirm my return ticket on the Caledonian sleeper for tonight's train to Glasgow?'

'Of course.'

'Thank you.' I consulted my watch. It had just gone midday, so I decided that a walk to Regency Street was in order.

CHAPTER 4
WEDNESDAY, 9 AUGUST 1922
HOLBORN

Wanda emerged from Blackfriars station into a City of London bathed in morning sunshine. She had phoned Miss Eunice Wade, the women's editor at the *Daily Chronicle*, yesterday afternoon and she had enthusiastically agreed to meet her at eleven at her office on Fleet Street. Ten minutes later she arrived at the *Daily Chronicle* and asked for Miss Wade at reception.

A few moments later a rather large lady came bounding down the stairs. Dressed in a slightly old-fashioned tweed suit and wearing brogues, she had a head of red curly hair that she obviously had trouble keeping under control.

'Miss Cushway, lovely to meet you,' she said as she approached Wanda at an alarming rate of knots, holding out her hand as she did so. Wanda took it and all but managed to suppress a yelp as Miss Eunice Wade crushed her hand in a vice-like grip.

'Miss Wade, lovely to meet you too.'

She was half expecting a slap on her back.

'Eunice, please. Now follow me to my sanctuary.' With that, she about-turned and marched back towards the stairs which she took two at a time. Wanda was almost having to break into a skip to keep up.

Eunice threw her office door open, and Wanda was greeted with what could be best described as an Aladdin's cave. There was a scent of old books and an underlying mustiness. Although the office was fairly big, it seemed cramped. A large leaded window looked down onto Fleet Street, in front of which was her desk, covered in files and newspaper and magazine cuttings. You could barely see her desktop. The walls on either side of the room were lined with floor-to-ceiling bookcases, with not a single space for another book. A second desk faced hers, which was the parallel opposite. It was neat and tidy with an ink blotter, ink and pen stand at its centre, and a lovely small Chinese vase to the right containing at least twenty sharpened pencils, and that was it.

'Please come in, Miss Cushway, and take a seat here at Florence's desk,' she said, pointing at the pristine desk. 'Tea?'

'Tea would be most welcome,' replied Wanda. 'Do you have Earl Grey?'

'But of course, coming right up. Make yourself comfortable.'

As Wanda settled in at Florence's desk, a shrill squawk made her jump out of her skin. 'Votes for women!' She spun around and in the corner was a large macaw on a stand. How she hadn't noticed it when she walked in she didn't know, but it was beautiful with its vivid blue, red and yellow plumage.

'Hello to you too, and what brings a beautiful macaw to the heart of Fleet Street?' she said as she walked over to get a closer look. 'And what's your name?'

'Tea!' Eunice announced as she marched back into her office with two cups of tea. 'Ah, I see you've met Emily P.'

'Emily P?'

'Yes, Emily P, as in Emily Pankhurst.'

To emphasise the point, Emily P squawked again. 'Votes for women.'

'Enough, Emily. Your tea, Miss Cushway. Milk?'

'Just a dash, and please call me Wanda.'

'Of course. This is an awful to-do. Florence has been missing for over six weeks now and the police seem to have given up. So when you phoned yesterday and said that your agency had been taken on by Sir Chester and Lady Eastoff to try and find her, I don't mind telling you I rejoiced. I will do anything in my power to assist you.'

'Thank you. What was she like?'

'She's extremely bright, with an engaging personality, very quick-witted and curious, which is a good trait to have in journalism. Her writing is first class, with a unique style, and she has a marvellous vocabulary. I keep telling her she should write a novel. Florence is one of the only people I know who actually loves Latin and would often use a phrase in her writing when she could, with hidden meanings that stretched her reader's mental powers.'

'Golly, she's a woman after my own heart. I absolutely adore Latin.'

'Good gracious, do you? You clever old thing. Now where was I? Ah yes, she was getting frustrated as she felt that she was being stereotyped and pigeonholed as a woman in that all she was allowed to do was write on women's issues. This wasn't true, of course; the women's desk on any newspaper fulfils an extremely important role and subtly ennobles us. But she never quite saw it that way and felt as though she was being thwarted as what she really wanted to do was investigative journalism. But as I have said to her on many occasions, what she was doing now was the best way to hone her skills and craft as a writer, and when a chance presented itself she would be in a position to grab it with both hands.'

'You paint a picture of a strong and determined woman.'

'I do, and she has a great future as a journalist and a writer.'

'The article she was working on before she disappeared: what was it about?'

'Oh, it was... now let me get the title right.' She rummaged around on her desk lifting several piles of paper until she had unearthed a notebook. She flicked through several pages. 'Right, here we are. Yes, it was called "What are the Influences of Continental Cooking on a Modern British Woman's Household?".'

Wanda smiled at this and made a mental note to explore if continental cooking was influencing her household.

'I see. Has her writing ever upset anyone?'

'Not to my knowledge. Her postbag has always been very supportive, and since her time here she has developed a loyal following of readers. There's always the odd letter of disagreement but never anything malicious.'

'Has she any enemies?'

'Not to my knowledge. She is one of the most likeable people I know. Yes, she is very forthright and a tenacious debater, and some of her colleagues are wary of her because of her quick temper; only I might add in her defence that they dither around her, and she can't abide ditherers. But I think the best description that encapsulates her character is as mischievous. She is highly intelligent, curious, fearless and has boundless enthusiasm. So, in answer to your question, she may rub some people up the wrong way, especially the ditherers of this world, but is not the sort of person to make enemies.'

Well, she has made an enemy of someone, hasn't she? Wanda thought.

'You mentioned to Inspector Finkelstein that on the evening before her disappearance she telephoned you about a call she had from a source, about a potential scandal at a Paris fashion house. Can you elaborate any more on that call?'

'Not really, but she was very excited. She didn't say who her source was, and I checked with our Paris correspondent the following week to see if there had been any scandals, but after some research he drew a blank. I told the inspector this.'

'What time did she call you?'

'I remember I'd just settled down to listen to my collection of Jerome Kern records when she called, and my mantel clock had just chimed nine o'clock.'

'I see. Is there anything else you can tell me?'

'No, not really, other than the fact that her disappearance is totally out of character.'

'I agree with you; what we have gleaned so far about her suggests that it is indeed totally out of character. It has been most useful to meet and talk to you. If you think of anything else, however trivial, please call me on this number.' Wanda handed her a business card.

'I will do, but I really feel I haven't been of much help at all.'

On balance that is true, Wanda thought. *But on the other hand, you don't get to meet a Miss Eunice Wade every day of the week.*

'Far from it, Eunice, you have been a great help in building a picture of how Florence thinks and acts, which is extremely useful.'

'Thank you, Wanda. For God's sake, please find her. She means a great deal to me and the office is so soulless without her.'

'We will leave no stone unturned. Now I must say goodbye to your feathered suffragette. Goodbye, Emily P, a pleasure to meet you.'

'Votes for women,' the macaw squawked. And with that, Eunice marched Wanda back down to the reception where they said their goodbyes. Wanda skilfully avoided another handshake, only to receive a hearty slap on the back instead.

CHAPTER 5
WEDNESDAY, 9 AUGUST 1922
WESTMINSTER

It was a pleasant walk beside the Thames en route to the Regency Café. As I neared the restaurant, however, I was surprised that Tony had selected a 'greasy spoon' for our lunch. As I entered I saw Tony sitting at a corner table, puffing away on his pipe. We greeted each other warmly.

'Wispy, you look more prosperous every time I see you. I think I'm in the wrong job. Have you eaten here before?'

'No, I haven't.'

'Well it's good honest fare. Are you peckish?'

'Yes, somewhat.'

'Good, then what takes your fancy?'

I viewed the daily menu chalked on a board above the counter and selected their liver, bacon, crispy fried onions, chips, peas and gravy.

'Sounds perfect, however not for me; I'll have the scrambled egg and smoked salmon. Sit down and make yourself comfortable, and I'll order.'

A few moments later he was back with two mugs of steaming tea.

'So, once again we find ourselves working on the same case. Please update me on where you are.'

I related all we had discovered since our telephone conversation yesterday. He sat and listened, concentration etched on his face, his eyes never wandering from mine, until we were interrupted by a booming cockney voice, which I assumed must be the proprietor of this dining establishment.

'One liver and bacon, one salmon and scrambled eggs!' Tony got up and returned with two wonderful-looking plates of food. I put a large dollop of Colman's mustard on the side of my plate and tucked in. I must say it was a gastronomic triumph.

I finished my summary and he sat for a few moments in contemplation.

'Well, Strangely and Constanza are off on their adventures again, *sur le continent*, or should that be *auf dem Continent?*'

'Indeed they are.'

'I understand their decision not to involve me. I don't agree with it, but I respect it. I'm pleased and to be frank, a little emotional that you have asked me to get involved despite the Eastoffs' wishes. What passes between us is of course in total confidence, you have my word on that. However, Wispy, I'm sure that you appreciate this collaboration is not without risk to myself, but that is a risk I'm happy to take. But oy vey iz mir if my commissioner finds out... I know you are the exception to the rule, but I've told you before of his aversion to private detective agencies. You are in his good books after the Leighton case, but that could change pretty rapidly if he gets wind of this – before I'm ready to tell him, that is.'

'Well mum's the word until then.'

'And when that moment arrives, yours truly and the might of Scotland Yard will be ready and waiting to spring into action. Let me get you another tea.'

'No, it's my shout.' I made my way to the counter and caught myself humming 'Pack Up Your Troubles'. I was happy he was on board – although Chester would no doubt take a somewhat different opinion when the time came to break the news.

'Very well, let's start with the ransom note,' he said.

I opened my briefcase and passed him the manila envelope, along with a set of Chester's and Strutton's prints. Wearing his own cotton gloves, he extracted the note and envelope and examined them thoroughly.

'What's this watermark: Brousses?'

'I'm intrigued by that, and I've got Ernest researching it.'

'Good. I fear this person or persons are deadly serious and mean business. It wouldn't surprise me if Sir Chester doesn't get another note in fairly short order. I agree with your assessment that this may unfold pretty rapidly. Let me get the note and envelope checked for fingerprints, but like you I doubt that we will find any other than Sir Chester's and his butler.'

'I'll arrange for the note to be returned as soon as I've had it checked.'

'No, just call me and I'll have Ernest pop over to the Yard and he can collect it.'

'Thank you.'

'Now I must go and throw a few things into an overnight bag for what will no doubt be a very invigorating meeting with the rather irascible and ill-mannered Mr Mungan MacCabe.'

'From what you've told me of him you are bound to get along like a house on fire. Wispy, it's good to be working together again, although be it at the moment in a slightly clandestine way. There's a saying: "He who kidnaps a man – whether he has sold him or is still holding him – shall be put to death". Have a good trip to Glasgow and I sincerely hope that Strangely isn't challenged to a duel in Bremen.'

'Let's hope not, I don't think he's known for his skills with an épée.'

With that, we both stood up. I thanked him for an excellent lunch, and we shook hands and went our separate ways.

I walked back to the office and arrived there shortly before four o'clock. Ernest confirmed my train reservation for later that evening and instructed me that I needed to be on board by nine thirty at the latest.

I updated Wanda on my meeting with Tony and she reported back on her meeting with the very eccentric Miss Eunice Wade, who sounded like a tour de force.

'I'm going home to pack an overnight bag and have dinner with Libby. Depending on what happens in Glasgow, I should be back here hopefully no later than Friday morning. Oh, and Wanda, can you contact Hubert Groves and find out as much as you can about that assistant gardener he dismissed in October 1919? Chester thinks there's nothing in it, but you never know.'

'I will try Groves now. I hope Mungan MacCabe is more pleasant face to face.'

'So do I, but somehow I wouldn't bank on it!'

I left Wanda to it and headed back to Salthouse.

*

'Mr Hubert Groves, please.'

'Speaking.'

'Mr Groves, please allow me to introduce myself. I'm Miss Cushway and I'm calling from Fescue's Detective Agency in London.'

'Sir Chester told me to expect a call. How can I be of assistance, Miss Cushway?'

'You dismissed an assistant gardener in October 1919. Can you please tell me everything you know about him?'

'Of course. His name was Frederick Renou, and he joined the staff here at the beginning of August 1919, the day after the summer bank holiday – the fourth of August, so his first day was Tuesday the fifth of August.'

'And why did you employ him?'

'Thomas Postlethwaite, our head gardener, needed a new assistant, so I placed an advertisement in the *Newcastle Evening Chronicle* and he applied for the position. We both interviewed him, and he came across as a very likeable young man.'

'Did you take up references?'

'Of course, and here's a coincidence: he was employed at Eastoff Shipbuilding Company as a chef and came with impeccable references, so naturally we took him on.'

'Why would a chef want a job as a gardener?'

'Thomas asked him that very question and his answer was that he felt confined in a kitchen and wanted a creative job in the great outdoors.'

'I see, and how old was he?'

'He was twenty-two.'

'Describe his character.'

'When he joined us, he was pleasant and engaging, but that soon changed and he started to show signs of arrogance, almost overconfident, cocksure of himself. The other staff were noticing it too. So I asked him to explain himself, and what came out was that he thought the job beneath him, and he wasn't born to work, as he put it, in servitude.'

'Really.'

'Yes. I have to say I stopped him in his tracks then and there, pointing out we were in service, not servitude. Servitude is more comparable to slavery, being tied to someone. Service, on the other hand, is about a free and intentional choice to help, support and give aid to another – in my case it is a career. It's about mutual respect. The Eastoffs have mutual respect for all of us and we for them. We are in fact employees.'

'And did he accept your rationale?'

'No, he didn't at all. He actually thought that it was wrong that the Eastoffs had such great wealth. I got a strong impression that he was forming some misplaced jealousy of the family. I talked to him again on several occasions about his attitude, which seemed to be hardening and he was starting to see himself as a slave. It was at our last meeting that I said unless he changed his ways immediately I would dismiss him. That last meeting was on the eighteenth of October and the next day, Sunday, he attacked Miss Florence.'

'Gosh!'

'Thomas frogmarched him straight to me, explaining what he had witnessed, and I dismissed him on the spot. With hindsight I should have called the police, but I was concerned about attracting unwarranted publicity to the Eastoffs. As Thomas and I escorted him off the premises, he threatened that he was going to seek revenge on… forgive me, Miss Cushway, I don't want to offend your ears.'

'Mr Groves, I can assure you I'm no shrinking violet.'

'He said he was going to seek revenge and destroy that slut!'

Wanda's normal serenity and calmness was starting to be pushed to its limits.

'And you thought not to mention this when Florence went missing?'

'My apologies, I know I should have mentioned it, but I wanted to protect my employers from such tasteless and offensive language and from the slur against Miss Florence. It would have hurt Lady Alberta to hear such language.'

Heaven forbid that Her Ladyship should be exposed to such an outrage, Wanda mused. *Whatever next? We'll be returning to the dark ages!*

'That, if I may say so, was a huge error on your part.'

'I can only apologise. I had the Eastoffs' best interests at heart.'

'Laudable, I'm sure, but totally wrong. Any other incidents involving Renou?'

'Yes, there were a couple.'

'A couple? Give me strength!'

'Sorry, Miss Cushway. After I dismissed him, Lady Alberta's lady's maid Lily Little came forward and said she too had been molested by him. It happened in our housekeeper's sitting room. Lily was concentrating on her sewing and hadn't heard him enter the room. The next thing she knew was that he had his arm around her neck and he was trying to kiss her. She struggled but his grip was too tight, so she plunged the sewing needle into his arm, and he let go in a cry of pain and ran off.'

'Why did she not report this at the time?'

'Because she was embarrassed. It was only when she heard about Miss Florence that she came forward.'

'When did this happen to Lily?'

'It happened on the Saturday afternoon, the fourth of October.'

'And the other incident?'

'The family has two chocolate Labradors, Marcus and Titus. They are a part of the family and have pretty much the freedom of the house, except for the bedrooms, and are much loved by all of us. But soon after Renou arrived, Thomas noticed that they gave him a wide berth, which he found odd, and shortly before the incident with Miss Florence he discovered why. Thomas caught him pinching them to the point they would yelp and cower from him. Thomas challenged him straight away and he said it was just a bit of good sport. Thomas said if he caught him doing that again he would know what a good bit of sport really meant!'

'Gracious. Do you have a picture of him?'

'In actual fact, I do. We have an annual staff photograph taken outside the main entrance of the house every September. It's on my office wall.'

'I will need that picture at some point, Mr Groves.'

'Certainly, shall I post it to you tomorrow?'

'No, hold off for now. Do you have an address for Renou?'

'Yes I do, it's actually his parents' address.'

Wanda wrote the address down. 'Fine, now I need to make a telephone call. Can I call you back later this evening?'

'Of course, and once again, my apologies.'

'Hindsight is a wonderful thing, Mr Groves. Goodbye for now.'

She found Inspector Finkelstein's number and called Scotland Yard. After what seemed an eternity, he answered.

'Wanda, what a pleasant surprise. Sorry, I was away from my desk, and you've just caught me as I was about to leave to return home to the delights of Mrs Finkelstein's cooking. I think she is preparing one of my favourites this evening, salt beef with potato latkes and her pickled cucumbers.'

'It sounds absolutely delightful, and I'm glad I caught you. My apologies if I'm about to delay your departure, but I need a favour.'

'If I can grant it, I will give it.'

She explained what she had found out about Renou and asked if he could check with the Northumberland constabulary to see if they had any records on him. He readily agreed to help and said he would call them right away and see what he could ascertain.

*

It wasn't until gone seven that he called her. 'I spoke to an Inspector Gleghorn, and he just called me back with the information on Renou. He does indeed have a criminal record; he was convicted for assault when he was fourteen and sent to borstal school. He attacked and seriously injured a lad three years his senior. His defence was that this seventeen-year-old looked at him the wrong way.'

'Gosh.'

'On his release from borstal he was hired by Eastoff Shipbuilding Company as a trainee chef in 1915, aged seventeen. The company hired him in line with their policy of employing reformed young offenders where appropriate.'

'Tony, this makes him a suspect. I must get to Eastoff's shipyards at Wallsend pronto. I'll see if I can get a train this evening.'

'Sorry, Wanda, there's no point.'

'Why?'

'He's dead.'

'Dead!'

'Yes, he was found on the sixth of August last year at Hold House Farm, near Black Callerton Hill. He had been gored to death by Hercules, the farm's English Longhorn bull.'

'What?'

'Exactly, that's what I said when Gleghorn told me. The most fascinating and interesting thing about his death is that he was wearing a matador's suit of lights complete with a cape. The inspector said the coroner's report into his death concluded that he must have lost his mind.'

'I'm flabbergasted. What a terrible way to die.'

'Oh, I don't know. If he was mad, it may have been the way he wanted to shuffle off this mortal coil and meet his maker as a matador.'

'Well that's certainly ruled out José Gómez Ortega.'

'Who?'

'The famous Spanish matador, Little Joe the Rooster. Gored to death in the ring at Talavera de la Reina on the sixteenth of May 1920.'

'Wanda, you never cease to amaze me.'

CHAPTER 6
THURSDAY, 10 AUGUST 1922
GLASGOW

The Caledonian pulled into Glasgow Central as I was finishing a rather nicely cooked breakfast. I took a final few sips of my Earl Grey tea before disembarking. As I walked through the ticket barrier, a chauffeur approached me.

'Sir William?'

'Yes.'

'Please kindly follow me.'

Well, if he is a sample of MacCabe's staff, they are blessed with better manners than their master.

The morning traffic was heavy, and it took thirty minutes to drive to Clydebank and the offices and shipyard of MacCabe Shipbuilders. I was shown into a large, well-furnished office. There was a window across the whole width of the office that looked out across the mighty shipyard. Four giant ships were at different stages of construction, and they were covered from bow to stern in steel scaffolding, giving them the appearance of being cocooned in a steel bird's nest. Towering over the four ships I counted eight massive cranes, which, set against the morning sky, looked like giant herons with their beaks poised to feed their creations below.

A large desk was in front of the window, along with a well-padded leather swivel chair facing inwards. The walls were covered with paintings and photographs of ships, and on the far wall hung two portraits. One I recognised as Mungan MacCabe, and the other one had the same features but was older. They were obviously father and son.

The door opened and in strode MacCabe. He was a giant of a man with an athletic build.

'Sir William, it's a long way to come to discover that I had absolutely nothing whatsoever to do with the disappearance of Miss Florence Eastoff. I also don't take kindly to having to reschedule my board meeting.'

'Let me be the judge of that, Mr MacCabe. And as to you having to reschedule your board meeting, I do not give a fig.'

'Bloody tosh. But in the interests of civility, can I offer you some refreshment?'

'In the interests of civility, I accept. May I have an Earl Grey tea?'

'Take a seat, Sir William.' He took his seat and pressed a buzzer on his desk. A few moments later, a rather skittish butler appeared and left hurriedly to prepare our beverages. He swivelled in his chair and looked out across the vast shipyard to the Clyde beyond.

'The Clyde is a mighty river, Sir William, and the shipbuilding industry on its banks serves the world. There are some big players based here but none bigger and more powerful than my shipbuilding empire.'

'Really, and is that why you threatened to destroy Sir Chester Eastoff's empire, which from my research is of a comparable size to yours?'

He turned around and stared at me as I took out my notebook. 'You seem to be a serial threatener, Mr MacCabe. When Sir Chester won his court case you threatened to destroy his business. Again, in late May this year, you threatened to hurt him beyond measure. Strong and pernicious words.'

There was a knock on the door. 'Enter!' I jumped as the command was shouted. The butler entered and with shaking hands set his tray of clattering crockery on the desk.

'Now get out!'

I thought he was obnoxious on the telephone, but in the flesh he is an utter bastard of the first order.

'Now, where were we before that idiot interrupted me? Ah yes, you were painting me as a serial threatener. I prefer to use the words "serial intimidator". I intimidate people, Sir William. I take after my father, and what was good enough for him is good enough for me. It has got me to where I am today, and that is at the bloody top of the pile.'

'You strike me as a bully, and you know what they say about bullies...'

'I don't give a damn what you think about me, you jumped-up prig of the realm. But what I do give a damn about is my bloody business being interfered with. The British India is my biggest client. I'm their first choice when it comes to ship construction. What I can't manufacture I subcontract out to Count von Delmenhorst's company Edle Schiffbaugesellschaft. We have a profitable understanding, and I do not under any circumstances tolerate that being interfered with.'

'Well, as a jumped-up prig of the realm, and with my limited understanding of the law, it appears to me that you are operating a cartel, which runs totally against our anti-competition laws.'

I saw it coming, so I didn't jump this time as he smashed both fists down onto his desk with such force that our beverages flew into the air and went everywhere.

'Never ever accuse me of being anti-competition. I love competition. I thrive on competition. That's what makes me a winner,' he shouted.

'Of course it does, Mr MacCabe, of course it does.'

I must admit I was quite enjoying myself. The arrogance of the man was extraordinary. If Sir Chester had a few enemies, this so-called gentleman must have legions of them.

'Mr MacCabe, where were you on the twenty-sixth and the twenty-seventh of June?'

'That's my business.'

'Well now it's my business too. I believe you had a hand in the disappearance of Miss Eastoff, and it is my intention to leave no stone unturned until I can prove your involvement.'

'You're talking utter crap, you stuck-up prig. But just to shut you up, I'll tell you where I was.'

He made a point of slowly opening his large desk diary and flicked through the pages.

'Ah, here we are. I was at my country estate, Alladale, in the Highlands. I arrived there on Saturday the twenty-fourth of June and returned the following Sunday, the second of July.'

'And you can prove you were there?'

'What an unintelligent question. Would I tell you something I can't prove, you imbecile? Send a telegram to my butler, Mr Breathnach, and he will confirm I was there.'

'I've no doubt whatsoever he will. You don't have a telephone there?'

'No, it's too remote.'

'How jolly convenient.'

'Look, you're nothing more than a jumped-up amateur sleuth. I'm surprised that you're not wearing an Inverness cape and sporting a bloody deerstalker with a calabash pipe stuck in that mouthy gob of yours! I've told you where I was. So, before I lose my temper completely, you'd better sod off out of my office.'

'Oh, I would hate to witness that. Very well, I would say it's been a pleasure to meet you, but unlike some people I've been brought up not to lie. But… how shall I put it? To my surprise I've found the experience quite invigorating and stimulating.'

'Are you bloody well accusing me of lying?'

'Would I, Mr MacCabe? I was just making the point that some people lie. God forbid me of accusing you of lying, or anything else for that matter. I wouldn't want to give my solicitor an unnecessary work burden. I've heard enough, so unless you have any other pearls of wisdom to impart I must be off.'

'I don't like your tone, Fescue.'

'The feeling's mutual, MacCabe. Now if you wouldn't mind, can you get your chauffeur to take me back to the station?'

'I'm afraid that's impossible, he is out and about running errands.' He pushed the buzzer on his desk and a few moments later the nervous butler appeared.

'Show Mr Fescue off the premises and point out the bus stop. He needs to get himself back to the station.' And with that, he swivelled around in his chair to gaze back over his empire.

*

I hadn't ridden on a bus for years, and I have to say I enjoyed sitting on the top deck and watching the different layers of Glasgow unfold all around me. It had just gone midday when I arrived back at Glasgow Central, and I managed to exchange my return ticket on the Caledonian for a first-class single to London.

The train didn't depart until just before one o'clock, so I called Libby and told her to expect me home at about nine thirty. I said I would have luncheon on the train, and could she arrange for Alice to cobble something together for when I arrived home.

Next, I phoned the office and talked to Wanda. She told me about the matador Frederick Renou, and I updated her on Mr Mungan MacCabe and how I wouldn't trust him as far as I could throw him. She said they had received a telegram this morning from Strangely in Paris, and they were about to board the train to Bremen. Inspector Finkelstein had been in touch and the only prints on the ransom note were Chester's and Strutton's.

I asked her to telegram Mr Breathnach to establish MacCabe's alibi, which was a fruitless but necessary chore because it would come back in the affirmative; even if he'd said he'd been for a week on the moon, that too would have come back in the affirmative.

The journey back to London gave me the opportunity to order my thoughts on MacCabe, whilst having a late lunch of *petite sole Colbert, noisette d'agneau Béarnaise,* and *poires Alma* to finish, accompanied by a half-bottle of 1911 Château Talbot.

CHAPTER 7
THURSDAY, 10 AUGUST 1922
BREMEN

The train pulled into Bremen Hauptbahnhof as the station clock struck seven. Strangely and Constanza disembarked and a porter followed, struggling with their large suitcases as they walked towards the ticket barrier. They were immediately drawn to a very tall gentleman wearing what appeared to be a full white dress uniform, complete with cavalry boots and helmet topped off with a large silver eagle. He was sporting a wonderful waxed moustache. As they neared him, they noticed his face was covered in scars and he was wearing an iron cross. The only thing he was missing was a monocle. Strangely was completely and utterly astonished at his appearance. He looked like he was about to take part in some elaborate military parade. He wondered if his steed was tethered outside the station.

'Count von Delmenhorst?'

'At your service, Herr Drye.'

'Marjorie, please.' The count didn't bat an eyelid.

'But of course, I'm Reinhardt.' They shook hands.

'Please allow me to introduce my wife, Constanza.'

'Enchanted.' Constanza offered her hand and the count kissed it. 'Did you have a pleasant journey?'

'Pleasant, yes, but also a tad tiring,' replied Constanza.

'Well in that case, my *schloss* is at your disposal. *Kommen sie!* He clicked his heels together, turned on the spot and marched out of the station. Strangely and Constanza had trouble keeping up. Outside was a Silver Mercedes-Benz Cyprus complete with a flag bearing a coat of arms on the left-hand wheel arch. The chauffeur held the door open.

About thirty minutes later they turned into the long tree-lined avenue to Schloss Delmenhorst. On their right was an airstrip with a windsock lightly blowing in the breeze and a hangar with two biplanes parked outside. 'They are my pride and joy, Marjorie, two Albatros C.X – a similar aeroplane to that of the Red Baron, Manfred von Richthofen.'

The castle looked magnificent, and it imposed itself on the surrounding countryside. They drove through a large gate into an impressive courtyard, drawing up adjacent to steps that led to huge solid wood double doors. A butler appeared with another member of staff and helped them out of the car.

'We will have dinner at nine o'clock, but now you must refresh yourselves. Please join me for a drink in the drawing room at eight thirty. Stein, please take Herr and Frau Drye to their room.'

Stein led them through the hall, which was lined with suits of armour and the walls were adorned in armaments from centuries gone by. The stairwell was covered in portraits of what they assumed were the count's ancestors. Stein showed them into a huge bedroom with large windows which looked out over the castle grounds and beyond into the estate. The walls were covered in more portraits and hunting scenes. In the centre of the room was a highly ornate four-poster bed; it looked incredibly old, maybe sixteenth century.

'Please push the bell here if you need anything.'

'Thank you, Stein, I will,' replied Strangely.

He shut the door behind him. 'Well, Connie, what do you make of our host?'

'Not what I was expecting at all. He's utterly charming. Doesn't strike me as the kidnapping sort.'

'Really, so what does strike you as the kidnapping sort?'

'Come on, darling, don't be tetchy, you know what I mean. But where on earth did all those scars come from?'

'I imagine they are duelling scars.'

'Gosh, how terribly exciting.'

Feeling much refreshed, and changed into their evening finery, they started to make their way to the drawing room.

'Do you think there's a Countess Delmenhorst and lots of little Delmenhorsts?' enquired Constanza.

'Oh, there's bound to be.'

They got lost a few times but eventually found the drawing room, which like the rest of the castle was on a grand scale. It was magnificent; the ceiling was high and painted with a scene depicting a Prussian cavalry charge led by who they thought must have been Frederick the Great. On the walls hung beautiful tapestries and more paintings of battles and hunting scenes. A huge fireplace at the end of the room had the family coat of arms above it, the same as that on the count's car: a silver key on a red shield supported by two lions rampant. The count was still in his dress uniform but had changed out of his boots into patent leather shoes.

'My dear Marjorie and Constanza, I trust your room is to your liking.'

'It is perfect,' replied Strangely.

'Good, now let me get you a drink. Constanza?'

'Thank you, Reinhardt, I'll have a gin and tonic.'

'Ah, a quintessential British drink; an excellent choice, but let me introduce you to the oldest gin distillery in the world, our famous Konig's Westphalian Gin. Ice and lemon?'

'Yes, please.'

'Coming up.'

He handed Constanza her gin. 'Now, Marjorie, we have a famous brewery here in Bremen called Becks, so let me get you one of their Pilsners.'

He went over to a large sideboard, and on the way there he stood in front of a full-length mirror and with his left index finger, checked that his moustache was as it should be. He pulled out two large bottles from a silver ice bucket and poured them into two pottery steins with pewter lids.

They raised their steins and glass to each other – *'Prost'* – and they clanged them together.

'Please sit.' They sat down on opposite sides of the fireplace. 'Did you have a good war?'

Well that was an interesting opening question, thought Strangely, but in the light of all the militaria maybe not a surprising one.

'A relatively good one. I got injured on the first day of the Battle of the Somme, but other than that I came through it largely unscathed.'

'Ah, the glories of the battlefield. And what rank were you?'

'When I left I had attained the rank of Captain.'

'You must be very proud of him, Constanza.'

'I am very proud, but most importantly he survived.'

'Quite. You see that painting there?' He pointed to a large painting which dominated the far end of the room. *'Kommen sie.'*

They walked over to the painting. It was a portrait of him astride a rearing cavalry horse that was readying for a charge, with him leaning forward in the stirrups, pointing his sword towards the enemy.

'My father had that painting commissioned when I joined the most elite regiment in the German army, the Gardes du Corps, in 1911. I was a captain then and rose to the rank of major. The honour of serving my glorious Reich was something that will stay with me until the day I die. My father was in the regiment when he was young and insisted that I joined too. However, all I wanted was to join Die Fliegertruppen des Deutschen Kaiserreiches, the aviation troops of the German Empire. I pointed out my aircraft when we drove in?'

'Yes, you did, very impressive,' replied Strangely.

'Thank you. Flying is my passion, but my father gave me little choice in the matter. Do you fly?'

'I'm afraid I don't. I prefer to have my feet well and truly planted on terra firma.'

'Marjorie, you don't know what you are missing. Unfortunately, my regiment was disbanded in 1918 along with the mighty Prussian army. But it's good to keep the traditions alive, hence I wear my uniform when the occasion permits, like today in your honour. I meet up as often as I can with my comrades for our regimental dinners.

'My beloved father was tragically killed in a hunting accident in 1920 – that's when I took over the running of the business. Do you like the beer?'

'It's excellent.'

'Then let me recharge your stein. Another gin, Constanza?'

'No, thank you, Reinhardt.'

They walked back to the fireplace and the count went over to the sideboard and poured two more Pilsners. Before he returned with them he stood in front of the mirror again and checked his moustache, straightened his uniform and clicked his heels. They heard him say, 'Sehr gut.'

'Now a toast: to brothers in arms. *Prost.* Tell me, have you a family?'

'No, it's just Constanza and me.'

'Ah, I have three children, two boys and a girl, so that the magnificent line of the Delmenhorsts can continue. I apologise they are not here to meet you, along with my beautiful wife, the countess. They are holidaying at my *schloss* in the Schwarzer Wald. I intend to join them next week.'

Well, that solves Constanza's earlier question, Strangely thought.

'Now, dinner. I have chosen a menu that gives you a flavour of our wonderful gastronomy.'

The dining room was another large room with the continuation of the military and hunting themes running through it. Again, the ceiling had been used as a canvas to illustrate the family's history in the shipping industry. There was another full-length mirror near the fireplace and the count went over to it and stood admiring himself with his usual gesture of straightening his moustache; however, this time he ran his fingers through his hair, pushing it back into place.

They sat at the end of an extremely long dining table; Strangely thought it would seat thirty comfortably. Stein served dinner. They had *Labskaus* to start, a local speciality from Bremen made with salt-cured beef, potatoes and onion. To follow they had *Schweinebraten* with *Stöcklkraut* and *Knödel*, roast pork with cabbage and dumplings. For dessert they had *Rote Grütze*, a mixed red berry dessert with cream. The cheeseboard was a new experience as well, with Allgäuer Emmentaler, Romadur, Allgäuer Bergkäse, and Limburger accompanied by pumpernickel. The count eulogised over the Allgäuer with its nutty finish.

The food was first class and served with a Schloss Johannisberg Riesling Bronzelack Trocken. They returned to the drawing room for coffee, and Strangely declined a cigar.

'So, you have travelled all this way to question me on the disappearance of Sir Chester Eastoff's daughter, Miss Florence. I am all yours, Marjorie.'

'Thank you. Where were you on the twenty-sixth and the twenty-seventh of June?'

'That from memory was a Monday and Tuesday. Am I not correct?'

'You are.'

'*Gut*, then my brain is as sharp as ever. I was here all week working at Edle Schiffbaugesellschaft and at home every evening with my beautiful family.'

'And you can prove that?'

'Do you doubt the word of a major of the Gardes du Corps? But if you must check my alibi, I chaired meetings on those days, so you are welcome to check the minutes that confirm my attendance.'

'Thank you, I will need to see those.'

'You can see them tomorrow when we visit the shipyard. I will arrange for my solicitor to have a signed affidavit from Stein that I was here all that week.'

'Thank you, Reinhardt.'

'I know metaphorically I've crossed swords with Sir Chester, but I hope and pray that his daughter is found. I may be ruthless in business, but away from that I too am a father, and family above all else means absolutely everything.'

'On the subject of crossing swords, why did you challenge Sir Chester to a duel?'

'He impinged my honour! I might be relentless in pursuit of business, but I most certainly do not, and I repeat do not, use

51

underhanded tactics. Remember, Marjorie, I am an officer of the Gardes du Corps!'

'How did you get so many scars?'

'Ah, you've noticed my duelling scars, my "smiles". Whilst at Heidelberg University I joined the academic fencing club, and they are my badges of honour.'

Constanza and Strangely glanced at each other, with Strangely giving her an indiscernible wink.

'Good gracious, what an awfully painful way of going about proving yourself. I trust it was worth it?' enquired Constanza.

'Yes, absolutely. The duelling helps to enhance one's character and personality, don't you think?'

'Really, it seems strange to want to disfigure one's face; however, each to his own,' added Strangely. 'Now, tell me about your relationship with Mr Mungan MacCabe.'

'In all honesty I can't stand the man. He has absolutely no etiquette and breeding whatsoever. My shipbuilding empire was bigger than his and more successful. However, after the war our international clients went elsewhere. Having said that, I'm in the process of tendering again for three vessels for two of my old clients, French Line CGT and Cunard. I have met them both again on several occasions; the noises they are making are extremely encouraging, and we are working on their tenders.

'His business has been built primarily around just one client, the British India Steam Navigation Company, and that, Marjorie, is not a good way to run a business. He approached me after the war ended to see if I would be interested in subcontracting, and because beggars can't be choosers, I accepted the crumbs from his table. I'm a proud man, but I'm not a fool. Foreign business at the moment is hard to come by.'

'It must have been very tough after the end of the war.'

'That's an understatement, but as I've just said, we are about to turn a corner.'

'So MacCabe helps to keep you afloat?'

'Yes. He doesn't like to turn business away, so when his yard is full and he doesn't close his advance order book, he still accepts orders.

I have spare capacity in my shipyard, so he subcontracts the orders to me and I manufacture the vessels. As long as I make my correct margins, the arrangement suits me, and when my clients return it will give me the greatest pleasure to kick him into the long grass. The man's a pagan and believe me, that's an insult to pagans!

'Good Lord, he didn't even have the courage to fight for king and country as you and I did. He used the fact that he was in a protected occupation to avoid going to war. The workforce in the shipyards were rightly protected, but not the owner's son. The man's a *hosenscheisser*, a coward.'

'You don't think that what you and MacCabe were doing was against fair competition?'

'Not from my point of view. The contract I entered into was a legal one between me and MacCabe. British India were welcome to visit my shipyards anytime they liked. What he told them is a different matter, but I suppose they didn't give a fig as long as they got their thirty-odd-thousand-tonne vessels delivered on time and at the right price.

'Now, tomorrow after breakfast I will take you to my shipbuilding empire and you can see for yourself two British India vessels under construction. But before we turn in for the evening, a nightcap might be in order, and can I challenge you to a game of billiards – if that's all right with you, Constanza?'

'Perfectly fine with me. I will turn in for the night; it's been a long day.'

'Then I bid you *Gute Nacht.*'

'I won't be too long, darling, just long enough to teach the count a lesson or two on the billiard table.'

'Ah, you have thrown down your gauntlet. Come, Marjorie, the billiard room beckons. Do you know what? I think, as you English say, we are beginning to rub along quite nicely.'

CHAPTER 8
FRIDAY, 11 AUGUST 1922
CHELSEA

Libby and I rose early and went down for breakfast at seven thirty. Eleanor had placed today's *Times* on my place setting, and I had just started to take in the headlines.

'Wispy, please take your head out of the paper and talk to me.'

'Sorry, darling, force of habit. So what plans do you have for today?'

'I've brought my sketch pad and notebook with me, and I'm going for a walk to see what draws my attention. I did enjoy finishing my painting of Waterloo station in the rush hour, which I'm going to submit for next year's Royal Academy Summer Exhibition, along with another one of my recent paintings which I've yet to choose. So, let's see where my mind and walk takes me.'

'I'm sure wherever your walk takes you your sketches will be as wonderful as always. I do wish I could draw just a tad, but I'm hopeless. I remember one of my school reports on the subject from Gresham's that has stuck with me. It went something along the lines of "Fescue's lack of ability in art is so apparent he should pursue other avenues for his creativity, namely on the cricket pitch, bowling his fast yorkers"!'

'Yes, your skills and abilities do lie in other directions, darling. Speaking of which, Eleanor informed me we are running low on your pickles.'

'Did she? God forbid having to eat shop-bought pickles. I will go into full production when we get back to Blakeney.'

There was a knock at the door and Eleanor walked in. 'Speak of the devil. Eleanor, you can rest assured that I will be averting your forthcoming pickle crisis.'

'Thank you, Sir William, that is indeed a weight off my mind. Sir Chester Eastoff is on the telephone for you.'

I got up and went into my study.

'Good morning, Chester.'

'There's nothing good about it, Wispy. I think we've received another ransom note.'

Well at least he called me Wispy, which is a distinct improvement.

'Have you opened it?'

'No, I bloody well haven't.'

'Good. I'm on my way.'

I glanced at my watch; it was just before eight. I hoped Wanda would be at the office.

'Libby, darling, there's been another ransom note so I must get over to Lennox Gardens straight away.'

I kissed her and dashed into my study, grabbed my briefcase, and headed to the garage and started my relatively new Bentley Gairn three-litre, which I had purchased last year. It came to life with a satisfying roar and as I drove out of the garage, the morning sun glinted off the deep burgundy body of the car. I pulled up outside the office and jumped out. I was in luck; Wanda was in. She picked up her bag and we were off the short distance to Lennox Gardens.

A rather rotund butler opened the door. 'Sir William, Sir Chester and Lady Eastoff are expecting you. Please follow me.' We went upstairs and he showed us into the drawing room.

Chester and Alberta were holding hands, staring out of a large pair of French windows that led onto a balcony overlooking the garden. They turned as we entered the room.

'Thank you for coming over so quickly.'

Well that's a first!

'Please allow me to introduce Miss Wanda Cushway.'

They both shook hands with her.

'Now where's the note?'

'It's on the table over there.'

We all crossed to the table and stared down at a parcel wrapped in brown paper. It was addressed to Sir Chester and Lady Eastoff, and the letters were of the same type as used on the first ransom note.

'Who has handled this?'

'Only Strutton, our butler. I instructed him to leave it on the table and called you straight away.'

'Good. Are you all right with me opening it?'

'Of course we're bloody all right with you opening it. You're the damned detective.'

'Chester! We've spoken about this.'

'Sorry, darling, I'm rather tense.'

I glanced at Wanda whilst I opened my briefcase, took out my penknife and put on my cotton gloves. I cut the string and unwrapped the parcel, then folded the brown paper neatly and put it to one side. We looked down on a white cardboard box, with the same type of cut-out lettering spelling out the words 'Open me to stare into your worst nightmare!'.

I lifted off the lid and placed that with the brown paper, and we saw two envelopes and another parcel, which was cylindrical and wrapped in the same brown paper. I lifted the two envelopes out and put them side by side on the table. The first one again had the same cut-out letters which spelt the words 'Your Instructions'. The second one was handwritten and read 'My dearest Mother and Father'. I heard Chester gasp, and Alberta started to sob.

'It's Florence's handwriting,' Chester confirmed.

I waited until Alberta had composed herself and then opened the first envelope. Placing the envelope with the other packaging, I unfolded the letter. Again the same cut-up typeface greeted me. I noticed the same watermark, Brousses, which reminded me to chase up Ernest. I read out loud:

'"Sir Chester and Lady Alberta, you haven't heard from me since Monday, so it is high time I laid out my terms so that you might once again be able to look upon the beautiful face of your daughter.

"'For that great privilege, which is now in my gift to grant, my terms are simple: I require ten thousand pounds in gold bullion in troy ounce bars, which I'm sure you can work out with your wonderful mathematical brain is two thousand, one hundred and forty-five bars.

"'Today is the eleventh of August, and as I am a generous man, you have until next Friday the eighteenth of August to deliver the gold to me. I will be in touch again to tell you where I wish my gold to be delivered.

"'I shouldn't have to, but I must stress once more that if the police are involved, you will never see Florence again. I thought you would enjoy reading her letter and receiving her precious gift to you both.

"'Until the next time!'"

I put the note down, and we all stood in silence for what seemed like several minutes.

'It won't be a problem organising the gold. I will call Lord Downham at Coutts to make the arrangements as a precautionary measure, in case all else fails.'

'Very wise, but only as a last resort.'

A wave of self-doubt hit me like a hammer blow. We had until next Friday to find her. A knot of fear gripped my stomach; God, I hoped it didn't show.

'Now to Florence's letter: would either of you like to open it?'

'No, you do it,' Alberta said, the strain etched in her quivering voice.

I took the letter out of the envelope and read:

"'My dearest Mother and Father,

"'Please accept my grandfather's signet ring, which I have worn ever since he left it to me on his deathbed. This ring is proof that I'm alive.

"'I am frightened and terrified of being butchered and left here. I had hoped to become a Lady and not a Carcas. I plead with you to pay whatever they arx demanding.

"'I miss you more than words can say.

"'Your loving daughter, Florence.'"

Alberta looked like she might collapse, and Chester helped her sit down on the sofa. He went over and pulled the bell pull, and a few moments later Strutton appeared.

'Strutton, a large glass of water as quick as you can.'

He disappeared and was back in fairly short order. Chester sat down next to her and helped her drink. Alberta's breathing had returned to normal, and Chester stood up. 'Now for the present.'

He went to grab the cylinder, and I stopped him in his tracks.

'No. I will open it. Please sit down with Alberta.' It came out more as an order than a request. He sat down. I put my gloves back on, picked up the present and carefully unwrapped it. I momentarily recoiled at its contents and hoped nobody noticed. I placed the object on the table in front of Alberta and Chester. They stared at what I had placed in front of them and their eyes slowly widened in abject horror.

Chester was the first to react and he let out a moan that sounded like a wounded animal. Alberta rose slowly and stood bolt upright, threw her arms behind her, tilted her head heavenwards like a winged angel, and let out a harrowing scream. It seemed to stem from her very soul and rose through her being, exploded into the room and punctured the whole house. She collapsed sobbing back onto the sofa. Chester drew her to him and enveloped her in a hug until the sobs abated.

What I had placed in front of them was a cylindrical specimen jar containing Florence's little finger in a clear liquid of some sort, which I guessed was an alcohol, and on that little finger was her grandfather's signet ring. Whoever did this act of butchery was no trained surgeon. I just prayed that for this act they would have been humane enough to administer some sort of anaesthetic first. But as God is my witness, we were dealing with a ruthless, sadistic, cowardly bastard.

Chester was the first to break the silence. 'My God, what our poor child must be going through I can only imagine. But understand this: mentally she is the strongest person I know, and she will not buckle.'

'No, she won't,' replied Alberta. 'She will rise to the challenge of survival, and that she will triumph I have not the slightest doubt. We must both be strong and totally focused on the job in hand. And that job is to get her back safe and sound where she belongs, and to crush her kidnapper.'

I must admit I hadn't expected this response, quite the opposite in fact. But the sight of Florence's finger seemed to have galvanised them into action. 'Bloody well said, both of you.'

'It's what us Eastoffs do, Wispy. It's no good moping around and feeling sorry for ourselves. What has happened we can't undo, but what we can do is prevent what might happen.'

'Chester, might I say something?'

'Yes, Wanda, please.'

'Mentally she is supremely strong and she's most definitely not about to buckle.' Wanda now had our undivided attention.

'What do you mean?' I said.

'Let me explain my reasoning. I have just taken the opportunity to have a closer look at Florence's letter.' She picked it up again in her gloved hands.

'The first paragraph: "Please accept my grandfather's signet ring, which I have worn since he left it to me on his deathbed. This ring is proof that I'm alive". This is factual, and I assume is correct, as a dead Florence is no use whatsoever to our kidnapper.'

I felt myself wincing as Wanda said this, but Alberta and Chester did not bat an eyelid.

'You are right, Wanda,' replied Alberta. 'She loved him dearly and that ring meant the world to her.'

'I understand,' continued Wanda. 'Now this is where it gets interesting. The second paragraph: "I am frightened and terrified of being butchered and being left here". It's an excellent use of the word "butchered" because when you butcher an animal, you are left with a carcass.'

We all stared at Wanda, hanging on her every syllable.

'Note how she uses the phrase "being left here". I think for the second use of "being" in the same sentence she's referring to a human being, and when she uses the word "here" she is about to tell us where she is.'

'Good God, Wanda—'

'Be quiet, Chester, and let her concentrate.'

He nodded an apology.

'Now, to the next sentence: "I had hoped to become a Lady and not a Carcas". The use of the word "Lady" and how she uses it in conjunction with the word "Carcas" is fascinating. She is definitely telling us where she is.'

'So where on bloody God's earth is she?'

'Chester!'

'I'm coming to that. Now this is genius: look how she has spelt the word "carcass". She has spelt it with a capital C and dropped the last s, followed by a full stop. If you take the word "Lady" and put it with "Carcas", we get "Lady Carcas". So where does that tell us she is?'

We all looked blankly at her.

'According to folklore, the ancient city of Carcassonne was saved from Charlemagne's five-year siege by Lady Carcas, and when the siege was lifted, the bells of the city rang out and the men of the city cried out "*Carcas sonne!*", which literally means "Carcas is ringing".

'The last sentence in the paragraph reads: "I plead with you to pay what they arx demanding". See how she has misspelt "are" and used the word "arx" instead?'

She pointed to the word on the page. '"*Arx*" in Latin means citadel, and a citadel is a fortress which typically is one that is on high ground above a city. Which, if we know our history, points to Europe's largest medieval fortified city, Carcassonne. This, I believe, is where Florence is being held, or somewhere nearby.'

We sat transfixed for what seemed like minutes absorbing what she had just said.

'Miss Wanda Cushway, you're a genius!' I said.

'Hardly, but a love of Latin and a BA in Classics and English has its uses.'

'It's absolutely amazing what can be conveyed in such a short letter,' said Alberta.

'Wanda, you have a bloody brilliant mind,' said Chester. 'But don't we need to get someone out there as quick as we can?'

'Leave that with me. Strangely and Constanza are in Bremen visiting Count von Delmenhorst and they can go from there. Can I use your telephone?'

'Bloody hell, Wispy, you don't hang about. You can use the one in my study. Follow me.'

He stood up and in his haste to get there nearly tripped over a chaise longue. 'Please make yourself comfortable.'

'Ernest, it's me. Can you send a telegram to Strangely at Edle Schiffbaugesellschaft and, hang on,' he checked his watch; it had just gone eleven o'clock, midday in Bremen, 'reading "Call me after two your time STOP Require you to travel to Carcassonne urgently".'

I returned to the drawing room. 'Thank you, Chester. Now, I need to get the ransom note, packaging, and unfortunately the specimen jar, which I assure you will be treated with the utmost dignity, checked for prints.'

*

We found a telephone box on Walton Street and I called Inspector Finkelstein at the Yard. He agreed to drop everything and meet us immediately at the Two Chairmen on Dartmouth Street, just off Birdcage Walk. Wanda and I jumped into the Bentley and five minutes later we walked into the pub. Tony was there already, sitting in a corner booth, smoking his pipe. He stood up. 'Shalom, Wanda, Shalom, Wispy. Let me get you a drink.'

With a pint of best bitter in front of me and an orange juice in front of Wanda, I relayed all the events of the morning and my visit to Glasgow.

'Of course, I'll get everything checked for prints but as we all know, we won't find any. However, Florence's finger has ratcheted this up to another level entirely. I now need to involve the commissioner. I will exp—'

'No, Tony. Can't you hold off for a little while longer?'

'If you will let me explain, Wispy. When we met on Wednesday I said to you at some point I will need to tell him, and that tipping point has just been reached. My relationship with him is such that I know I can convince him that you can run with the case. He knows how you operate and despite his natural instincts to mistrust private detectives, he accepts that you and your team are good at what you do and are the exception to the rule, and more to the point, trustworthy.'

'I'm still not convinced.'

'But knowing what we now know, it can only be beneficial to the case to get me officially involved, and it will make your job easier knowing that I'm available to you night and day with the blessing of the commissioner. You must see that?'

I took a large pull on my pint. 'Yes, I do. You are right, and it will make things a lot easier rather than acting in this clandestine way. Wanda?'

'I'm absolutely in agreement, and I will feel a lot more comfortable knowing you're officially involved. However, the Eastoffs must not know of your involvement until the right moment.'

'Exactly, and we will all know when that moment arrives,' replied the inspector. 'The other benefit is that all the red tape will be in place to allow me to move quickly. We only have a week to find her, and at the moment we don't have too many solid suspects. The obnoxious Mungan MacCabe has an alibi, we are waiting for Strangely's verdict on the duelling Count von Delmenhorst, and we have yet to track down the architect Mr Walderne Smithers. What we do know is whoever we are dealing with is utterly ruthless – and I believe will have absolutely no compunction to kill – but what we don't have on our side is time.'

Thanks for stating the obvious. 'Agreed.'

'You know my involvement will be confidential. I will seek the commissioner's blessing when I get back to the Yard.'

'Thank you, I actually feel relieved.'

'If it's any consolation, so do I. Now, Wanda, can I congratulate you on your brilliant deductions from studying the ransom note? I'm sure with your intellect and insight there's a job of serious gravitas with your name on it at Scotland Yard.'

'Thank you, but I rather like where I am.'

'I know you do and so you should. Rather like the commissioner, I have a built-in aversion to private investigators, but as I just said, you are the exceptions to the rule and I'm glad to be working with you again. Cheers!'

We raised our glasses.

CHAPTER 9
FRIDAY, 11 AUGUST 1922
AUDE

Florence thought it was totally unjust and against any semblance of natural justice to be shackled in a vault underneath such a beautiful and peaceful place. The only light she had came from a candle, and she longed to feel the warmth of the sun on her face again.

The pain from the wound after her little finger had been hacked off came and went in waves of such intensity that she nearly passed out every time one flooded over her and left her feeling nauseous.

Her main concern was to prevent infection, which might lead to the onset of gangrene. Her captors had bandaged her left hand, and although blood had soaked to the surface of the bandage and had dried, she managed to keep the dressing dry and so far the hand smelt fine.

One of her captors, the shorter and more rotund of the two, who she nicknamed Napoleon, brought a pail of well water every day for her to wash as best as she could without soap. She had tried to wash her hair at the start of her captivity, but gave up because she had no means of drying it, and she could feel it turning into a tangled oily mess. How she longed for a bath.

Napoleon was her clock and calendar; she had lost all sense of whether it was day or night, or what day of the week it was.

Her companion was her mind, and in it she kept a daily diary of everything that had happened both physically and mentally, as well as her thoughts and ideas. These would then be turned into a series of articles, which she could visualise on the printed page in her mind's eye for the *Chronicle* and which she hoped would capture the imagination of the British public. In turn, they would increase circulation figures and finally make the paper's editor prick his ears up to her true potential as an investigative journalist.

And if her mind wasn't full enough, she started to formulate ideas for her first novel, a murder mystery. Her main protagonist was a character called Miss Edwina Whybrow, who resided in York near the Minster and was a local second-hand bookshop proprietor and amateur sleuth.

CHAPTER 10
FRIDAY, 11 AUGUST 1922
BREMEN

'*Guten Morgen*, I trust you slept well?'

'Yes, like a baby, Reinhardt,' replied Constanza.

The count was more soberly attired this morning in a chalk-stripe double-breasted suit.

'Excellent, I see you two both share my eye for style and elegance.'

Strangely had also dressed in a similar suit but with a charcoal stripe, and Constanza wore a pale-yellow silk barontine dress.

'Help yourself to breakfast. I had Chef prepare *Weisswurst* and Grandma's bacon pancakes, *Speckpfannkuchen*, with the addition of cheese and onions. Oh, and make sure you have some of his pickled cucumbers; they are delicious.'

Strangely and Constanza would have happily settled for toast and marmalade, but as they tucked in, they cast aside their wish as the food was exceptional.

'More coffee?'

'Yes, please, I could manage another.'

The count rang his bell again and Stein appeared in an instant. 'Another pot of coffee, please, for Herr Drye, and can you ask Schmidt to have the car outside for eight thirty?'

It was a perfect summer's day with hardly a cloud in the sky as they drove to the shipyard. The yard was huge and a hive of activity as they surveyed the scene from the count's vast office, which continued his theme of military glories and hunting, with paintings and artefacts adorning the walls, bookshelves and desk.

'Here are the minutes of the meetings I chaired here on the twenty-sixth and twenty-seventh of June.'

Strangely sat down and read the minutes, and they did indeed confirm that he chaired the two meetings. 'Thank you, Reinhardt. You have an alibi for the dates when Florence disappeared, and I must say I'm rather jolly well relieved.'

'As I said yesterday, I have had my differences with Sir Chester, but I wouldn't wish what has befallen him and Lady Alberta. I have my solicitor visiting Stein at the *schloss* to take his sworn affidavit this morning. Now come, both of you!'

On the way out, he checked himself in a full-length mirror by the door, straightening his moustache. '*Augezeichnet! Kommen Sie.*' They couldn't help smiling to each other as he clicked his heels.

The count took them out onto the ground level of the yard. The noise was deafening, and towering above them were two massive vessels under construction. The count had to shout to make himself heard. 'These two cargo ships were subcontracted to me by MacCabe in April 1921. They are due for completion and delivery next April. If you look there,' he pointed off to his right, 'you will see three large barges being manufactured that will be bound for service on the Rhine. Come.'

The count took them on a tour of the yard, and they both sensed the enormous pride he had in his business. They returned an hour later to his office and coffee and pastries were served.

'You know, Marjorie, I often sit here and ponder why MacCabe used to keep winning the British India Company tenders. Was it because they liked him for his irresistible charm and impeccable manners? I doubt it. Was it because his ship construction is better than anyone else's in the world? I doubt it. Did he understand the tendering process better than any of us? I doubt it. Did his procurement department purchase steel and every other component part to build a ship at a more favourable price than any of us could buy it for? I doubt it. So, I ask you the question, why did Mungan MacCabe keep winning their tenders?'

'Because he is corrupt,' replied Constanza.

'That is exactly the right answer. He is absolutely corrupt and rotten to the core. I have turned a blind eye and have conveniently accepted his business to keep mine on a firm footing. I'm the innocent subcontractor; what he gets up to to secure these contracts has nothing whatsoever to do with me. But your visit has brought into sharp focus the duty of an officer of the Gardes du Corps. The motto on my helmet is *Summ Cuique* – each to his own. Which is very laudable but not so when you are dealing with someone who is so dishonourable.'

'So, if MacCabe is corrupt, how do we expose him?' Strangely asked.

'Well, you're the detective, not me, having been brought in to find Florence, which I can't help you with but I dearly wish I could. However, as part of your ongoing investigation you might want to lift a few stones on MacCabe's business activities and see what crawls out, and I may be able to point you in the right direction.'

'That would be exceedingly helpful.'

'Last night whilst I was thrashing you at billiards – correct me, Marjorie, if I'm wrong, but I believe I was up four frames to nil at the time – you told me how Sir Chester personally oversaw a tender and delivered it into the hands of the chairman of the British India Company himself, and that he subsequently won the tender. After which we had that rather unfortunate court case.'

'You're correct that you were giving me an abject lesson in the art of playing billiards.'

'*Sehr Gut*, quite so. Then you told me that he subsequently launched an internal inquiry into his whole tendering process, after which he won another British India Company contract. What does that tell you?'

'It tells me he has a problem in his procurement department.'

'Exactly, but more specifically it tells me that someone inside the Eastoff Shipbuilding Company had been working actively to prevent the company winning tenders, until Sir Chester personally stepped in. And whoever that person is, I would lay odds on, will lead you to MacCabe's front door.'

'Bloody hell. Fraud.'

'Yes, I believe so, and not a very honourable state of affairs.'

There was a knock on the door.

'*Kommen Sie.*'

A lady entered and handed the count an envelope.

'It's for you, Marjorie.'

'Thank you.' He read the contents of the telegram. 'I need to telephone Sir William in London. Would it be possible for you to arrange a call? I will pay for it, of course.'

'Nonsense, I will not hear of taking any payment. Give me the number and I will arrange the call. You can take it in here as I need to go and talk to my general manager. Give me a few moments.'

After about five minutes the phone on the count's desk started to ring as he entered the room. 'Marjorie, you pick it up; it is your call to London. I will be about half an hour and as it's just gone one o'clock, I think by then we will have earned some lunch. I pride myself on the culinary excellence of my staff canteen: my army marches on its stomach.'

With that, he clicked his heels, about-turned and left the room.

Strangely picked up the receiver. 'Ernest, may I speak to Wispy.'

Wispy brought him up to date on his meeting with MacCabe and his earlier meeting that morning with the Eastoffs.

'Bloody hell, we're dealing with a psychopath!'

'We certainly are, and we haven't got long to find him. I realise that at the moment, as far as Carcassonne is concerned you are looking for a needle in a haystack. But we are all certain here that Wanda is spot on, and that Florence is there or near there. So, you being there gives us a head start.'

'I can only marvel at Wanda's abilities,' said Strangely. 'The train to Paris leaves tomorrow morning at nine, so we will be on that.'

'You will also need assistance in Carcassonne so I'm going to contact Fabrice Barsalou to see if he can spare the time.'

'Ah, Fabrice. Try stopping him! He'll be absolutely bursting to get involved.'

Monsieur Fabrice Barsalou was the hotel proprietor of the Hôtel L'Enclos de L'Evêché in Boulogne-sur-Mer. He had been invaluable on their last case and saw himself as an amateur sleuth, and he had become a good friend.

'And how are you getting on with the count?'

'Exceedingly well in actual fact, a rather interesting fellow, and Constanza and I are quite warming to him. He's becoming more of an ally than an adversary.' He recounted their trip so far.

'I see, so the count looks like he's a non-runner.'

'Yes, at the moment he hasn't even left the stables.'

'So, from what you've just told me, Wanda and I should already be in Wallsend. I'll call Chester as soon as we finish and make the necessary arrangements. If I get hold of Fabrice and if he can help, I'll send you a telegram as confirmation.'

'Thanks, and Wispy?'

'Yes.'

'Brush up on your Geordie.'

'I've already started!'

The count returned and Strangely explained that they needed to leave for Paris in the morning.

'I will get you a reservation on tomorrow morning's train when we return from lunch, and I very much look forward to spending another evening with you. I think after dinner a fencing bout might be in order to see how good your conversation is!'

'I think Marjorie would prefer sticking to billiards, wouldn't you, darling?' Constanza said.

'Oh, I don't know, Connie, I rather fancy myself as a musketeer. Maybe D'Artagnan.'

'Really, darling. D'Artagnan wasn't a musketeer.'

'Oh?'

'No, he was a member of Des Essart's guards. I see you more as Aramis.'

'Right, Aramis it is. Reinhardt, prepare to be taught a lesson in the art of fencing.'

Constanza rolled her eyes heavenwards. 'On your head be it.'

'Come, Constanza, where's the sport in you? Marjorie will be fine.'

'Promise me, Reinhardt.'

'Of course. I can assure you no harm will befall him. You never know, I might give him a smile as a permanent memento of your stay at Schloss Delmenhorst.'

'I don't like the sound of that,' Constanza replied.

CHAPTER 11
FRIDAY, 11 AUGUST 1922
CHELSEA

Wanda and I needed to get to the Eastoff Shipbuilding Company PDQ. She went off to pack for a few days' stay and I sent Ernest off to make reservations on the Newcastle train for later that afternoon.

'Sir Chester, please, Strutton. It's Sir William.'

'One moment, Sir William.'

Chester came on the line, and I explained Strangely and the count's suspicions.

'Bloody Delmenhorst, he can keep his meddling aristocratic nose out of my business.'

'That's as may be but he makes some very pertinent points. When you won that contract to build those two cargo ships for the British India Company, did any staff involved in the tendering or procurement process leave?'

'How in God's name would I know? The tendering process was dealt with by my general manager, Mr Eamonn Babbage. I really only get involved at director level, so you'll have to ask him as he and his team deal with all staff-related issues.'

Maybe if he spent a little time looking under stones, he might find some answers. Let's hope he hasn't left it too late.

'I see. And after you launched your internal inquiry into the whole tendering process, did anyone leave?'

'How the hell do I know? I've just told you I don't get involved. It's way below my sphere of responsibility. You'll have to ask Babbage.'

'That I intend to do. Wanda and I are going to travel to Newcastle this afternoon. Can you call Babbage and tell him to expect us tomorrow morning, and can you recommend a hotel?'

'I will call him now and get him to look into any staff that might have left around the time when I won the first contract, and again when I launched the inquiry. That way you won't be wasting time when you get to the shipyard. As to staying in a hotel, I won't hear of it; you will stay at Eastoff House. Let me know the train you are on, and I will call Groves to meet you off it. I will also have my car at your disposal for the duration of your stay.'

Well, that is definitely an improvement.

'Thank you, that will certainly help make our time there as productive as it can be. I will call you once I know what train we are on.'

'Is that it?'

'Yes.' The line went dead. *Charming – maybe not such an improvement after all.*

Now, onto Fabrice.

'*Bonjour, puis-je parler à* Monsieur Barsalou?'

'*Qui puis-je dire appelle?*'

'Sir William Fescue.'

'*Juste un moment.*'

'Wispy, lovely to hear from you. It's only five minutes since we said goodbye to you in your wonderful village of Blakeney. So, to what do I owe this honour?'

I related the story so far.

'I can't leave Strangely and his lovely wife to the mercies of my fellow countrymen; I will travel to Paris tomorrow in plenty of time to meet him off the train from Bremen.'

'Thank you, Fabrice, good to have you on board.'

'The pleasure is all mine.'

As I put the receiver down, the telephone rang almost immediately. It was Tony.

'I've spoken to the commissioner and he is fully in agreement with our decision-making and, I might add, is extremely impressed with Wanda. Would you believe it, he even sends his regards.'

Well, dear Father, what do you make of that!

'Excellent news.' I related my conversation with Strangely.

'So, the French arm of your agency has swung into action.'

'It most certainly has.'

We said our goodbyes. I consulted my watch and it had just gone one thirty, time for lunch and to pack my case. Libby was in her studio at the top of the house. Its windows afforded wonderful views over the River Thames, with the Albert Bridge to our left, extending to Battersea Park beyond and Battersea Bridge on our right. The windows allowed the maximum amount of light to flood in, ideal for painting. She hadn't heard me enter and I kissed her on top of her head. 'Did you have a productive walk, darling?'

'Yes, I did. What do you think?'

She handed me her sketchbook. There were ten pencil sketches of a Chelsea Pensioner from all different angles.

Gosh, I wish I had her talent.

'They are superb. What an amazing face.'

'It is, and it tells its own story. I walked past the Royal Hospital and noticed him sitting on a bench outside the front, soaking up the sun's rays. I asked the guard on the main gate if I could go and talk to him, and he let me in. His name is Sergeant Major Gulliver Saxby, known as Gully, and he saw action in the Second Boer War. And he allowed me the privilege of sketching him.'

'I look forward to seeing how you transform your sketches into a portrait. Now, are you ready for some lunch?'

'I could eat something.'

'Well in which case I'll get Alice to make us some sandwiches. What do you fancy?'

'Do you know what I fancy right at this moment? Cold roast chicken with stuffing, a grind of pepper and some sea salt, a few tomatoes and game chips, and some of her home-made lemonade.'

'My mouth is watering already. I'll order the sandwiches and see you downstairs in twenty minutes as I need to go and throw a few things into a suitcase.'

'What?'

I sat down and went through the case to date.

'Well, just stay out of trouble.'

'Of course, Libby, you know me.'

'That's the point, I know you so well.'

The sandwiches hit the spot. We said our goodbyes with a hug and I promised to call later that evening. Wanda was back at the office and Ernest had booked us onto the ten past four to Newcastle, which was scheduled to arrive in Newcastle Central just after nine thirty. It had already gone three fifteen and I dispatched Ernest to go and find a cab. He returned ten minutes later.

As we were getting in, I remembered something that had been nagging me. 'Ernest, any results on the Brousses watermark?'

'No, Sir William. I've checked a few stationery suppliers and they've never heard of it, but don't you worry, I'll track it down.'

'Jolly good. Oh, and can you call Sir Chester and let him know our arrival time into Newcastle?' With that, we were off to King's Cross.

*

We pulled into Newcastle at nine forty having dined on the train. A porter assisted us with our luggage. As we left the platform, we noticed a man in a very smart butler's uniform. He was slightly greying, middle-aged, with a military bearing.

'Mr Groves?'

'Welcome to Newcastle, Sir William, Miss Cushway. I trust you had a pleasant journey?'

'We did indeed, Groves.'

We were soon seated in the comfort of the Eastoffs' Rolls-Royce Silver Ghost and on our way to the Eastoff estate near the village of Rothbury, some thirty-two miles north of Newcastle. The sun was starting to set as we arrived at the estate and we had our first glimpse of the house. It was certainly spectacular; although not necessarily to my taste, it certainly made a statement. Wanda described it as Germanic in appearance, worthy of a setting for one of Wagner's operas.

Groves showed us to our rooms. Wanda was given the Owl bedroom and I was in the Red bedroom. He said that cook had prepared a few sandwiches and when we were ready to come along to the drawing room.

The sandwiches were just what we needed. Groves informed us that breakfast would be at seven thirty, which would enable us to get to the shipyard for nine o'clock.

CHAPTER 12
SATURDAY, 12 AUGUST 1922
BREMEN

'*Guten Morgen*, I see your smile has already started to heal.'
Strangely's hand automatically touched the wound on his right cheek that he sustained in the lesson he received in the noble art of fencing, given to him by the count yesterday evening after dinner.

'Stop touching it and it will heal perfectly. Aren't you proud of him, Constanza?'

'I am proud of most of his achievements, but I'm not so sure of this one. I'm thankful that you only inflicted the smile, as you put it, and mercifully it's a small one, but I'm not happy, Reinhardt.'

'Oh, come, Constanza, it's his badge of honour. But I see you are not happy with me. Can you find it in your heart to forgive me?'

She looked at Strangely, who smiled at her and gave an implicit nod.

'Very well, I forgive you, on one condition.'

'Anything?'

'You never fence with my husband again.'

'You have my word as an officer.'

'In that case, I forgive you.'

'Thank you. Now, for breakfast I have had Chef prepare *Bauernomelett*, an omelette of bacon, onions and potatoes seasoned to perfection, which will set you up for your long journey. Oh, and a telegram arrived first thing for you, Marjorie, it's by your place setting. Coffee?'

The count rang his little bell and Stein entered the dining room almost immediately. 'Coffee for Herr and Frau Drye, please, and can you ask Chef to prepare a hamper for our guests' journey to Paris?'

Strangely slit the telegram open: 'Fabrice on board STOP Will meet you off your train in Paris.'

A broad smile spread across his face.

'Good news?'

'Yes, a friend of ours is meeting us in Paris.'

'*Sehr Gut*, then you can show off your duelling scar.'

Stein returned with the coffee, and they finished breakfast in a companionable conversation about field sports.

'Right, it's time to get you to the station.'

The count stood up, walked over to the full-length mirror, straightened his moustache and clicked his heels. '*Großartig! Kommen.*' Then he marched out of the room with Strangely and Constanza in his wake.

It was a beautiful sunny morning for a drive, with high cirrus clouds in the sky. At the station, a porter met them and followed them to their carriage and stowed the luggage on the train. The count escorted them into their first-class compartment and placed the hamper on the seat opposite. 'I wish you well in your attempts to find Florence Eastoff and trust you will find her safe and well. When you see Sir Chester, please give him my regards. I assure you I bear him no ill will, and in actual fact I have a grudging admiration for him. I have enjoyed your company and hopefully in the not-too-distant future we may be fortunate in that our paths will cross again.'

'I most certainly hope so,' replied Strangely.

The count shook his hand and kissed Constanza's and left the compartment. He waited on the platform and as the train started to pull away, he stood to attention and saluted. Strangely returned the compliment.

CHAPTER 13
SATURDAY, 12 AUGUST 1922
ROTHBURY

I walked into the dining room shortly before seven thirty, and Wanda was already there. I helped myself to a tomato juice, adding Worcestershire sauce, a splash of tabasco, a pinch of celery salt and a grind of black pepper. I sat down opposite her.

'Did you notice the portrait above the fireplace?' Wanda said.

'No, I didn't.' I got up and walked over to the painting. It was a portrait of Florence in what I would describe as a relaxed and soft style. The artist had caught her elegance.

'Have you seen who it's by?'

I took a closer look, and in the left-hand bottom corner was the signature Henri Matisse. 'Good Lord.'

Strutton entered. 'Good morning, Sir William, Miss Cushway. I trust you slept well. I see you are admiring our painting of Florence.'

'Yes, it's rather wonderful.'

'Quite, sir.'

'Really, Strutton. Might I suggest you keep your views to yourself in case Sir Chester gets wind of them?'

He gave me a perceptive nod accompanied by a nervous smile and took our beverage orders.

'Please help yourself to breakfast. I strongly recommend the kippers; they are smoked locally in Craster. William Robson bought the smokehouse off the Craster family in 1906 and is doing very well.'

The kippers were indeed very good, but not to Wanda's taste as she opted for scrambled eggs and smoked salmon.

*

Groves saw us off with a hamper for lunch and hoped for a successful day ahead of us. It was another beautiful day, and the drive through the picturesque rolling countryside, villages and farms was good for the soul. We arrived at the shipyard gates just before nine o'clock and were ushered straight through, pulling up outside a rather grand building. Wanda informed me that it was built in the Gothic Revival style, and I have to say it reminded me of the Palace of Westminster. On the steps leading up to the entrance stood a tall, bespectacled man with his arms behind his back, and if first impressions were anything to go by, he looked rather full of himself.

'Sir William, Miss Cushway, welcome to Eastoff Shipbuilding Company, alas under this terrible cloud of Miss Florence's disappearance. I'm Mr Babbage, general manager of all you see before you. Please follow me.'

Clearly modesty is not Babbage's strong suit – 'of all you see before you'! I wasn't aware we were in the presence of Charlemagne, Emperor of the Romans.

He showed us into his office which had views over his empire, and we accepted the offer of tea, which arrived in fairly short order.

'Sir Chester telephoned me yesterday and explained the situation. I assured him that on my watch I was one hundred per cent certain that nothing untoward had happened.'

'Please, let us be the judge—'

'Don't interrupt, Sir William. My tenure here as general manager is in its eleventh year, and nothing whatsoever escapes my attention, I can assure you. I run a very tight ship, if you pardon the pun, and Sir Chester holds me in the highest regard. My position here also gives me status in the local community, which allows me to influence—'

'Desist, Babbage, we are not interested in your status. What did Sir Chester ask you to do?'

He clasped both hands together and cleared his throat. 'He asked me to look into any staff that might have left around the time we won the first contract for the British India Company and when we launched the internal inquiry into our tendering process. Which, I might add, I led, and we found not one jot of evidence that our tendering process had been compromised.'

Gosh, why doesn't that surprise me?

'And did any staff leave?'

'Well in actual fact, yes, two did. Well, not so much as left but disappeared, on the first of March, the day after I started my inquiry. They failed to turn up for work and that was it, never to be seen again – puff, and they vanished into thin air. However, they were of absolutely no consequence whatsoever.'

'I see, and didn't that whet your managerial instincts that something may not have been quite right?'

'No, it didn't. As I've just said, they were of no consequence and as I said, I run a—'

'What did these two people of no consequence do, Mr Babbage?'

He cleared his throat again. 'They were clerks in the procurement department.'

'I'm assuming that these clerks, as they were of no consequence, had absolutely no authority. Am I correct in that assumption?'

'Umm, well, not exactly.' I noticed beads of sweat had started to appear across his forehead.

'How not exactly, Mr Babbage?'

'They were my number one and two in the department, my two most senior clerks in the office.'

'Good Lord, Babbage, your incompetence astounds me. And was Sir Chester not made aware of their sudden departure?'

'No, he wasn't.'

'And you saw fit not to mention this to him?'

'Sir Chester only deals with matters at director level.'

I must admit I am getting seriously annoyed with the excuse of matters not being discussed at director level. God, do the directors really not know what is going on in their business?

81

'I understand that, but surely two senior staff disappearing just as you were starting your inquiry might have sounded little alarm bells in that big head of yours, Mr Babbage?'

He stood up and walked over to the window and looked out across the shipyard.

'Mr Babbage, I'm waiting.'

He turned around, nervousness etched across his face. 'No, it didn't sound alarm bells. As I mentioned, they were of no—'

'You surprise me. You of course mentioned their disappearance in your inquiry findings?'

'No, I didn't.'

'Sit down, Babbage!'

He looked everywhere but at us. We stared at him for what must have been a minute. His discomfort was palpable.

'So, who exactly were these two people of no consequence?'

'A Mr Jack Potts and a Mr Florian Boutroux.'

He sat down and pushed their staff files across his desk.

'Thank you. May we borrow these for a while?'

'I'd rather they stayed here.'

'I'm sure you would, but I was trying to be polite. It is not a request, Babbage, it's more of a command.'

I put them into my briefcase. 'You mentioned they were your number one and two. Which was which?'

'Boutroux was the senior of the two.'

'I see, and did these two have any disciplinary marks against their names?'

'No, they had exemplary records.'

'And you didn't investigate their disappearance?'

'No, I didn't. If they had returned to work, I would have fired them for gross misconduct, and there's no shortage of applicants for their jobs. I actually promoted two internal junior clerks. Who, I might add, are doing an excellent job under my guidance.'

'Bloody Norah, why does that not surprise me? Is there anything more you've conveniently forgotten to mention and wish to add now?'

'No, I haven't anything more to add other than I wish you well in your search for Miss Eastoff.'

'Well on your present performance you seem to be more of a hindrance than a help. One last thing: do you have any recent pictures of either of them?'

'As a matter of fact, I do. We took some pictures at last year's annual procurement Christmas dinner and there's a couple on the wall in the department. If you'll bear with me, I'll go and get them.'

He returned with two framed pictures. 'There you go. Mr Boutroux is on the back row far left, just there, and the rotund Mr Potts is here, sitting next to me. Incidentally I gave a very amusing speech that evening which was well received.'

Good Lord, is there no end to the man's talent? Not only are we in the presence of a management guru, but a talented comedian as well. I am truly in awe!

'Really, well I don't think Sir Chester will find a single jot of amusement in your performance, far from it. He might even take a stick of celery to you, as Bloody Norah did back in the seventeenth century!'

We left a nonplussed Babbage with his mouth agape.

*

On the steps of the *porte cochère*, I turned to Wanda. 'I wouldn't trust Babbage as far as I could throw him. I'm going to get Ernest to do some digging into his background.'

Sitting in the back of Sir Chester's Silver Ghost, we read the two staff files. Jack Potts's address was Magpie Cottage, Church Bank, Newburn. Florian Boutroux's address was Pennine House, The Towne Gate, Heddon-on-the-Wall. We didn't know the local area at all and I asked Treadway, our chauffeur, where they were.

'They are two small parishes. Newburn is just over six miles away, whilst Heddon is over ten miles away.'

'In which case, Treadway, let's start with Potts.'

We arrived in Newburn, and Treadway sought directions to Church Bank. We must have stuck out like a sore thumb in the Rolls-

Royce and we were attracting a good deal of attention as we drove along. Eventually we pulled up in front of Magpie Cottage.

The cottage was quite large and in good order with a well-maintained front garden. It was covered in a beautiful, vivid pink climbing rose and as we neared the front door we were greeted by a wonderful fragrance. I knocked, and a few moments later a harassed woman opened the door, with two young children clinging to her skirt.

'Mrs Potts?'

'Yes?' I saw her eyes flicker nervously from me to Wanda and then to the Silver Ghost.

'Is Mr Potts in?'

'No, he isn't, so I must request that you leave.'

'Mrs Potts, we need to talk to you about your husband. We know he hasn't been to work since the first of March.'

She looked crestfallen and stared down at the front doorstep.

'You'd better come in.'

She led us through to a lovely kitchen. Everything was in its place and spotless. The outside door was open, letting the midday sun flood in. I caught a glimpse of the back garden and it too mirrored the front garden in being well tended and cared for.

'Please, sit down.'

We sat at the kitchen table and she pulled a chair out. 'Now, you two, run along outside as Mummy needs to talk to these people, and remember, play nicely.' They reluctantly left her side and went out into the garden.

'Mrs Potts, please allow me to introduce myself. I'm Sir William Fescue and this is Miss Wanda Cushway, and we urgently need to talk to your husband.'

'I urgently need to talk to him too. I haven't seen or heard from him since the evening of the twenty-eighth of February. He said he was going for a pint at the Boathouse and he never returned. I've been worried sick ever since. It's not like Jack at all. He loves his kids and me; we had a perfect life. Oh my God, help me, please. Where is he?'

She buried her head on her lap and started to cry. Wanda put her arm around her and hugged her.

God, I hated this. The poor woman was desperate and we were intruding on her distress. A wave of self-doubt hit me again; was I really cut out for this?

Right, Wispy, do something useful. Tea, that's what is required.

I got up and went over to the stove, grabbed the kettle, filled it and put it on the heat. I found the teapot and caddie and soon had a pot of tea brewing. By the time I placed a cup of tea in front of Mrs Potts, Wanda had managed to comfort her and she sat dabbing her eyes with Wanda's handkerchief.

'I'm sorry. I've tried to remain strong for the children but it's so hard. I'm scared. The mortgage hasn't been paid since March and I'm desperate as I'm now faced with eviction. Where on earth is he? And what have I done wrong to deserve this? My life was perfect until he disappeared. Now it's slowly being destroyed.'

'You've done nothing wrong, Mrs Potts. But have you any idea where he might be?' Wanda asked.

'No, I haven't. He's never done anything like this before. We've been married for over ten years and it is absolutely out of character. I reported him missing to the police the next morning after he didn't return from the Boathouse.'

'And what did they make of his disappearance?' I asked.

'They said from what I've told them it sounded out of character. They visited Eastoff Shipbuilding Company and interviewed the general manager, a Mr Babbage, who told them he couldn't explain his disappearance as he seemed totally content at work.'

So why didn't bloody Babbage mention that? He'll be lucky to have an empire left after this if I have anything to do with it!

I looked at Wanda and she raised an eyebrow.

'And have the police been in touch again?'

'Yes. Initially they called in often, but the visits tailed off and now he is just listed as a missing person. It sounds pathetic: "just listed as a missing person". That person is my husband, with his own personality, his own history, his own family and his own devoted wife. He's not just another statistic, he's a kind and gentle man.'

'Mrs Potts, did your husband ever mention a Mr Florian Boutroux?'

'Yes, he did, but only occasionally in passing as a senior work colleague. I've never met him and as far as I'm aware, they never socialised away from work. But can I ask why you are interested in talking to my Jack?'

'We've been engaged by Sir Chester Eastoff to investigate various issues, and one of these is to look into the role of his procurement department. We found it odd that Jack didn't show up for work on the first of March and we want to find out why.'

'If only I knew. But please, for the love of God, I implore you to find my Jack. He is the centre of our universe and we are struggling to carry on without him.'

'Mrs Potts, we will do whatever we can to find your husband. Did he ever mention a Mr Mungan MacCabe or MacCabe Shipbuilders on the Clyde?'

'No, he didn't.'

'Very well. In that case, Mrs Potts, we have no further questions, and I promise we will do our best to bring him back safely.'

She went into the garden with the children and we saw ourselves out.

*

Treadway suggested stopping for lunch and he pulled off the road onto an unmade track that led into a wood, and found a glade where he parked the car. He opened the boot and set up a picnic table and chairs, complete with a fine damask tablecloth and napkins. He set the table and placed the hamper on it. 'Mrs Harbottle is an excellent cook. Enjoy your lunch.'

'Please, Treadway, join us.'

'I'm perfectly well catered for, Sir William. Mrs Harbottle has prepared me a packed lunch.'

And with that, he returned to the car.

The picnic was a triumph, consisting of a raised pork pie with English mustard, quiche Lorraine, egg and cress sandwiches, potato salad, and a crisp green salad with vinaigrette, accompanied by pickled onions, pickled beetroot and pickled mushrooms; not quite in my league, but good nonetheless. To drink we had a choice of Pimm's or ginger beer, and to finish, a good slice of Keen's Cheddar, a Colston Bassett Stilton and biscuits. A perfect luncheon in a perfect setting.

We discussed the plight of Mrs Potts and her two children over our lunch. If her description of her husband was to be believed, he did not fit the profile of a psychopathic kidnapper.

We sat back and enjoyed the rays of the sun filtering through the surrounding trees.

'Look there,' said Wanda.

'Look at what, where?'

'Just there on the Stilton: a *Psyllobora vigintiduopuntata*.'

'A what?'

'A twenty-two-spot ladybird.' Wanda delved into her bag and brought out her sketchbook, coloured pencils and her magnifying glass. 'Here, take a look.'

I did; it was a beautiful yellow ladybird. 'I thought ladybirds were red?'

'There are fifty species of ladybirds in Britain and only three are yellow.' She opened her sketchbook and with great speed drew the insect.

'There,' she said, turning the book to me.

'Wanda, you've caught the likeness exactly.'

'Thank you. When I get home I will produce a far more detailed set of pictures and some watercolours of it.'

'I would love one of the watercolours if possible.'

'It will be my pleasure.'

Treadway returned shortly before two and packed away the picnic, and we were soon on our way to Heddon-on-the-Wall. Again, after seeking directions we found our way to Pennine

House, which struck us both as being much grander than the Potts's cottage.

Wanda knocked and immediately some dogs started barking. A few minutes later we were greeted by a woman in her dressing gown, smoking a cigarette and her hair in curlers, accompanied by two miniature poodles.

'Mrs Boutroux?'

'Who's asking?'

Charming!

'Allow me to introduce myself. I'm Sir William Fescue and this is Miss Wanda Cushway.'

'We don't often get knights of the bleeding realm visiting. What do you want?'

'We wish to speak to Mr Boutroux.'

'You and me both. He's not here. Well, not only is he not here, but I haven't seen the lazy wastrel since the twenty-eighth of February.'

'Might we come in?'

'I suppose so, if you must. Follow me.' She led us along the hall and into a drawing room, which was the complete opposite to Mrs Potts's kitchen. It was an untidy mess with magazines strewn all over the place, used coffee cups, full ashtrays, and a half-eaten plate of food that had congealed and was the focal point of a couple of bluebottles.

'Move some of those mags and sit yourselves down on the sofa.'

The sofa looked as though we might stick to it.

'Thank you, but we prefer to stand.'

'Suit yourself.' She stubbed her cigarette out and promptly lit another one.

'Have you any idea where he has gone?'

'Before I answer that, why are you interested in Florian?'

'We've been engaged by Sir Chester Eastoff to investigate various issues, and one of these is to look into the role of his procurement department. We found it odd that Mr Boutroux didn't show up for work on the first of March and we want to find out why.'

'I see. No, I haven't got a clue as to his whereabouts.'

'Did you report him missing to the police?'

'No, I most certainly didn't. As far as I'm concerned, it's good riddance to bad rubbish. He was bloody useless and I'm better off without him. The only sensible things he achieved were to buy this place outright and buy me my business in Newcastle, Boutroux's Poodle Emporium. I have a very extensive client list, you know, and am famed for my coloured tints.'

I'm sure she is, whatever she's talking about, but I did notice that her two poodles had a pink tinge to them.

'Really? How terribly fascinating. What was he like?'

'He was very boring, unadventurous, but good at figures and analysis. Hence his job, I suppose. I can't quite remember what attracted me to him. It wasn't his looks, I can assure you, but maybe it was his money. We've only been married two years and that's been the longest two years of my life. Since his disappearance I've made my mind up and I'm going to seek a divorce.'

'Did he ever mention a Mr Mungan MacCabe or MacCabe Shipbuilders on the Clyde?'

'No, he didn't.'

'Boutroux: is that a French name?'

'It is.'

'And what part of France did he hail from?'

'Hail from! He was born and bred a bleeding Geordie. He claims he can speak French but as far as I'm aware, the only French he knows are the numbers from one to ten and the song "Sur le Pont d' Avignon", which his mother taught him.'

'So, you don't know the part of France his family came from?'

'No, I don't. You'll have to ask his father.'

'We will. Can you please give us his address?'

'No, I can't. I only met him once and that was at our wedding. Florian doesn't get on with him on account he divorced his mother years ago and he has never forgiven him. He used to work at Eastoff Shipbuilding so I assume they would have a record of him.'

'Did he ever mention a Jack Potts?'

'Yes, often, and he was always derisory about him, saying he was a fat lump of lard and a little goody two shoes.'

Wanda and I exchanged glances. 'And what do you think he meant by that?'

'He used to say that he was far too diligent in his work and lacked ambition.'

'Interesting. Is there anything else you can tell us about Florian?'

'Not really, but if you do find him, tell him not to bother coming home. Oh, and tell him I'm applying to the court for a divorce.'

'Thank you, Mrs Boutroux, you've been remarkably helpful.'

She lit another cigarette and blew the smoke at them, which Wanda wafted away. 'Anything to get that bleeding wastrel out of my life. Now, I must get on and do some housework.'

'Really, it's so nice to meet someone who is so house proud. Goodbye.'

Wanda and I walked slowly back to the car.

'Well, what do you make of that?' I asked.

'We know one new fact about him and that is he has money, far more money than a senior clerk would earn.'

'Exactly. Now we need to find out why. I need to get hold of Babbage.'

*

Treadway pulled the car over at a telephone box and I phoned the shipyard. I got back in and handed him an address in Whitley Bay.

'We're off to the seaside.'

It took us an hour to drive there and we drove in along the promenade and past the Pleasure Gardens. The town was bursting with holidaymakers and day trippers. We pulled up outside a terraced house in Warkworth Avenue.

An extremely rotund man answered the door; his shirt was bursting at the buttons trying to contain his large belly. He shielded his eyes from the sun and squinted at us.

'Mr Boutroux?'

'That's me. What do you want?' His accent was an interesting mix of French and Geordie.

'We're trying to find your son. He's been missing since the twenty-eighth of February.'

'I haven't seen or heard from him since his wedding day, two years ago.'

'Can we come in?'

'I suppose so, but I doubt I'll be able to help.'

He turned around and wheezed his way down the hall into his drawing room, which was neat and tidy. A strong sickly sweet odour of mothballs greeted us, which I'm sure was contributing to his wheezing.

'You have an advantage over me. You know my name, but I don't know yours. Please, sit down.'

'I'm Sir William Fescue and this is Miss Wanda Cushway. I'll cut to the chase, Mr Boutroux. We need to find Florian PDQ. Would you have the slightest inkling as to where he might have gone?'

'No, I wouldn't have a clue. As I said, I haven't seen him in ages. Our relationship was somewhat strained. I would actually say we are estranged. He worshipped the ground his mother walked on, and after we divorced when he was ten years old, she walked out and he never forgave me. He tolerated me and we were companionable when required to be. He only invited me to the wedding because Mabel, his fiancée, insisted on inviting me.'

'Boutroux is a French surname, is it not?'

'It most certainly is.'

'When did you arrive here in Britain?'

'It was in April 1884 that my wife and I moved here for me to seek better employment. Monique was pregnant at the time and Florian was born here in August.'

'You got a job at the Eastoff Shipbuilding Company?'

'Yes, I did, as a fitter. I was fully qualified and did my apprenticeship in the Port of Carcassonne on the Canal du Midi.'

I glanced at Wanda and a slight smile crossed her lips.

'You lived in Carcassonne?'

'No, we didn't. Monique and I rented a smallholding near Montlaur under the shadow of the Alaric mountain, which was some twenty-four kilometres from Carcassonne. She worked on the smallholding, whilst I cycled into Carcassonne six days a week to work in the port. It was a tough existence, and when the landlord put the rent up we could no longer make ends meet, so we chose to move to Newcastle where we knew there were jobs for skilled workers in the shipyards. It was me who made the decision to move. Monique never wanted to leave; she was young, just turned eighteen.'

'I read in Florian's personnel file that he followed in your footsteps as an apprentice fitter at Eastoff's.'

'Then you will have read that he had a bad accident and lost the sight in his left eye when a fragment of a red-hot rivet embedded itself in it. He eventually returned to work but could no longer manage to do the job as a fitter, so he was given a desk job in the procurement department.'

'And excelled there,' said Wanda.

'He did. He was naturally bright and good with figures.'

'How would you describe your son's character?' she continued.

'He was always quiet and thoughtful, but when his mother left he withdrew into himself, into his own world, and after the accident he was prone to mood swings.'

'I see. Where do you think Monique went?'

'She always wanted to live in Paris, so she may have gone there, but in all honesty, I don't know.'

'Is there anything else you could tell us about your son?'

'Not really, only that I wish things could have worked out differently.'

We both noticed that tears were slowly running down his cheeks. So, we quietly stood up and left him to his thoughts in his armchair and let ourselves out.

It was good to be outside again in the early evening sun. We walked to the car where Treadway had gathered a small crowd of boys. He had the bonnet up and was pointing out various parts of the engine. I consulted my watch; it was past six o'clock.

'I see you've got quite a fan club, Treadway.'

'Yes, Sir William, they are as keen as mustard to know everything about the car. Right, lads, you'd better run along as we need to get going.'

They all stood back as he opened the door for Wanda and we climbed in. We gave the boys a cheery wave and we were off back to Eastoff House.

I called Libby before dinner and she relayed her conversation with Fabrice about the arrangements he had put in place so far in Carcassonne, and I brought her up to date with where we were. She was genuinely amazed that I hadn't sustained any injuries so far. I said I hoped to be back by mid to late afternoon tomorrow depending on the vagaries of the Sunday rail timetables.

Next, I telephoned Tony. We were discussing today's developments when I heard Mrs Finkelstein calling his name. He explained that the wonderful Mrs Finkelstein was in the process of serving his dinner of matzo ball soup and her home-made dill pickles. We finished our conversation and Tony promised to bring me a jar of her pickles on Monday morning, when we were to meet at eight o'clock in the Regency Café.

CHAPTER 14
SATURDAY, 12 AUGUST 1922
PARIS

The train pulled into Paris at seven o'clock that evening. The journey was tedious, but Strangely and Constanza were buoyed up by the excellent hamper of fine meats, cheeses, pickles, bread and fruit that the count's chef had prepared and had kept them company through the long journey.

A porter struggled to load their cases onto his barrow, and followed them along the platform. Fabrice was there at the ticket barrier and they greeted each other warmly.

'*Mon Dieu!* What is happening to your face?'

'I sustained it in a duel with Count von Delmenhorst yesterday evening.'

'*Quelle folie!*'

'Yes, I know, Fabrice. It was, as you rightly point out, a mad thing to do, but I must say once it is fully healed I think it will add a certain *je ne sais quoi*, don't you think?'

'If you say so, but what do you think, Constanza?'

'I think that it will give him bragging rights for years to come, but I'm still not happy.'

They made their way across Paris to Gare Montparnasse and boarded a train to Bordeaux Saint-Jean, changing there for the train to Carcassonne. They arrived the following morning, shortly before seven thirty, and took a taxi to the Hôtel de la Cité.

Fabrice explained that a good hotelier friend of his, Monsieur

Gaillot, had with great foresight left Boulogne in 1908 after purchasing a former bishop's residence that formed part of the south-west wall of the Cité. It was next to the Basilica Saint-Nazaire.

They entered the hotel and were assailed by a wonderful mix of neo-Gothic and art deco styles. Monsieur Gaillot was behind the reception desk and warmly greeted his old friend Fabrice, and introductions were made.

Monsieur Gaillot showed them into the restaurant where they had a breakfast of a selection of viennoiseries, tartine with butter and the hotel's wild blueberry conserve, and coffee. Then they retired to their rooms for a well-earned rest.

CHAPTER 15
SUNDAY, 13 AUGUST 1922
ROTHBURY

Groves had made reservations on the ten past ten train to London, and we met for breakfast at seven thirty. At eight he informed me my telephone call was connected to the Hôtel de la Cité and I went into Chester's study to take it.

'Bonjour. Monsieur Drye, s'il vous plait.'

'Qui dois-je dire appelle?'

'Sir William Fescue.'

'Un instant, Sir William, j'irai le chercher.'

After about five minutes Strangely came on the line. 'Sorry about that, Wispy, Constanza and I were just recharging the batteries. It's been a long twenty-four hours.'

'Blast, sorry to disturb, you must be exhausted, but Wanda and I are leaving for the station shortly and I've got some important information for you to get your teeth into today.'

I related the events of yesterday.

'Very well, we'll get out to the village of Montlaur and find this smallholding.'

'Take care. Did you remember your revolver?'

'Of course, on both counts. I'll call you at home this evening with any updates.'

'Excellent, because I'm meeting Tony tomorrow morning at eight o'clock.'

We said our farewell to Groves and thanked him for looking after us. He said he would pray for a successful conclusion to our hunt for Florence and hoped to welcome us here again in less traumatic times.

Treadway drove us to Newcastle Central station, and we thanked him for his sterling driving efforts the day before.

I got back to Salthouse, caught up with Libby and took a long hot bath, which rejuvenated me and lifted my spirits slightly as my little friend self-doubt had been sitting on my shoulder, nagging me that as today was drawing to a close, it only left five days in which to find Florence.

Libby took me to her studio and showed me the start she had made on the portrait of Sergeant Major Gulliver Saxby. She had been experimenting with modernism for some time now, and this was going to be her first portrait embracing the new style. I liked what I was looking at and gave her a hug. She sensed something was wrong and I told her of my doubts.

She grabbed me by the hand. 'Come on, what we need is a large gin and tonic and a chat.' We went down to the drawing room and she prepared the drinks.

By the time we had finished talking, my anxieties and self-doubt had been kicked into the long grass, and I was looking forward to the challenges of the week ahead. She had arranged that supper would be served informally where we were, and I was delighted that Alice had prepared one of my favourite comfort foods of Cumberland sausages, mashed potato, cabbage and lashings of onion gravy. Bloody marvellous.

We had just settled down to listen to a few of our latest jazz records when Eleanor knocked and came in. 'Excuse me, Sir William, Lady Fescue, Mr Drye's on the telephone. Where would you like to take the call?'

'I'll take it in my study.'

I sat down at my desk and picked up the receiver.

CHAPTER 16
SUNDAY, 13 AUGUST 1922
CARCASSONNE

Although tired after their long journey, Strangely and Constanza were itching to get on with the job in hand.

Strangely knocked on Fabrice's door and summarised his call with Wispy and the need to get to Montlaur PDQ. They agreed to meet in reception at ten o'clock.

Strangely put the agency's fairly new 35mm American Tourist Multiple camera in his well-worn leather satchel along with his binoculars, notebook, sunglasses and revolver. He was wearing a cream linen suit which could have done with an iron and sporting a panama hat that had seen better days. Constanza, on the other hand, looked immaculate, dressed in a yellow silk summer dress, with white sandals on her feet and a wide-brimmed white floppy hat with a matching yellow silk ribbon tied around it that flowed down her back. It was just before ten when they headed downstairs.

Fabrice was already there, poring over a map with Monsieur Gaillot.

'Bastien has put his car at our disposal for as long as we need it, and his chef is just finishing preparing a picnic hamper. Here, look at the map. We're here and this is the village of Montlaur. It should take us about an hour to get there.'

The chef appeared and handed the hamper to Bastien. 'Come, your chariot awaits.'

His car, a Citroën B Torpedo, was parked outside the front of the hotel with the top down and he placed the hamper in the back. 'Enjoy your trip to Montlaur.'

Fabrice drove and as they passed through the communes of Trèbes, Fonties d'Aude and Monze, he explained that they were renowned for their truffles. They arrived in Montlaur and headed north towards the Alaric mountain, and as they approached the foothills they spotted a large farmhouse in the distance at the end of a valley, about half a mile away. They parked and surveyed the scene.

'Look there.' Strangely handed Constanza his binoculars.

'Got it, and there's a copse on the right about two hundred yards from the farmhouse, where we should be able to observe it without being seen.'

'Right, let's go,' said Fabrice.

A short track led into the copse where they parked the car out of sight and found a spot that had an unrestricted view of the farm and the river beyond. There were about twenty Gascon cows grazing, and moving skittishly amongst them was a herd of goats. Off to the left of the farmhouse was a pigsty, and chickens were roaming all over the smallholding, scratching and pecking at the ground. The scene looked idyllic.

They made themselves comfortable at the edge of the copse behind some bushes, which successfully camouflaged them. Strangely surveyed the scene through his binoculars and other than the farm animals there was no sign of life.

An early lunch was in order as breakfast had been a while ago. Fabrice spread out a tablecloth and laid out three ramekins containing rillettes of pork, three individual quiche Lorraines, a tomato and red onion salad, a radicchio and frisée salad, a jar of cornichons, a jar of vinaigrette, Roquefort and a Tomme des Pyrénées. This was accompanied by a large, freshly baked baguette and a bottle of Chardonnay from the local vineyard of Domaine de Domneuve, which Fabrice informed us was literally a couple of kilometres up the road.

This was all very pleasurable but time was pushing on. The church clock in Montlaur was striking the hour of four when they heard the sound of a tractor in the distance. It grew louder as it passed behind them on the road and reappeared shortly afterwards on the track to the farm. It was towing a flatbed trailer. A woman emerged from the farmhouse to greet the man driving the tractor. Strangely trained his binoculars on her and she appeared to be in her mid-fifties, tall with strong features. The man seemed of a similar age and very muscular. They greeted each other warmly with a kiss and went back inside the farmhouse.

A few moments later they came back out and started to walk up the field towards the herd of Gascon cows, which was about ten yards away from their observation post. Strangely managed to take several pictures of them before they started to herd the cows back down the field towards what they assumed was the milking parlour.

'Blast, that's not what I was expecting.'

'No, it's not,' replied Constanza. 'Wispy was right: we are looking for a needle in a haystack, and we might have found the haystack over there, but certainly no needle!'

'Just a middle-aged couple running their smallholding. Bloody hell, this is absolutely useless.'

'Shall we return to Carcassonne?' enquired Fabrice.

'Not yet. Let them finish the milking and we'll pay them a visit. We know this is the smallholding that was once farmed by the Boutrouxs, despite it being over thirty-eight years ago. You never know, they might be able to tell us something of its history, but I fear we are grasping at straws.'

The church clock had just struck the half hour and it was five thirty when the cows filed out of the milking parlour and wandered back up the field.

'Very well, let's pay them a visit.'

They drove down the track and pulled up outside the farmhouse. The front door was wide open. Fabrice knocked on the door.

'Bonjour,' Fabrice called out.

'Bonjour, bonjour,' came the reply as the large muscular man strode with purpose down the hallway to meet them. 'What brings you good people to our farm on this lovely Sunday evening? Shouldn't you be worshipping the Lord at evensong?'

'Not really. We'd like to ask you a few questions about your farm.'

'Really? Well, I can tell you straight away it's not for sale.' He kept up the hail-fellow-well-met tone to his voice, but they noticed a flicker of concern cross his face.

'I can assure you we have no interest in purchasing your farm. We are looking for a missing person.'

'A missing person? I can't see how we can help, but you'd better come in. I'm Jean-Pascal Lacroix. Come, come.' He led them down the hallway into a huge area more like a restaurant kitchen than a domestic one. Dried herbs hung from the rafters, and on the massive pine dresser, jars of spices formed a line from one end to the other. A butcher's block stood in the corner and a large floor-standing mincer stood next to it, both spotlessly clean.

'Darling, we have visitors. Please allow me to introduce my wife, Odette. And you are?'

'Please allow me to introduce Monsieur and Madame Drye, and I'm Monsieur Fabrice Barsalou.'

'You are most welcome. Darling, glasses for our visitors, please, and I will open a bottle of my own red wine. Give me a moment and I will go down to the cellar. Please take a seat.'

As they sat down at the large pine table in the middle of the room, Constanza noticed six watercolours on one of the walls and went over and studied each one. Jean-Pascal returned with a bottle of wine in his hand.

'Ah, I see you are admiring Odette's lovely paintings; just another of her many talents.'

'You are very gifted, Odette,' said Constanza. She didn't reply to the compliment, but just nodded and smiled nervously.

'*Ta bonne santé.*' Jean-Pascal raised his glass.

Strangely and Constanza exchanged glances before gingerly taking a sip, fearing the worst, but were both pleasantly surprised; it was very good.

'Ah, I see you were expecting vinegar! I pride myself on the wine I produce and have won many plaudits at our local wine festival. So, you are here about a missing person. Why, might I ask?'

'We are looking for a Florian Boutroux,' replied Fabrice. 'Our research has revealed that his parents worked this smallholding for a while up until April 1884, when they moved to Newcastle in England. Florian was born there, and he went missing on the twenty-eighth of February this year. It's vital that we find him.'

'How very intriguing. But alas, we can't help you. We moved here twenty years ago. My trade is as a butcher and we own a shop in Carcassonne. We started to sell our own range of charcuterie and it took off. We didn't have enough room to produce our range so we bought this place. My brother and his wife run the butcher's shop for us, allowing Odette and myself to produce our range of charcuterie here. We also produce our own cheese, which has won many awards and which we mature in the caves high up on the hill not too far from here. It's the air passing through the caves that helps that process. Our shop sells our range of products, whilst we visit the surrounding towns on their respective market days doing the same. It's hard work but very rewarding.'

'It sounds fascinating and if we had more time, it would be most interesting to watch you make your charcuterie and cheese. Maybe at some point in the future that could be arranged?'

'It would be our pleasure.'

'Thank you, Jean-Pascal, Odette. It's been nice meeting you and thank you for your hospitality, but now we must be going.'

'Sorry we could not be of more help.'

They stood and waved as they headed back up the track to the road, where they turned left towards Montlaur and the road back to Carcassonne. The evening sunshine was pleasant but it failed to lift their spirits.

'Well, what did you make of the Lacroixs?' Constanza asked.

'He seemed a pleasant fellow and obviously they are hardworking, and I imagine quite successful. I found it slightly odd that Odette did not utter one word, even when you complimented her on her watercolours,' replied Strangely.

'Yes, I found that strange, and I thought his demeanour was slightly forced,' said Fabrice.

'Maybe she's just used to him talking ten to the dozen and has decided that there's no point in joining in.'

'A fair point, Connie. However, we are back to square one. "I wasted time and now time doth waste me!" I wonder if Sir Chester could buy us more time, because at this rate we're never going to find her.'

They arrived back at their hotel, and Strangely arranged a call to Wispy before they sat down to dinner. The last two days were beginning to catch up with them, but a long soak in the bath had the desired effect of restoring their spirits. They went down to reception shortly before nine and he was directed to a telephone box where the call was connected to London.

Wispy picked up the receiver and Strangely appraised him of their day. Despite the setback and the pressure of the sands of time running against them, they both managed to convince themselves they were on the right track.

CHAPTER 17
MONDAY, 14 AUGUST 1922
CARCASSONNE

Strangely and Constanza went down for breakfast, having slept the sleep of the dead. When they had woken, something was bothering her but for the life of her she couldn't put her finger on it. Fabrice was already down, and they joined him and ordered eggs and bacon and a pot of coffee. The restaurant was fairly full and as Constanza looked about her, she noticed a few interesting paintings on the wall. Then it dawned on her. Odette's watercolours. She explained her thoughts, and straight away after an excellent breakfast they were heading back to the village of Montlaur.

*

They pulled up outside the farmhouse and Strangely knocked on the door. There was no answer so he knocked harder, but still no answer, so they circuited the house, peering into windows. No sign of life. They noticed the cows were showing signs of distress because they hadn't been milked. They found themselves outside the kitchen where they had sat yesterday and drunk Lacroix's wine. Again, there was no sign of life from within. They tried the back door but it was locked.

'Very well, Fabrice, we need to break in.'

The back door was a solid affair and in the end they both took a run at it and shoulder-charged into it. It gave way with a large crack of splintering wood, and they ended up sprawling on the floor. Constanza walked in across the flattened door and went over to the watercolours.

'Chop, chop, you two, now's not the time to lay down on the job. Come here.' They got up and dusted themselves down and joined her.

'You see this picture here?' She pointed at a lovely, well-executed watercolour of a bridge with a stream flowing under it and beautiful, vivid green foliage tumbling down the sides of the steep riverbanks. 'Strangely, tell me where that is.'

He peered at the painting for a few moments then shrugged his shoulders.

'Darling, sorry, I haven't a clue.'

'That is Jesmond Dene, a famous park in Newcastle if I'm not mistaken.'

She took the picture down and turned it over. 'There, it's titled *Jesmond Dene* by Odette Lacroix. And look at this one; this is a painting of the well-preserved narrow medieval alleyways and lanes of Newcastle. Look again; it's titled *The Old City Chares* by Odette Lacroix. Now why would there be two paintings of scenes of Newcastle hanging on their kitchen wall?'

'I don't know, darling.'

'Oh, come on, Strangely, exercise that grey matter of yours.'

'Very well. Odette has connections to Newcastle.'

'Good. Let me float an idea: is there a possibility that in another life Odette is none other than Monique Boutroux?'

'That is indeed a possibility. You clever old thing.'

'Less of the old.'

'Sorry, darling. Let me get some pictures of them.' He took out the American Tourist Multiple and photographed the two paintings front and back and replaced them on the wall.

'Right, let's search the place for any clues as to their whereabouts.'

They found what looked like an office and methodically went through all the paperwork on the desk and then through the drawers one by one. It was all mostly business related. They emptied the contents of the bottom drawer, again all business related.

Strangely took the drawer out. 'Look at this; there's a false bottom to it. See, if I put my thumb at the top of the drawer and my index finger at the bottom, it measures five inches. Now if I do the same on the outside, it measures six inches.'

'Gosh, you're right, darling.'

'Fabrice, please can you get me a knife from the kitchen?'

'Coming up.'

Strangely took the knife and used it to lever up the false bottom until he could get his fingers underneath, and lifted it out. They were greeted by an empty compartment.

'Bloody hell, what's the point of a false drawer with nothing in it? Damn and blast the thing!' He replaced the false bottom and the contents of the drawer. 'What now?'

'Look at this picture.'

Strangely and Fabrice wandered across to Constanza who was looking intently at a painting on the wall opposite the desk.

'What grabs your attention?'

They both stared at the painting. 'Well, darling, it looks like another well-executed watercolour by Odette Lacroix of a restaurant on a busy street.'

'It is, but what grabs your attention?' They both peered again at the painting. 'Fabrice?'

'It's twice the size of the watercolours in the kitchen.'

'Yes, that's correct, but what else strikes you?'

They both re-examined the painting.

'Look!' Strangely took the painting off the wall. 'The depth of the frame is far too big.'

'Bravo. See if you can find me a pair of pliers.' They turned and sprinted from the room, managing to both get stuck in the door frame as they tried to go through it together. They returned a few moments later with their prize.

Constanza had used the knife to cut away the framing tape and now used the pliers to remove the pins holding the backing board. She lifted the board out, but instead of being greeted by the back of the watercolour, their eyes met a black leather portfolio. She carefully extracted it, opened it, and removed a couple of what looked like legal documents. She passed them to Strangely who then passed them to Fabrice.

'What we have here is an *Acte Authentique*, which is a deed of sale, and an *Attestation*, which is a certificate of purchase of property. The property in question is Apartment 14, 5–7 Rue de la Bastille, Paris. The date of purchase was May the nineteenth, 1910.'

'So, their butchery and charcuterie business obviously has its rewards. An apartment in the capital, no less. We need to get to Paris *tout de suite*.' Strangely took out his notebook and wrote all the details down. He then photographed the deeds and the frame, front and back, before handing them to Constanza, who replaced them in the picture frame.

They went through all the downstairs rooms and then the first floor, but found nothing more of interest and ended up back in the kitchen. They pulled out drawers and looked in cupboards, with no results. Just as they were about to give up, Strangely noticed something. Hanging from a hook on the dresser was an ancient iron key with a label attached. He took it off the hook.

'"The top barn, Château Domaine de Domneuve". We need to find this place. But before we do, those cows out there need our help; they desperately need milking.'

'Well, we can kill two birds with one stone. Let's go to the *mairie* to report the disappearance of the Lacroixs and get help for the cows, and they can give us directions to Château Domneuve.'

'Very logical, Connie, I'm impressed.'

'So you should be.'

*

They secured the back door as best they could and headed into Montlaur and parked outside the *mairie*. Thirty-odd minutes later and after wading through much bureaucracy they were on their way to the château.

The château was situated at the end of an avenue of plane trees surrounded on either side by vineyards rising away up the gentle

107

slope of a hill. They drove slowly up the hill and as they neared the apex, a château came into view on their right. As they passed it, they noticed a sign over the gates: 'Domaine de Domneuve'. They drove on.

'Look there, at the top of the hill.' Strangely pointed.

'Yes, I see it. Let me pull the car over into these woods so it's out of sight.'

At the top of the hill five hundred yards further on was a barn. Strangely grabbed his satchel and they made their way up through the woods to its edge, where they had a clear view of the barn. He trained his binoculars over the building: nothing. He passed them across to Constanza.

They had been watching for a few minutes when the sound of the Montlaur church clock carried to them, announcing the hour of midday.

Strangely took his revolver out of his satchel. 'Right, Connie, wait here. When it's clear I'll call you up. Come on, Fabrice.'

They both ran the thirty yards in a crouched position until they reached the wall of the barn. The arrow slits were too high to peer through. They slowly edged their way towards the large, heavy door. 'I will unlock the door and then on my count of three I will fling it open and we'll both run in, screaming and raging for all we're worth, and dive for the nearest bit of cover. Are you all right with that?'

Fabrice gave the thumbs up.

Strangely edged the last few yards to the door and to his amazement there was no lock. It looked like it had been recently removed. There was a large iron ring which he grabbed with his left hand. He checked his revolver in his right hand, and in no more than a whisper counted one, two, three. He flung the door open and the pair of them, sounding like screaming banshees, hurtled headlong into the barn. Fabrice dived behind a tractor and Strangely threw himself behind some bales of hay.

Total and utter silence. Strangely poked his head over the top of the bales and surveyed the scene.

There were two large grape presses in the middle of the barn and two large wooden vats sited on each side of the building. Light streamed in through the arrow slits on the opposite wall and dust motes were dancing in the light. Another large door was set into the far wall. Above them was a mezzanine which covered half the building and was accessed by a wooden ladder. Strangely stood up and tucked his revolver into its holster, then went back outside and waved to Constanza to join them.

'There's no one here, Connie.'

'So why did the Lacroixs have a key to this barn?'

'That's an interesting question, darling, considering there's no lock on the door.'

'Well, the key must fit a lock somewhere.'

'It must, but not here.'

They proceeded to search the ground floor and discovered the usual accoutrements of agriculture: spades, forks, rakes, hoes, pitchforks and scythes. Fabrice climbed the ladder to the mezzanine floor.

'Nothing up here except sacks of wheat seeds.'

'So, in God's name why do they have a key to the top barn? This is the bloody top barn, and there's not a single sign of anyone using it for anything other than tending the vineyards.'

'As I said, darling, the key must fit a lock somewhere. Come on, let's regroup outside in the warmth of the sun.'

They stood and surveyed their surroundings: nothing except dense woods to the right and left. They walked around the back of the barn and the vineyards stretched out into the distance to more woods beyond. As they returned to the front of the barn, the church clock struck the half hour.

'Look there!' Strangely pointed to the woods on the right. 'A small path. Can you see it?'

'Yes,' replied Constanza.

'Come on, let's see where it leads to.'

They set off, and once into the wood, the density of the overhead canopy cut off most of the sunlight, with just dappled light breaking through and playing tricks as it danced on the woodland floor. The path ran level for about fifty yards then descended rapidly. After another two hundred-odd yards, Strangely suddenly stopped, held his hand up and motioned them off the path and into the wood.

In an urgent, hushed whisper, he said, 'There's another barn down there at the bottom of the hill, in a glade.' He led them through the wood to the edge of the glade where they had a good view of the barn without being observed. It was similar to the top barn but completely covered in ivy. There was no sign of an entrance on the side of the building. Along the top, underneath the eaves was a row of four round windows. He passed his binoculars to Constanza.

'I can't see any sign of life. This time we'll use stealth. Fabrice, you go clockwise around the edge of the glade, and we'll go the other way and meet you at the far side.'

They stared at the same ivy-clad walls, again with four round windows underneath the eaves. A wide run of stone steps led up to a pair of rusted wrought-iron gates that filled a large stone arched doorway, beyond which was a whitewashed vestibule. Above the doorway was a black Cathar cross. They stood and listened for any sounds of life, but all they heard was the chatter of birds and in the distance the cawing of a murder of crows.

'Come on,' Strangely whispered, and they broke cover and walked out into the sunlit glade. They stood at the bottom of the stone steps and listened intently, but couldn't detect any sounds from inside the building so they approached the stone steps. There was no lock on the gates and they protested at being pushed open. At the end of the vestibule on the right-hand side was a heavy wooden door.

'Look there, that looks like it doesn't belong,' Constanza said, pointing at the lock on the door.

'You're right, darling. It appears that it has recently been fitted.'

Strangely took the key from his briefcase and after some initial resistance, the lock opened. He pushed the door open and the three of them stood in astonished silence and awe. What greeted them was a chapel with a beautiful vaulted ceiling covered in exquisite religious scenes. The walls were adorned in iconic images of the stations of the cross. They noticed a foetid smell hanging in the air. Entering, their focus was drawn to the altar, but there was no crucifix or candlesticks upon it. As they approached, they noticed cans of food consisting mostly of corned beef, haricot beans, cannellini beans, tinned tomatoes and fruit. There was a large sack of potatoes leaning against the side of the altar, and the floor was strewn with discarded tins that had attracted the attention of many flies, who were now angrily buzzing around after being disturbed. At one end of the altar was a Primus stove and various pots, pans, enamel plates and mugs that looked as though they had never been washed. Behind the altar they discovered a crucifix and candlesticks up against the wall and two filthy mattresses spread out on the floor.

'Well, it would appear that someone has been living here, and whoever they are must have been known to the Lacroixs. Right, let's start at the back of the chapel and see if we can shed any light on who was here.'

They spread out. Constanza took the right side, Fabrice the left and Strangely the middle. They looked under every pew and tuffet, moved the lectern, looked under the priest's stone sedilia and the altar, but found nothing.

'Here, Fabrice, give me a hand to move these foul-smelling mattresses.'

What greeted them was a square wooden trapdoor, hinged on both sides, with two large iron rings set into the centre of each door. They each grabbed a ring and pulled the doors up and lowered them carefully onto the floor. The three of them stared into a dark abyss, with stone steps leading down into it.

'Fabrice, grab those two candlesticks and light them, please.'

Strangely led the way, followed by Constanza, with Fabrice bringing up the rear, and they descended the steps. The light from their candles danced off a vaulted ceiling; this time it was plain but nonetheless beautiful in its simplicity. As they reached the bottom of the steps, it was apparent they had entered a crypt. On both sides four stone ledges ran the length of the crypt, and every space was taken up with coffins from centuries ago. They slowly walked towards the end wall and their candles started to pick out a simple stone altar with a Cathar cross on top.

They stopped in their tracks, frozen, and stared in abject horror. They had found Florence's prison.

A manacle with a fairly lengthy chain was threaded through an iron ring set into the altar front. To the side stood a small table with a chipped enamel washing-up bowl and several filthy flannels and towels on top, and a chair. On the other side was a portable latrine, and placed on the altar was a cat-o'-nine-tails. They stood there motionless for at least two minutes, taking in the enormity of the scene.

Strangely broke the silence. 'My God, the absolute barbaric bastards. She must have been held down here in total darkness. There's no sign of a candle or any other source of light. And the worst of it is, when we left the Lacroixs yesterday they must have warned the kidnappers and they are long gone. Damn and blast it.'

'Good God, we were only a few kilometres from her yesterday and we couldn't help the poor girl. She must be absolutely petrified,' Constanza said in no more than a whisper.

'She must be, but she's made of sterner stuff and has already proved her mettle, and if I were a betting man, the kidnappers will have unwittingly met their match. Now let's see if the crypt can reveal any secrets. Fabrice, you take that side, and we'll take this side.'

Strangely examined the manacles. The chain they were attached to was long enough for someone to move to each side of the crypt. They examined the altar and then turned their attention to the coffins within reach of the length of chain. They could just about reach the top coffin and they worked their way to the fourth coffin on the bottom shelf, kneeling down to examine it.

'Look there, Connie.' He pointed to the head end of the coffin. 'Something has been scratched into the wood.'

"Fréthun, Caletum, domum fidelem, Maison Hugo."

'Here, Fabrice, have a look at this.' He pointed to the message on the coffin.

'My schoolboy Latin tells me *domum fidelem* means "safe house", "Maison Hugo" is the name of a house, but what is *Fréthun* and *Caletum?*'

'Let me enlighten you: *Caletum* is the Latin name for Calais and *Fréthun* is a small village near there,' said Fabrice.

'You clever, clever girl. "Fréthun, safe house, Maison Hugo." She's a bloody genius. I told you she was a match for her captors. Right, I need to make detailed notes of everything down here and take photographs of the chapel.'

They worked methodically and it took them a good couple of hours to get all the pictures and information Strangely needed. They swept the whole chapel and crypt again to make sure they hadn't missed anything, and locked the door behind them.

*

Strangely wanted to check at the château to see if anyone had seen or heard anything unusual around the chapel over the past few months, and especially the previous evening. Fabrice pulled the car up at the entrance. A large bell was mounted on top of a grand pair of intricate wrought-iron gates. He tugged on the rope and the sound of the bell echoed around the courtyard. A dog was immediately galvanised into action and sprung up from its slumber from under a tree, barking and bounding up to the gates.

A butler emerged from a set of double doors and asked what their business was. Fabrice explained, and the butler about-turned and went back inside. A few moments later he returned and asked them to follow him. Accompanied by the dog, which the butler informed them was a Pyrenean sheepdog who went by the name of Angus, they entered the house. The entrance hall was magnificent, with two huge crystal chandeliers suspended from the ceiling, and the yellow walls made the room warm and most welcoming.

The butler showed them into the drawing room, where a tall man was standing next to a woman, both looking out of the French windows. The butler cleared his throat and they turned. The man was elegantly attired in a coral linen suit with a white open-neck shirt, sporting a cravat. He had a deep tan. She was wearing a gingham tan midi with red check trimming and a red check skirt. 'You are most welcome. Please allow me to introduce my wife, Baroness Maria-Françoise Gascoigne, and myself, Baron Pierre-Édouard Gascoigne. To whom do I have the pleasure?'

'This is Monsieur Marjorie Drye, Madame Constanza Drye, and I'm Monsieur Fabrice Barsalou.'

They shook hands. '*Un plaisir de vous rencontrer*,' said Strangely.

'Ah, I detect an English accent.'

'You are correct.'

'Then I can practise my English. So how may we be of help?'

'What can you tell us about the Lacroixs?'

'They produce the best charcuterie this side of the Pyrenees. Jean-Pascal delivers here every couple of weeks.'

'What were they doing with the key to your barn at the top of the hill?'

The baron raised a quizzical eyebrow. 'They are renting it from me for storage of various commodities they use in their business. I offered to have it cleared out – the wine presses and vats are old, and we have relocated our vinification process to a new, much larger, state-of-the-art building on the estate – but they said there was no need as all they needed was the mezzanine level. We agreed a year's rental from the first of June this year, payable at the end of each month.'

'My Lord, I have to—'

'Pierre, please.'

'Pierre, I have to inform you they weren't using your barn.'

'Really? Why on earth not?'

'Because they removed the lock and refitted it to the chapel door down in the glade.'

'*Bon Dieu*, the Chapel of Saint Vincent of Saragossa. How dare they? And what the hell were they doing in there?'

'Might I come to that in a minute? How often did they visit the barn?'

'I heard his motorcycle go by at least two or three times a week. Funnily enough, I heard it yesterday evening at about seven o'clock and thought what a strange time to visit on a Sunday.'

'Did you see any other people coming and going?'

'No, I didn't, but might I enquire as to your interest in the Lacroixs and my barn, sorry, chapel?'

'You might. We are trying to find a missing person, a Florian Boutroux. We believe he is related to Madame Lacroix, and our suspicion is that he was holed up in your chapel but has now fled. I also doubt very much you will be seeing much of the Lacroixs in the near future, and I fear you will not be getting any more rental money.'

'Good God, what has this Boutroux chap done?'

'That is a very good question and one that I'm afraid I can't answer at the moment, for the protection of an innocent victim who we believe he and an associate wish to harm. But in the meantime, here is your key. I have locked the chapel, and you should keep it that way as it is the scene of a major crime.'

'A crime scene? How absolutely awful. I've been duped, and to think I've been doing business with them for years.'

'No, you haven't been duped. The Lacroixs are an exceedingly plausible couple.'

'I see. I will of course make sure it is kept locked and that the estate workers keep an eye on it.'

'Thank you. Does anyone use the chapel?'

'Not anymore. The Roman Catholic Bishop of Carcassonne deconsecrated it early last century as there were some peculiar goings-on. It was a shame, really, as it was our family chapel. We look after it and I'm actually in discussion with the current bishop to see if it can be reconsecrated.'

'So why does it look like a barn?'

'To hide it from the Catholics. You see, the chapel goes back to the late eleventh century, and its origins were Cathar – hence the Cathar cross above the outer gates and in the crypt. The Catholics took the chapel over in the fourteenth century.'

'I thought the Catholics hated the Cathars?'

'They did, and they persecuted them.'

'So why is there still a Cathar cross on the building?'

'There's a local suspicion that if the cross is removed, the vines will fail. That's why the Catholic Church named the chapel after Saint Vincent of Saragossa; he's the patron saint of winegrowers.'

'Fascinating. Now, we must be off. But speaking of wine, can I compliment you on your excellent Chardonnay? We had a bottle yesterday with our picnic whilst staking out the Lacroixs' smallholding.'

'Really? How exciting. Is it normal to picnic whilst one is spying?'

'Absolutely a must.'

'I say, how very civilised. Now let us walk you to the gate.' He had a quiet word with his butler who scuttled off. As we walked to the gate, we were joined again by Angus, who was running around madly with a stick in his mouth in the hope someone might throw it for him. At the gate the butler came hurrying back with a wooden box.

'Compliments of the château, and when you are in Carcassonne again please be sure to look us up.'

'We certainly will, and thank you for the wine, that's extremely generous of you.'

'Not at all, and make sure to let us know when you get that Boutroux fellow!'

'I certainly will.'

*

Strangely consulted his watch. It was already past three thirty and he was desperate to get back to the hotel to call Wispy, but he wanted to check on the smallholding on the remote chance that the Lacroixs had returned.

Pulling up outside the front door, the place still looked deserted. He knocked on the front door and there was no answer. The back door had been repaired, so the mayor had obviously rallied some locals. The cows were grazing contentedly, and he assumed that the village would take care of the welfare of the animals. The Lacroixs had fled.

Fabrice opened the Torpedo up as much as the roads allowed, and they pulled up in front of the Hôtel de la Cité shortly before five o'clock. Fabrice went straight to reception to arrange tickets for the overnight train to Paris, and Constanza steered Strangely into the lounge.

'I need to talk to you, darling.'

'Of course, what is it?'

'First, let's order a drink.'

Strangely attracted the attention of a waiter and they decided on a gin and French. The waiter placed their drinks in front of them. They raised their glasses and clinked them together.

'I love you very much, Strangely.'

'And I love you from the bottom of my heart.'

'What I witnessed today in that grotesque horror chamber has shaken me to the core. Those evil, pathetic people will, I believe, stop at nothing; they are barbaric. But I ask a simple question: why oh why can a human being inflict so much hurt and pain on a fellow human being?'

'Because, my love, they are depraved.'

'So when we travel to Paris tonight, it is vital that I continue on to get those films back, so Wispy and Tony can understand exactly what they are up against. They can also ask Florian Boutroux's father to see if he can identify Odette Lacroix, which is now of paramount importance.'

'Connie, you are the wisest and most beautiful person I know. I'm sorry it didn't occur to me, but you are right and those films need to be en route PDQ. Come here.'

They gave each other a hug and raised their glasses. 'To Florence.'

CHAPTER 18
MONDAY, 14 AUGUST 1922
WESTMINSTER

I walked to the Regency Café and arrived shortly before eight o'clock. Tony was already ensconced at a table with a mug of tea.

'*Boker tov*, Wispy.'

'And a good morning to you.'

We both ordered, and as tempted as I was to have a large traditional English breakfast, I opted for poached eggs on toast with mushrooms. I relayed the events of Strangely's Sunday trip to Montlaur.

'Well it was worth a try, but Wanda's analysis of Florence's note is spot on; we've found the haystack, now it's the difficult matter of finding the needle.'

'Blast, Tony, I just feel that the kidnapper is holding all the cards.'

'Not all the cards, he doesn't want the police involved, but look, here I am, and our strongest suit is Florence herself. She is one hell of a formidable opponent, and I wager her kidnapper hasn't got a clue what he's up against.'

'Not forgetting the jokers in the pack, Fescue's Detective Agency, another formidable player.'

'Hallelujah and amen to that! Now, I promised you a jar of Mrs Finkelstein's pickled dills the other day, so here you are.'

'Please give my regards to Mrs Finkelstein and thank her very much for the wonderful pickles.'

'I will, Wispy.'

'Right, let's see what today brings.' I paid the bill, and we went our separate ways.

*

Wanda was in the office and I appraised her of Sunday's news. I checked my watch. 'No sign of Ernest?'

'No, I haven't seen him yet.'

'It's just gone nine thirty. I'll have to have a word about his timekeeping; he lives opposite the office, for goodness' sake. Now how about a cup of tea?'

I went into the kitchen and put the kettle on, and we soon each had a cup of Earl Grey tea, at which point Ernest arrived clutching his notebook.

'You must have heard me making the tea. I'll put the kettle back on.'

'Thank you, Sir William, and then I can tell you about my visit to Harrods this morning.'

'Harrods!'

'Yes, I arranged to meet the stationery department manager at eight thirty.'

Well done, Wispy, you nearly put your size nines in it!

'Really. Let me make your tea first, then you can explain.'

I put a steaming mug of Assam in front of him. 'Now, Ernest, please enlighten us on your findings at Harrods.'

'On Friday after you left to travel to Newcastle, I called the stationery department there and the person I spoke to suggested I came in this morning to speak to the departmental manager.

'He was extremely knowledgeable and I doubt there's much he doesn't know about paper. The paper is produced by Brousses Paper Mill, which is located in the village of Brousses-et-Villaret in the Aude. It is seventeen miles north and slightly to the west of Carcassonne. The paper is mostly sold by stationers in the local area.'

'Good work, Ernest. This certainly indicates that Florence's kidnappers are in the Carcassonne area. All we have to do is find the needle. I must let Strangely know. But before I do, I need you to do some digging into the background of Mr Eamonn Babbage, the general manager of the Eastoff Shipbuilding Company.'

After about ten minutes I was connected to the Hôtel de la Cité, only to find Strangely had left the hotel earlier that morning. I left a message for him to call me on his return. As I replaced the receiver, the phone rang again.

'Just one moment, Sir Chester, I will pass you over,' said Ernest.

'Wispy, we've had another note. Strutton has just answered the door and it was lying on the doormat.'

'Right, we're on our way.'

I replaced the receiver. 'Come on, Wanda, Sir Chester has just received another note from our kidnapper.'

We grabbed our bags and I gunned the Bentley into life.

*

'The note is on the table there and before you ask, no one has bloody touched it since Strutton picked it up fifteen minutes ago wearing gloves!'

'Chester, for goodness' sake.'

'Sorry, I'm feeling absolutely dead beat this morning. No excuse though, so apologies.'

'Thank you, Chester. Now for the note.' I put my cotton gloves on and picked it up. It was the same typeface as before and addressed to Lady and Sir Eastoff. I slit the envelope open with my penknife and unfolded the letter, noting straight away the Brousses watermark. I read it out loud.

'"My dearest Lady Alberta and Sir Chester,

'"I trust you are both well and enjoying this wonderful summer weather. I do so enjoy this time of year. Florence sends her love, and you will be delighted to know that through my skill, where I severed her finger, the wound is healing nicely with no signs of infection.

'"Now onto practicalities. According to my calculations the gold will weigh one hundred and forty-seven pounds. That's ten and a half stone.

These bars must be packaged evenly between four wooden ammunition boxes. This is not only for my benefit but yours as they will be required to be taken on a lengthy journey to make the rendezvous with me, where my precious cargo can be exchanged for your precious cargo.

"'I will contact you again at some point on Thursday, allowing you ample time to travel to my rendezvous. I will then reveal in detail your instructions. Again, if I as much as merely sniff the presence of the police, you will never hear from me again, and as for your daughter, I won't need to use an anaesthetic this time!

"'Try to relax and conserve your energy because by Friday every sinew and nerve end in both your bodies will be screaming out in such pain and hurt, your desperation will be palpable.

"'In eager anticipation.

"'Yours affectionately,

"'YOUR WORST NIGHTMARE'".

I folded the letter, placed it back in the envelope, put it in my briefcase and sat down. No one spoke for what seemed ages. Chester comforted Alberta who was gently sobbing. He broke the silence first.

'So bloody cards-on-the-table time: what are the realistic chances of seeing her alive again? Ten per cent? Twenty per cent? For Christ's sake, what bloody per cent? Give me some odds!'

'Chester, stop. How could you? Our daughter's life is not something that can be weighed and measured in percentages.'

'Alberta, please forgive…' Chester broke down, clasping his head in his hands and rocking gently back and forth. Alberta drew him to her as he started to cry.

Again, silence descended. The mantel clock marked the passing of time and slowly, with Alberta's comfort and soothing words, Chester started to regain his composure.

'I'm terribly sorry…'

I held my hand out. 'Please stop, Chester, there is no need to apologise. All he's focused on is the gold – that's what motivates him. As to what drives him, we can only guess. Therefore, if we are prepared to do exactly what he requests, you will see her alive.'

Bloody hell, listen to me: 'if we are prepared to do exactly what he requests'. For heaven's sake, I've got the most senior policeman in the land involved. One slip and this will only end one way.

'I believe that gold will be his downfall.'

And more than likely mine, and with it, my agency and the livelihood of Wanda and Ernest. Christ, I'm seriously in peril!

'Right, what you've got to concentrate on are the practicalities of the situation, and that is getting the gold exactly how he wants it, the security in place to guard it, and the means of transporting it when we get our marching orders.'

'Very well, I will have a word with Lord Ryston at Coutts and have everything ready to be moved by Thursday morning.'

'Thank you.' I pointed out the watermark and told them the origin of the paper. Then I brought them up to date on how Strangely's investigations were going.

'So, you've achieved the fantastic feat of discovering the paper comes from the same region as Carcassonne. Bloody marvellous. I think even I might have managed that! Strangely's down there kicking his heels with some Frenchman who helped you on your last case, and we are four days away from handing over the ransom. Bloody well done, a brilliant job!'

Well that's a tad harsh, but he might have a point!

'I said at the outset that our relationship must be built on mutual respect. You are fulfilling your part – the ransom – and if all else fails, it will be exchanged for your daughter's life. Now four days is a long time, so please give me and my agency some credit. What do you think we've been doing? That Strangely and Constanza have been on a cultural trip to Bremen and Carcassonne, taking in the sights, whilst Wanda and I have discovered the delights of hiking in the north-east, visiting ruined monasteries and sampling the local cuisine?'

'I know I'm not helping the situation.' Alberta held his hand. 'But we feel so utterly helpless.'

'I understand, I really do, but just concentrate on what you can control, and I know it's easy for me to say, stop speculating.'

Listen to me with my demons of self-doubt sitting on my shoulders.

'We need to go now, but rest assured as soon as we know of any developments we will inform you immediately.'

*

It had gone one o'clock when we arrived back at the office, and I dispatched Ernest off to Scotland Yard with the ransom note in an envelope for Tony.

'Wanda, I'm going back to Salthouse for lunch with Libby. Would you like a sandwich?'

'Yes, please. I was going out, but I'll mind the fort while Ernest is gone.'

'I'll get Eleanor to bring it around.'

Alice had prepared potted beef sandwiches, her Scotch eggs that knocked the socks off any shop-bought, a dollop of English mustard and some game chips, accompanied by a jug of her iced Earl Grey tea. I shared my frustration in dealing with Sir Chester with Libby.

'Darling, I think you have the measure of him. You just have to accept that he has spent most of his life being angry, for whatever reason, and the present situation has exemplified that anger. But put ourselves in their shoes and I think that we too would be exceedingly angry.'

'You're right, but it does feel like I'm treading on eggshells every time I'm with him.'

'Well you have to break a few eggs to make an omelette.'

'How true. At least Alberta's got the measure of him.'

'Where would we be in this world without strong women!'

'I don't know the answer to that, but what I do know is I wouldn't be where I am today without a strong woman beside me.'

She gave me a playful nudge.

'But I'm getting frustrated. Despite all our efforts we seem to be stalling, we're losing momentum. I know I told the Eastoffs four days is a long time, but in reality we're running out of time.'

'"It is not in the stars to hold our destiny but in ourselves." Trust yourself and your judgement, darling, and all will be well.'

'Thank you, darling, you've just kicked my little demon into the long grass. Now I fancy a walk. Would you care to join me?'

'What a lovely idea.' She gave me a hug. 'Come on, you.'

*

I returned to the office shortly before four and as I walked in, I sensed a feeling of lethargy had descended. I sat down at my desk and after a few moments I found myself aimlessly doodling in my notebook. I was pulled out of my daydream when the telephone started to ring and Ernest answered it.

'Sir William, it's Mr Drye.'

'Strangely, how's Carcassonne?'

'Carcassonne is as delightful as ever, but the village of Montlaur has revealed a grotesque secret. We've found where the needle was. You will need your notebook to hand.'

I grabbed my notebook and listened intently to Strangely recalling the events of his day. I had to keep interrupting him to make sure I had accurately written down what he was saying. Wanda and Ernest were picking up on my side of the conversation, and I could sense the atmosphere in the office changing by the second and the energy starting to flood back with a vengeance.

'Although horrific, this is the breakthrough we've been waiting for. Hang on a minute.' I checked my watch: five thirty. 'Wanda, can you call Tony at the Yard and say we need to see him immediately?'

'Of course.'

'Now, how are we going to handle this? You can't be in two places at the same time; you're on your way to Paris, and I will head for Calais and the village of Fréthun *tout de suite*, hopefully with Tony in tow.'

'Agreed. We will be departing for Paris later tonight. Connie was going to travel on to London with the films, but I will ask her to meet you in Calais with them. You can then get the photographic evidence we have gathered developed there.'

'Excellent. Wanda and I will meet Tony PDQ and appraise him of everything you've discovered, and I think now is the time to reveal

Tony's involvement to the Eastoffs. I will call you from Scotland Yard with what actions we have agreed, before you head to Paris.'

'Good luck.'

'Thanks. I think we might need it.'

I replaced the receiver and exhaled loudly. Wanda had got hold of Tony and he had cleared the decks and was expecting us as soon as we could get there. I recounted what Strangely had told me using my notes. Ernest agreed to stay on until we knew exactly what our plans were. Then I called Libby and explained I might be in for a long evening, and that there was a possibility of me travelling to Calais. She said she would get Alice to arrange some cold cuts and salad and would eat with me when I returned. Then Wanda and I headed to Scotland Yard.

CHAPTER 19
MONDAY, 14 AUGUST 1922
WESTMINSTER

Tony came bounding down the stairs. 'Good evening. Come, come.'

We followed in his wake up to his first-floor office and he put his Ritz Hotel 'Do not Disturb' sign on the outside of his door.

'So there have been developments?'

'You could say that.' I took out my notebook and recounted in sequence Strangely's day. Tony sat in silence but his facial expressions gave away his surprise. When I finished, he banged his fists on his desk.

'Oy oy oy! Your agency is a loss to Scotland Yard, and come to that so is Florence. I'm in total agreement with your strategy that Strangely should track down the Lacroixs to Paris and we should travel to Calais. I took the precaution of warning the commissioner that you might have some news. He's meant to be attending a dinner at the Commons, but he said this is far more important and is waiting in his office for me to brief him. Between you, me and the gatepost, it's hosted by the new Home Secretary, whom he finds incredibly dull, so he's glad of an excuse not to attend. Mind you, as you were so effective in getting his predecessor removed from office, he may well want to enlist your help with this incumbent. Now, if you will excuse me for a moment, I'll go and brief him.'

'Before you do that, I will need to update the Eastoffs on these developments, and I think now is the time for me to reveal your involvement.'

'Oy vey! You're a brave man, Sir William, but of course you are right.'

'And I want you there when I do, to totally reassure them that your involvement will in no way whatsoever endanger Florence; in actual fact, you can demonstrate that it will be a benefit to her and them.'

'Of course I will. I can assure them that my and the commissioner's involvement to date has been in total confidence and will remain so until exactly the right moment. However, I will have to observe the political niceties, and the commissioner will need to inform the chief of police in Calais that we will be travelling to his jurisdiction. We will need his help in arresting Florence's captors; as you know, I have no jurisdiction or powers of arrest in France.

'So, this is our main chance to put this sorry tale to bed, and with any luck we should have all this sorted out in the next few days, which will please Mrs Finkelstein as she doesn't like me being away from home for too long. Now, if you will excuse me…'

*

It had just gone seven when he bustled back into the office.

'Sorry, my moment turned into several, but we needed to make sure the i's were dotted and the t's crossed. The commissioner spoke to the chief inspector of the Calais police, a Monsieur Raphael Bombelles, and he has offered his total cooperation. As we speak, he is deploying his small team of undercover officers to the village of Fréthun to set up surveillance on Maison Hugo. He has given us his guarantee that the occupants of the cottage will not be aware in the slightest that they are being observed. And unless he is forced to, he will not make any moves until our arrival.

'The commissioner felt that due to the delicacy of the operation, it would be prudent to keep our presence discreet to avoid any possibility of the kidnappers getting wind of our arrival. Chief Inspector Bombelles assured him this will be the case.'

'Excellent.'

'And he also sends his warmest regards and compliments on your progress so far, which as you are no doubt aware is high praise indeed.'

'I feel blessed. Do you think we can tell future clients that we are fully endorsed by the commissioner of Scotland Yard no less? That should do wonders for business.'

'And it would certainly add a degree of gravitas too,' added Wanda.

'You both know the answer to that.'

'We do, but if you don't ask the question, you will never get an answer. Now I need to call Strangely. Can you get me this number in Carcassonne?'

'Of course.'

After five minutes I had Strangely on the line. 'The commissioner has approved our plan of action.'

'Good. There's a train to Bordeaux Saint-Jean leaving here at eleven fifteen, so with the change there we should be in Paris tomorrow morning at about ten.'

'You're becoming quite the expert on continental railways. Oh, and by the way the commissioner sends his regards.'

'Does he, by Jove. Maybe an endorsement to our young but burgeoning CV.'

'My thoughts entirely, but alas not the commissioner's. Now we must go and visit the Eastoffs and break the news that Tony is officially on board.'

'Good luck with that, old boy. Can I suggest it might be prudent to take a bodyguard with you?'

'No need, I'm sure his bark is worse than his bite.'

'I wouldn't bank on it, Wispy.'

My next call I wasn't looking forward to making, and it didn't disappoint. The result of which I thought my ear would bleed due to the decibels of my rebuttal, and I was left hoping that his bark was indeed worse than his bite.

*

It was just before eight o'clock when we arrived at Lennox Gardens. Strutton showed us into the drawing room and said that Sir Chester was working in his study and he would go and fetch him. Lady Alberta was dealing with some domestic issues but would join us shortly. As we were standing there waiting for him to appear, I must confess to a feeling of slight apprehension as to how he would react. I didn't have to wait long.

The door was flung open with such force it went back as far as it could, and we heard the splintering of the door frame as hinges were ripped from it. A few seconds later the door crashed to the floor.

'I bloody well told you I didn't want the police within one hundred miles of this, you bloody blithering idiot!' He spat the words with such venom that he was physically shaking with rage and his face was turning a deep puce.

'You will have my daughter's blood on your hands, you arrogant prig!' he screamed, and stepped forward a few paces into the room, then burst into a full bloody charge. I didn't have time to react and he felled me with an enormous arching haymaker.

I came to lying on the sofa, with Alberta administrating to me and Wanda peering down at me with concern. She had placed a home-made ice pack over my right eye. My head was thumping and the room was spinning. I hadn't a clue how long I'd been unconscious. I attempted to raise my head, but the searing pain persuaded me otherwise.

'Don't move, Wispy, Doctor Primrose will be here in a minute.' Right on cue we heard the front doorbell. Strutton showed him in and Alberta told him exactly what had happened. Primrose held two fingers up and at least I got the right number.

'You'll live, but you're going to have an almighty shiner on your right eye. Here, take these aspirin and repeat again in four hours.' He and Alberta managed to get me sitting upright.

'Where are Chester and Inspector Finkelstein?' I enquired.

'They have gone for a little tête-à-tête in Chester's study,' replied Alberta.

Blimey, I'd love to be a fly on the wall for that conversation. I wonder if Tony's arresting him for assault? No, he wouldn't be doing that, would he? We've got a case to solve.

'Right, let's get you onto your feet,' Alberta said, and she and Wanda helped me up.

'Let's take a walk around the room.' I still felt groggy but managed to complete the circuit successfully, albeit with the use of only one eye as my right eye had completely closed. I gulped down the rest of my glass of water. The doctor gave me a bottle of aspirin and reassuringly patted me on the back as Strutton showed him out.

A few moments later Tony came back into the room, followed by a rather chastened Chester. He walked straight over to me and shook my hand. 'Wispy, what can I say? What I did was unforgivable. Christ, what is happening to me? This is the second time I've done this.

'I know you must think my apologies are hollow, but can you find it in you to accept my heartfelt apology? I'm totally embarrassed about my behaviour and when this is all over, I intend to seek help in understanding and dealing with my anger.'

What a splendid idea. It would make my job a tad safer!

'I accept your apology, but it would have been far better for you to have listened to the explanation as to why Inspector Finkelstein is here in the first place.'

'I know it would, and what the inspector has just told me has compounded my behaviour and taught me a huge lesson.' He went over to Alberta and gave her a hug and a kiss. 'Darling, please sit down with me and allow Inspector Finkelstein to bring you up to date with everything Wispy and his agency have uncovered.'

Tony went through absolutely everything that had happened in Carcassonne and our plans going forward. He emphasised his and the commissioner's total commitment to confidentiality and praised my judgement for involving him when I did.

Alberta stood up. 'I can see now that having you involved was the right thing to do. It has saved valuable time.' She turned to face me and Wanda. 'But this news is absolutely the best news we've had since

Florence disappeared. You've found her, now you're off to rescue her. I just can't wait to hold her in my arms again.'

I don't think it's going to be that straightforward. There's the smidge of a problem of overcoming two psychopathic kidnappers first! But in essence, she is correct about the plan.

'However, Alberta, Chester, you both still need to be focused on the practicalities of getting the ransom together and being in a position to move it securely at a moment's notice. I doubt that it will now be required, but we need to be prepared for every eventuality.'

'Very well, I spoke to Lord Ryston earlier and it should all be ready by Thursday morning.'

'Excellent.' I focused on my watch with my good eye; time was marching on as it had just gone nine thirty. 'Right, we must get going, but before we go you mentioned that this was the second time you have had a violent outburst. When was the first?'

'That was about six months ago, and in my mind he deserved what he got.'

So much for changing his ways.

'Who deserved what he got?'

'A Mr Clement Featherstonehaugh. An acquaintance of mine introduced me to him as he knew I was in the market to purchase a ball bearing factory.'

'I see, and he owned such a manufacturing operation?'

'Purportedly.'

'What happened?'

'I spent a considerable amount of time researching the venture, and the more I dug, or should I say my solicitor dug, it was abundantly clear that the business was first class. The accounts showed a highly profitable company. It seemed too good to be true. Why in blaze's name would you sell a company that was outstanding? You wouldn't, would you? So, I decided to walk away. I met with him and nicely, I thought for me, informed him I was not going to buy his company. At which point he became quite angry and threatened me with all kinds of retribution.'

'Gosh, then what happened?'

'I decided if he was going to be seeking retribution, he'd better have something tangible to seek it on, so with one very satisfying punch I broke his nose.'

'And you failed to mention this at our second meeting when I asked you to think of anyone who had a grudge against you?'

'He is such a weak and ineffectual man, frightened of his own shadow, that I didn't even consider mentioning him as you'd have been wasting your time investigating him.'

'Let me be the judge of that. Weak and ineffectual people are often the most sinister, devious and dangerous. Can you let me have his details?'

'Certainly, give me a moment.'

A few moments later he was back with the information.

'Thank you.'

*

The three of us spent ten minutes chatting on the pavement outside the Eastoffs'. My head had stopped aching but my right eye had almost closed, and another difficult conversation with Libby beckoned.

'Wanda, can you tackle this Clement Featherstonehaugh chap?'

'I will try and contact him as soon as I get home. Luther arrived in town yesterday for a few days to meet with some editors who are interested in commissioning him to write a column on fly fishing and gardening. I thought I would ask him to join me if he's free.'

Good for you.

Wanda and Luther Spaulding met fairly recently whilst she was investigating our last case. He's a fascinating man with a very interesting history, slightly eccentric, which adds to his charm, and an all-round good egg.

'I'm sure he will jump at the opportunity.'

I arranged to meet Tony at Victoria station at six thirty the following morning, and he was going to organise the train and ferry tickets for the nine o'clock sailing from Dover to Calais. He would send a telegram to Chief Inspector Bombelles with our estimated time of arrival and a request to arrange a hotel.

We said our goodnights and I shared a taxi with Wanda as far as Cheyne Walk before she headed off to Clapham.

*

I rang the bell and a few moments later Eleanor answered. She was considerably taken aback by my appearance.

'Good gracious me, you've been in the wars again, Sir William. Lady Elizabeth is not going to be happy.'

'Thank you, Eleanor, for stating the obvious.'

'Not at all, Sir William. I've arranged a light supper which I can serve in the drawing room, or would you prefer the dining room?'

'The drawing room is fine, and we can have a tray each.'

'Alice will have it ready in fifteen minutes.'

'Thank you, I could eat a horse.' I was feeling weary as I trudged up the stairs and entered the drawing room. Libby was concentrating on her sketchbook. I walked over to her and put my arms around her and kissed the top of her head.

'Hello, you. You must be exhausted. Now go and fix us both a drink, and then you can tell me all about the rest of your day.'

I walked over to the drinks cabinet and made her a Tanqueray and tonic and a pink gin for myself. I turned around. 'Here we go, darling.' She stood up and turned to face me.

She looked at me with a mortified expression. 'Good gracious, William, what on hell's earth has happened to you? Why oh why on heaven's earth is it always you that gets hurt?'

'Well, darling, he has slight difficulties with his temper.'

'Who has slight difficulties with his temper?'

'Sir Chester.' And I explained exactly how it happened.

'So, because he has slight difficulties with his temper, that makes it all right?'

'Oh, come on, darling, you know it doesn't. Apparently he's going to seek help.'

'Really. Well at least you've been seen by a doctor. Come and sit down and let me have a closer look at you.' She examined my eye, then kissed me. 'There, that should make it better. And it's a vast improvement on your last case – you were only four days into it when you sustained your first black eye, and by my calculations you are already eight days into this case, so I take a little comfort from that. Now, tell me all of your news.'

Eleanor came in with our supper. Alice had prepared Scotch woodcock, accompanied by my crispy pickled red cabbage and a few of my pickled walnuts, followed by her charlotte russe with Cointreau. I explained I had an early start in the morning and would have tea, toast and marmalade in our room at five o'clock.

I went through all the events of that afternoon and evening.

'Gosh, Wispy, you've all made huge progress; you could have it all wrapped up by Wednesday. And fingers crossed for Wanda and Luther.'

'Yes, fingers crossed.'

'These two kidnappers have proven they are ruthless and psychotic, so no heroics in Calais, Wispy. I want you back in one piece.'

'No heroics, darling, I promise.'

'Where have I heard that before? Now, I will help man the office, and it will be nice to have Constanza back.'

'Thank you. Do you know what?'

'No, darling, I don't know what.'

'I couldn't do any of these things without you.'

'Of course you couldn't, you're a man. Now come on, you, off to bed.'

134

CHAPTER 20
TUESDAY, 15 AUGUST 1922
CHELSEA

Libby came down to see me off. Eleanor had gone to hail a cab on Oakley Street and she returned with it.

'Remember what I said?'

'Of course, darling. No heroics.'

'I mean it, Wispy. Now *bonne chance!*'

'Thank you, darling. Let's hope we don't need it.'

We hugged and then I was off to Victoria.

Tony and I boarded the six forty-five train to Dover and we comfortably caught the nine o'clock sailing to Calais, enjoying a hearty breakfast whilst crossing the Dover Strait. We docked at just after midday French time. As we went out on deck, we were greeted by a fantastic scene. On the docks below was a rather splendid police car polished to within an inch of its life, sporting the flag of Calais on its left front wheel arch. A chauffeur was standing by the rear door. To the right of the car were three ranks of gendarmes, all in what looked like their ceremonial uniforms. In the middle was a red carpet, and to the left a full band of gendarmes.

As we stepped onto the gangplank, the chauffeur opened the rear door and a rather portly – well, more than rather portly – little man struggled to get out of the car and managed to snag his sword in the door. The chauffeur came to his rescue and managed to extricate him. This must be the chief inspector, Monsieur Raphael Bombelles. He was wearing a full-blown dress uniform with as much aiguillette as

I've ever seen on any uniform, accompanied by at least eight medals pinned to his left breast. As he made it onto the red carpet, the band struck up 'La Marseillaise'.

The three ranks of gendarmes snapped to attention, turned their heads towards us and saluted. When we reached the bottom of the gangplank we stood side by side on the red carpet, putting down our overnight bags and briefcases. At this point 'La Marseillaise' had finished. The conductor tapped the music stand with his baton and the band broke into 'God Save the King'.

Blimey, if this is a discreet welcome, God alone knows what a full-blown welcome would be like!

When our national anthem had finished, he walked towards us. 'I'm Chief Inspector Bombelles. Welcome to the beautiful city of Calais, which I have the honour of serving. Sir William?' I took one step forward and shook his hand. 'Inspector Finkelstein.' Tony stepped forward and they shook hands.

'It is my great honour to welcome the private detective and the inspector who solved the case of Miss Josephine Leighton on French soil – *un triomphe!* As a nation we are proud of the part we played in apprehending the perpetrators of that villainous crime. It falls upon me as the representative of the citizens of Calais to assist you in your quest to arrest these two monsters and help you to bring them to justice, whilst releasing Miss Florence Eastoff, a true heroine, from the torment of her villainous captivity.'

He certainly has a vivid vocabulary, but a bit flowery for my taste!

I didn't quite know what to make of Monsieur Bombelles. Was he a caricature of a man full of self-importance, or was he a man of genuine values wanting to do his utmost to embrace the 1904 understanding between our two nations of entente cordiale? Either way, I'd better come up with an appropriate response.

'On behalf of the Fescue Detective Agency and Scotland Yard, we thank you for the wonderful honour you have afforded me and my colleague Inspector Finkelstein from Scotland Yard in welcoming us to your captivating and charming city. We are most excited to be here and look forward immensely to working jointly with you and your colleagues.'

Less flowery, but hopefully that should have struck the right tone.

'Thank you, Sir William, most gracious of you. Now please, gentlemen, follow me.' As we walked towards the car, the ranks of gendarmes saluted again. The chauffeur had opened the rear doors and we helped the struggling inspector in. Once the doors were shut, four gendarme outriders pulled up alongside us and escorted us away into Calais.

'Sir William, do you mind if I ask a rather personal question?'

'Ask away, Chief Inspector.'

'How did you come by such a fabulous black eye?'

'Ah, you've noticed.'

'It is difficult not to.'

'My client disagreed with, how shall I say, the direction I wanted to take our investigation.'

'*Mon Dieu!* And what did you do?'

'Do, Chief Inspector? He was persuaded to see the error of his ways.'

'Really? How fascinating. Now, I have booked you into the Hôtel Meurice de Calais, where you can refresh yourselves after your journey, and then at one thirty I will take you to the commune of Fréthun.'

We pulled up outside the hotel and there was a hive of activity as three bellboys helped us out of the car and took away our luggage. At the entrance a tall, elegantly dressed man introduced himself as the general manager and warmly welcomed us, then personally escorted us to our rooms.

*

Refreshed, bathed and changed, I strapped on my revolver and went down to the reception shortly before one and was joined soon after by Tony. At one o'clock precisely I recognised the chauffeur, who now appeared to be dressed as a mechanic. He held open the hotel door and in walked the chief inspector. We stared wide-eyed in astonishment. Gone was the full-blown dress uniform, and in its stead he was wearing a farmer's smock, light-brown corduroy trousers, clogs and a large straw hat. The disguise was finished off with a church warden's pipe clenched between his teeth.

I felt somewhat overdressed in my cream linen suit and white shirt with a red polka-dot cravat matching my socks. On my feet were white nubuck loafers, and in my hand I held my well-worn panama.

'Good, you are ready. The commune of Fréthun, it is six kilometres from here. My men have been observing Maison Hugo since nine o'clock last night. Unfortunately we cannot see in as heavy curtains are drawn across every window. However, we did notice a glow of light coming from one of the downstairs rooms and from two of the upstairs rooms. I have commandeered two homes nearby which afford us views of the back and front of their hideout. What I suggest is once you've seen Maison Hugo from all sides, I can seek your views and then discuss my proposed plan of action.'

'Excellent,' Tony said. 'You have secured the area, so they have nowhere to go. Trapped in their own safe house. Perfect!'

'Thank you, Inspector. Our initial investigation has revealed the cottage is owned by a local farmer, a Monsieur Peyronnet. He had tenant farmers in there until recently who upped sticks and left. He placed an advertisement in the local paper and a Monsieur Lacroix took out a year's rental on it in early June. We've had no joy in finding this Lacroix chap as he paid for the first six months' rental in cash. Peyronnet never bothered with paperwork once he had the cash in his hand, and never saw him again.'

'Really.' I glanced at Tony and he raised an eyebrow.

'Now, gentlemen, let's depart.'

Outside the hotel the highly polished limousine had gone, replaced by an old, rusting Citroën. Fifteen minutes later we drove into the village and passed the impressive town hall. We drew up at the back gate of a cottage and walked up the garden path. The chief inspector knocked slowly four times, followed by two quick knocks on the back door, and it was opened by a gendarme wearing camouflage fatigues and sporting a beret. We entered and he showed us into the front room of the cottage. Net curtains were drawn across the window, enabling us to view the cottage opposite without being seen. I took out my binoculars and trained them on the cottage. There were blackout curtains across every window which gave the whole building a sinister air. Tony too had his binoculars trained on the cottage. Not a sign of life.

Then we were taken on a circuitous route and arrived in the back garden of another cottage. The chief inspector used the same coded sequence of knocks and the door was opened. We stared at the back of the cottage; again, no sign of life.

We left the cottage and were driven to Fréthun station. The chief inspector led us along the platform and we entered the station café. It was gone two o'clock but it was still fairly busy with workers having their lunch. A waiter arrived at our table and we decided to have the *plat du jour*, and what an excellent choice it was: a rustic rabbit stew. The flavours were delicious and enhanced by the inclusion of Dijon mustard and crème fraîche, accompanied by a large glass of local cider.

The chief inspector dabbed delicately at the sides of his mouth with his serviette, then neatly folded it and replaced it on his side plate. 'Gentlemen, I have a plan in place: "Operation to Rescue a Nightingale".'

I was just taking a sip of my cider and it was all I could do to stop spitting it out as I tried to stifle a laugh.

'Operation to Rescue a Nightingale' – a tad on the dramatic side, what?

'Now that you have viewed the cottage, I would like to hear your thoughts first.'

'Inspector Finkelstein, what would you propose?' I asked.

'Although since nine o'clock last night no one has been sighted, we know that someone is in there as the lights are on. As we have the cottage under total surveillance, they cannot leave without being seen. I would suggest we give it until mid-morning tomorrow, say eleven o'clock, and then we enter the building.

'However, at some point soon they are going to have to move Florence for the ransom exchange, and when they do that they are going to be at their most guarded and dangerous, and she will be at the most risk of being harmed. We have the element of surprise on our side and we must use that to our advantage. I doubt that they will move her before early tomorrow afternoon, but we can't afford to leave it any later than that.'

'Thank you, Inspector. Sir William?'

'I agree with you, this is our main chance of complete surprise. They will not be expecting anything and hopefully we will catch them with their guard down. Chief Inspector, please can we hear your plan, umm, as in your "Operation to Rescue a Nightingale"? Just before you do that, why the name?'

'I would have thought that patently obvious, Sir William. "Nightingale", as in your famous lady with the lamp, Florence Nightingale, and the fact we are here to rescue—'

'Of course, silly me, you must think me stupid. An inspired choice, genius. Please continue.'

'I thought so too. I concur with you and agree with Inspector Finkelstein that we make our move at eleven. My eight officers are all highly trained and all ex-army. As soon as you requested our help, I got the team together and we travelled to the cottage. I took a draughtsman with us who sketched the cottage and I returned with him to our headquarters. He drew up plans for a replica cottage with the help of a nearby neighbour whose building is roughly the same as our kidnappers' cottage.

'Once the plans were ready, I assembled a team of ten local craftsmen who worked through the night to build a wooden mock-up of the cottage on our parade ground. That was completed by ten o'clock this morning.'

'I'm impressed.'

'Thank you, Sir William. One of my inspectors, D'Arras, returned to our two observation posts and split the team into two. Two from each post returned to the headquarters, where we trained the first four men on the operation at the front of the cottage. They spent a total of three hours rehearsing and they know the drill off pat.'

I exchanged a glance with Tony and he nodded back.

'One of them will pose as a postman and cycle up to the cottage gate, walk down the path and knock on the door. When the door is answered, the postman will have a telegram that he insists will need to be signed for. Whilst he is distracted by having to sign the postman's chit, the three other men will rush in, screaming for all they are worth, and drag him out of the cottage. They will have handcuffs on him before he knows what the hell is happening.'

Well, the chief inspector is certainly proving to be a mercurial character.

'He then swapped the teams around, and as we sit here, the rear section is training. As soon as they hear the front team screaming, two of them will use a heavy iron ram and smash the door down, and the four of them will storm the building, making enough noise to wake the dead, and apprehend the second kidnapper.

'Once their training is finished, they will return to their posts, where they will take shifts watching for the rest of the day and night. When they are not on a shift they will make sure they are well rested.

'Assuming the kidnappers don't make a move before eleven tomorrow morning, at ten forty-five they will be deployed to their positions, armed with their revolvers and combat knives. The postman will deliver his surprise telegram at eleven o'clock. I think that just about covers everything. Have you any observations or questions?'

'Just a couple of observations. I'm very impressed with your plans and how quickly you have put them into operation. You run a well-oiled machine. Bravo, Chief Inspector.'

'Thank you, Sir William.'

'I think it's highly unlikely they will make their move, but what plans have you in place if they do so before eleven?'

'Wherever they go, my men will follow at a distance and unobserved. We obviously don't know the location for the ransom exchange, but wherever it is they can't escape the attentions of my men; it will be an impossibility.'

I wouldn't be so sure.

'I have arranged for a fully crewed naval frigate to be at my disposal if it becomes apparent they intend to cross the Channel.'

'Excellent, Chief Inspector, you seem to have covered all eventualities.'

'And I would just add we couldn't have asked for more. Scotland Yard is in your debt.'

'I am honoured, Inspector. Now let me settle our account here before we head back to the observation posts to receive any further updates, then back to your hotel. By the way, I will be hosting a dinner there this evening in your honour, to which I will be bringing a few dignitaries.'

'That is most kind, but I'm afraid we've only packed with a view of undercover surveillance, not a black-tie dinner, so alas we must decline as we do not have the requisite attire.'

'Nonsense, Sir William, we too will dress casually.'

Blast. The last thing we need is a formal dinner. Bloody hell, we are trying to rescue Florence, not here as some delegation to cement our mutual cooperation. But we need him more than he needs us, so I suppose one will just have to grin and bear it.

'Thank you, Chief Inspector. We very much look forward to this evening.'

'Bon!'

CHAPTER 21
TUESDAY, 15 AUGUST 1922
PARIS

Strangely's train pulled into Gare Montparnasse at ten o'clock on the dot, and he and Constanza found their way onto the platform for the metro to the Gare du Nord.

'Now promise me that you will stay safe.'

'Connie, don't worry, I intend to.'

They hugged each other as the train screeched into the station. He saw her onto it and tried to keep up with it as it drew away, blowing her a kiss.

Strangely and Fabrice then made their way onto another metro line and emerged into the Paris sunshine from the Brégret-Sabin metro station. Although it was a short walk to Rue de la Bastille, they hailed a taxi due to the weight of Strangely's suitcase and the fact they didn't want to be spotted.

They pulled up outside 5–7 Rue de la Bastille. The whole of the ground floor was a restaurant, Brasserie Bofinger; the first and second floors were apartments and on the third floor, attic apartments. Opposite the building was a small hotel, the Bastille. Fabrice instructed the driver to turn around and to park outside the hotel. They got out without submitting to the temptation to glance over their shoulders at the apartments and entered the reception. There were quite a few vacancies and they managed to get a twin room overlooking the apartments, on the hotel's second floor.

'So which one is number fourteen?'

'Your guess is as good as mine,' replied Fabrice.

'Well in which case we're going to need to go into the building and find it without being observed, and the only way we can do that is in disguise, which we don't have.'

'Leave that to me.' Fabrice pulled his panama down and put on his sunglasses. 'There's bound to be somewhere I might be able to pick up some useful items to disguise ourselves.'

He set off, leaving Strangely watching each apartment through his binoculars. He found his way to the Saint-Ouen flea market and returned several hours later with a large blanket tied to a staff, which he carried on his shoulder. He looked like Dick Whittington setting off to London to find his fortune. In his other hand he carried a carpenter's toolbox.

Strangely had just ordered two *jambon* and Emmental baguettes with some tomatoes and a few hard-boiled eggs, accompanied by two bottles of lemonade, from *service de chambre*. He reported that there had been no sightings of the Lacroixs in any of the apartment windows. They both sat looking at the apartment block whilst eating their lunch.

'It's a pity we can't go across the road and have a *plat du jour* in Brasserie Bofinger. It is a very good restaurant which opened its doors in 1864.'

'Maybe after this is over, we could organise a long weekend here with the girls and have dinner there?'

'An excellent idea, and I can be your guide to the parts of Paris I know and love. Now, let's try on our costumes for size.'

Fabrice had visited a few second-hand clothes stalls and had managed to assemble the following items: two cotton twill chore jackets, two pairs of dungarees, two collarless shirts, two flat hats and two pairs of well-worn leather workman's boots.

'I think we look quite the part,' said Fabrice.

'I do, but there's something missing.'

'What's that?'

'Dirt.'

'Dirt?'

'Yes, dirt. We look too clean. We need a bit of muck on our faces and grime under our fingernails.'

Looking around the room there wasn't anything obvious, then Strangely spotted a flowerbox that ran the length of their window on the outside sill. 'There's our answer.' He opened the window, reached down and scooped up some soil in both hands, and took it to the sink in the bathroom, where he added some water until he achieved the consistency he needed. 'There, our very own camouflage paint.'

Having applied the mud pie all over their faces, they lightly washed it off, leaving vague streaks of dirt which gave the air of general grubbiness. Then they worked their hands into the mud, paying particular attention to get plenty under their fingernails. They looked in the mirror and both gave a nod of approval.

On their way out, they handed their key to the receptionist who had checked them in some three hours ago, who raised an eyebrow of surprise at their appearance. They wished him a *bonne après-midi* and left the hotel and crossed the street. The entrance to the apartments was on the right-hand side of the restaurant, where they entered the lobby. There on the left-hand wall were all the postboxes in numerical order, and bingo, there it was: 'Appartement 14, Monsieur et Madame Lacroix, 2ème étage'.

'Bang on, Fabrice, we've found them. We deserve a well-earned pat on the back, don't you think?'

'I do, maybe a celebratory bottle of something with our dinner this evening whilst watching their apartment.'

'I can hardly contain my excitement at the thought of it. Now let's go and find it.'

There was a lift next to the stairs at the far end of the lobby. They slid back the caged lift door, then the inner cage door, and just about fitted in with their carpenter's toolbox. Fabrice pressed the button for the second floor. The lift came to a sudden jolt as it reached its destination. Number fourteen was at the far end of the corridor. They stood and stared at the door for several minutes, straining to hear if they could detect any noise coming from within. Not a peep.

'What shall we do now?' Fabrice said in a whisper.

'Well, we can't very well knock and say we've got a few more questions, can we? So I suggest returning to our hotel and taking shifts to watch their apartment and the entrance lobby.'

As they turned and started to walk back to the lift, it sprang into life and descended. They both looked down the caged lift shaft and saw it had returned to the ground floor, where they heard the lift doors being slid back then closed. It started to ascend and stopped with the same sudden jolt exactly where they were standing. The inner door was slid back, then the outer one, and they were confronted with the Lacroixs.

'*Bonne après-midi, monsieur et madame,*' said Fabrice, touching the peak of his hat. Strangely did the same and noticed that Fabrice's accent had totally changed.

'And a good afternoon to you both. What brings two carpenters to our apartment block?'

'The door on number nine was not closing as it should. It had dropped so we rehung it.'

'And is it fixed?'

'But of course. We are skilled craftsmen.'

'I don't doubt it for a second. Now if you will excuse us.' We both stood back and they exited the lift, and Odette even smiled at them. They watched them walk towards their apartment, and with relief took the lift down to the lobby. Once outside they both exhaled loudly.

'Bloody hell, that was close. Do you think they recognised us?' asked Fabrice.

'It's hard to know, but their facial expressions didn't give anything away so they are either damned good actors or they didn't recognise us. I'm inclined to think they fall into the latter bracket. But can I just say I was bloody impressed with your performance, and where did that accent come from?'

'It was my impression of a working man's northern French accent. They would have recognised my normal voice, so I hope it convinced them.'

'Well it damn well convinced me. Come on, it's now imperative we watch their apartment like hawks. If they move, we move. But before we do, we need to make sure there's no other means by which they can exit.'

Having satisfied themselves that there was only the one exit, they returned to their hotel. It had gone four o'clock as they sat and looked through the net curtains at the far left-hand apartment on the second floor. They plainly saw the Lacroixs occasionally moving from room to room.

'Why can't we contact the Paris gendarmerie and get them arrested?' suggested Fabrice.

'One, we can't take the risk of them warning Boutroux and Potts; that would put Florence's life at stake. And two, at the moment all we have on them is circumstantial evidence. We do not have any direct evidence, and that's why we need to hang onto their coat-tails until they slip up.'

'Understood.'

'Now I must get a message to Wispy.'

*

It had gone six thirty when there was a knock at the door. Fabrice answered. It was the bellboy informing them that Wispy was on a call at reception.

'So, by this time tomorrow you will have Boutroux and Potts under lock and key?'

'Yes, and as soon as they are in custody, I will get Chief Inspector Bombelles to contact his counterpart in Paris to arrest the Lacroixs. I will contact you as soon as that call is made.'

'Very good. Another one for our CV, all wrapped up with two days to spare!'

'Well it sure as hell beats rounding up Jersey cows. I will call the Eastoffs as soon as Florence is freed, and they can make their way here to be reunited with her.'

'Excellent. Well, you have a good evening being entertained by Chief Inspector Bombelles.'

'I can hardly contain my excitement!'

CHAPTER 22
TUESDAY, 15 AUGUST 1922
BRIGHTON

Wanda had contacted Mr Clement Featherstonehaugh late the previous evening. After the initial difficulty in pronouncing his name correctly, she learnt it should be Fanshawe. He refused to meet her, but she had persuaded him that failure to do so would mean a visit from Scotland Yard, so he reluctantly agreed. She left early, dressed for a day out by the seaside, wearing a light turquoise skirt, a white silk blouse, a saffron-yellow jacket and a pair of black Oxfords. She met Luther at a quarter past seven at Victoria station. They boarded the seven-thirty train to Brighton and breakfasted on the way down.

Featherstonehaugh lived in Hove, in a property on Westbourne Villas named Villa Xanadu, literally a two-minute stroll from the beach. The villa was a beautiful, well-appointed property, and as they approached the front door, they concluded that owning a ball bearing factory had its perks.

Wanda rang the doorbell and it was answered by someone who she assumed was his housekeeper.

'Please come in. Mr Featherstonehaugh is expecting you but he's on a telephone call at the moment. Let me show you into the drawing room. Can I offer you some refreshment?'

'A cup of Earl Grey tea, please. Luther?'

'Oh, Earl Grey, yes, that would be perfect.'

'Please make yourselves comfortable.'

They looked around the room. It was light and airy and had a pleasant, welcoming feel. It was tastefully decorated with many paintings hanging on the walls, two of which caught Wanda's attention.

'Look, Luther, don't they remind you of the cubism style of Picasso?'

Luther clasped his hands behind his back and peered intently at them. 'By Jove, I think you're right.'

They both stood in silence admiring them for several minutes.

'Do you know what? Unless I'm very much mistaken, I think they are the genuine articles,' said Wanda.

'Obviously our Mr Featherstonehaugh has a good eye and likes to surround himself with the finer things in life.'

'If that's the case, why does he want to sell the golden goose?'

'A good point, Wanda.'

They headed off in opposite directions around the room, studying the various paintings. Wanda's attention was drawn to an architect's hand-drawn layout, written beautifully in art deco italic writing. Above the plan Wanda recognised an exquisite sketch of Featherstonehaugh's villa. In the bottom right-hand corner, she read: 'Design and sketch of Villa Xanadu. Walderne Smithers, RIBA, Wren Cottage, West Dean.'

'Luther, here, quickly,' Wanda said in a shouted stage whisper across the room.

Luther headed across the room, but before he could join her the door opened and in came the housekeeper with their beverages. 'Ah, I see you're admiring Mr Featherstonehaugh's paintings. I don't see the point in them whatsoever. It's not art, is it? If you ask me, a child could do better. Look at this one.' She put the tea tray down and marched across the room and pointed at a painting. Wanda and Luther joined her. 'That's by someone called Henri Rousseau. Mr Featherstonehaugh says it's a great example of his primitive surrealism, whatever that is. Give me *The Hay Wain* any day of the week.'

As they stood looking at the Rousseau, the door opened and Mr Clement Featherstonehaugh entered, accompanied by two Pekingese dogs following in his wake.

'Thank you, Dorothy, that will be all.' Dorothy did a slight curtsey and scuttled off.

'Miss Cushway, sorry for my tardiness, and welcome to my humble abode. I see you are admiring my Rousseau.' He crossed the room and held out his hand, which Wanda shook. He was very dapper and dressed in a red velvet smoking jacket, open-collared white silk shirt, finished off at the neck with a bright-yellow silk cravat. His slim-fitting trousers were made of yellow and black MacLachlan tartan and on his feet he wore red velvet slippers. He was smoking a cigarette that was held in a rather long black lacquered holder.

'May I apologise firstly for snapping at you for the wrong pronunciation of my name; everyone gets it wrong the first time. And secondly, for my reluctance last night in agreeing to meet you. Purely nervousness on my part because my experience of dealing with Sir Chester Eastoff has somewhat clouded my judgement. My nose will never be quite the same again. Having said that, the disappearance of his daughter must be absolutely devastating for him and his wife, and I wouldn't wish that on them. And who might I have the honour?'

'Please allow me to introduce a colleague, Mr Luther Spaulding.'

'A delight to meet you.' Again, he held out his hand which Luther shook.

This really wasn't what the two of them expected. Where was the weak and ineffectual man that Chester had portrayed? What faced them was a self-assured, confident man. 'Please, sit down and let me pour your tea. And call me Clement – I insist.'

'Clement it is. And thank you for agreeing to see us.'

'It is my absolute pleasure; I am all yours.'

Wanda took out her notebook.

'We've just been admiring your two Picassos; they are quite something.'

'Why, thank you. They are my utter delights, and with my Rousseau they are my three pieces of utter perfection.'

'They must be a good investment for you?'

'Miss Cushway, one can't put a price on art; to do so would be vulgar.'

'Really? Well, hopefully you won't find me too vulgar if I ask you a simple question as to why you were trying to sell your highly successful ball bearing manufacturing company to Sir Chester Eastoff?'

'A good question, Miss Cushway, and one with a very simple answer. I got bored with it. You see, the humble ball bearing isn't, how shall I put it, exactly very stimulating for the grey matter, and the manufacturing process is somewhat tedious. I'm looking for more excitement in my life, more adventure, more passion, so I decided to sell.'

'The manufacturing of the humble ball bearing might be tedious, but it's what keeps the world turning,' Luther said. 'I'm always trying to broaden my knowledge of industrial processes, so as an expert, would you be able to answer a question I've always wanted the answer to about the manufacture of ball bearings?'

'Ah, I like an enquiring mind, Mr Spaulding, fire away.'

'Why do you use slugs in their manufacture?'

'A pertinent question. Nasty blighters, slugs, but they have their uses. We use their slime; it has certain chemical properties that we use when polishing our ball bearings.'

Wanda looked at Luther in absolute astonishment.

'Most enlightening, Clement. I'm a keen gardener and I've written several articles on the subject of our gastropod mollusc as garden pests and how to control them, but I've never heard them being used in the manufacture of ball bearings.'

'I'm always glad when I'm able to increase someone's depth of knowledge.'

'Thank you, and as a kindness please allow me to increase yours. Ball bearings are manufactured from steel wires or steel rods. This is the first step in the process and these wires or rods are cut up into small pieces, and I'm sure you'll be surprised to learn these are called slugs.'

Clement coloured and wandered over to an occasional table where he opened a cigarette box, inserted a new cigarette into his holder and lit it. He inhaled deeply and blew the smoke out. 'I see I've been well and truly rumbled.'

'You have indeed. Now, might I enquire as to how you really earn a living?' asked Wanda.

'Must you?'

'I must.'

'I'm just a plain, honest art dealer.'

'Really. In which case, why were you in a position to sell a ball bearing factory?'

'Oh golly gosh, this might prove to be a little bit problematic.'

'For you, maybe, but engrossing for us. Now please answer the question.'

'Well, in a sort of way it was mine to sell.'

'You intrigue me. What sort of way?'

'Well, in the sort of way that I acquired it.'

'And how does one acquire a ball bearing factory?'

'Well, um, it was given to me as a present.'

'A present. Gosh. And who might be the bearer of such a generous gift?'

'Oh, damn and blast, to hell with it, you might as well know. Two years ago, I meet a Mr Mungan MacCabe.'

'As in MacCabe Shipbuilders?'

'The very same, and a hail-fellow-well-met he was not. He'd approached me as a reputable art dealer because he wanted to make a foray into the world of art and buy a painting as an investment. I knew that there was a Juan Gris coming onto the market and suggested that it would indeed make a sound investment. He said he didn't care who the hell the artist was. In actual fact, the man was a complete philistine, a peasant.'

'So, you sold him the Gris?'

'Yes, I found out who the vendor was and I approached her privately and we agreed a price. I then sold it to MacCabe.'

'That all seems straightforward. So where does the ball bearing factory come into the equation?'

'It comes into the equation because a year later, and don't ask me how, he found out how much I had paid for the blasted painting. And more to the point he didn't like the profit I had made. Coupled

152

with the fact that he'd found out a few of my deals involved selling fakes. Despite my protestations on both counts, he felt that a three-hundred-per-cent margin was a touch on the extortionate side.'

'I thought you said a few moments ago that it was vulgar to put a price on art.'

'It is for the art I purchase for myself. When I purchase for clients I make as much money as I think I can squeeze out of them. Unfortunately, MacCabe took great exception to my squeezing.'

'Really, Clement, you surprise me.' Wanda glanced at Luther, who winked at her. 'Surely your reputation as a reputable dealer preceded you.'

'My thoughts exactly. But he didn't quite see it that way and demanded the margin on the Gris be returned, and worst of all he said he would let the purchasers of the fakes know that the paintings they had bought from me weren't worth as much as they had thought, unless I did him a favour. And that favour was to pose as a factory owner to sell his blasted ball bearing factory to Sir Chester Eastoff.'

'And why did he want to sell his factory?'

'He knew that Sir Chester was looking at buying such a factory and saw it as a way of hurting the man that he loathes.'

'Hurting him how?'

'Prior to the purchase, MacCabe was going to strip out all the assets of the company, so Sir Chester would end up buying a worthless shell.'

'I see, this is now starting to make sense. So why did you threaten Sir Chester?'

'Because I knew I had failed and that failure might cost me a lot of money, so that made me mardy and I don't like being mardy. So I threatened him, which as it turned out was not such a smart move on my part, because he broke my nose.'

'What did MacCabe do?'

'He was furious that Sir Chester had walked away.'

'Where were you on the twenty-sixth and twenty-seventh of June this year?'

'I can't remember.'

'Oh come on, Clement, even in your mad world you must remember where you were seven and a half weeks ago,' Luther ventured.

'Let me think. No, sorry, my mind is a total blank.'

'Is it really? Let me see if I can help you to think with a bit more clarity. At some point over those two days, Miss Florence Eastoff went missing. So, unless you can account for your whereabouts, Scotland Yard will be extremely interested in talking to you in relation to her disappearance, especially in the light of your threat to Sir Chester.'

'You make your point very succinctly, Miss Cushway, and in the light of that, and my desire for self-preservation, I must tell you that I was visiting the Alladale estate.'

'Ah, the family estate of Mr Mungan MacCabe in the Highlands of Scotland.' Wanda inclined her head. 'I take it you weren't there to shoot grouse?'

'No, I wasn't. He wanted me to help commission a painting at cost to celebrate the achievement of, as he put it, a forthcoming victory.'

'Why you, after what you did to him before?'

'Because if I didn't help him, he had it in his gift to ruin me.'

'And what forthcoming victory was this?'

'He didn't say, and I didn't ask.'

'I see. What was the subject matter?'

'He wanted a realistic painting depicting Exodus 21:23–37.'

'Gosh, how fascinating, and who are you going to commission to paint such a work.'

'I've got some feelers out on my behalf who are approaching Edvard Munch.'

Wanda looked at Luther and suppressed the urge to smile.

'Thank you, Clement, this had been most illuminating. Would you be happy to assist the police with their enquiries?'

'I don't suppose I have much choice.'

'No, you haven't. Now unless you have anything more to add we must be on our way.'

Clement smiled weakly but looked utterly dejected and shook his head. Wanda checked her watch. It had just gone one thirty, so they about-turned and left him to his thoughts, seeing themselves out.

'Well done! Where did that information on the slug come from? That was inspired.'

'And well done to you too! I wouldn't like to get on the wrong side of you in a debate; mind you, I knew that already. On the subject of slugs, a lot of our mining equipment has ball bearings as an integral part, so out of my natural curiosity I made it a point to understand how the equipment worked and was manufactured.'

'How fascinating, now I've learnt something new. Now, Luther, what does Exodus 21:23–37 mean to you?'

'I haven't been to church for a while, but from my Sunday school days, learning to recite scriptures, it went: "An eye for an eye, and a tooth for a tooth".'

'Correct: reciprocal justice. Now what did I learn from my trip to Rothbury?'

'That Florian Boutroux lost the sight in his left eye, after a piece of a red-hot rivet embedded itself.'

'Exactly. Now we're off to the village of West Dean near Chichester to pay a visit to a certain Mr Walderne Smithers.'

'As in the architect of Sir Chester's new wing?'

'The very same.' Wanda explained about the architect's drawing and sketch she'd studied whilst they were looking at Featherstonehaugh's works of art.

'Why didn't you question Featherstonehaugh about the drawing and his relationship to Smithers?'

'Because if there is a connection between the two, I didn't want him warning Smithers.'

'Gosh, you're good at this.'

Wanda gave Luther a broad smile and a little nudge.

'So, you think there might be a connection between them?'

'There's only one way to find out, but before we do, I fancy a walk along the seafront.'

Wanda put her arm through Luther's and they enjoyed the warmth of the sun as they absorbed what they had learnt from

Clement Featherstonehaugh. They passed a busy fish and chip shop and as they were at the seaside, decided that a treat of cod, chips with mushy peas, bread and butter, and a cup of tea was the order of the day.

Dessert was eaten al fresco on the way back to Brighton station: a cornet full of the creamiest vanilla ice cream each.

CHAPTER 23
TUESDAY, 15 AUGUST 1922
WEST DEAN

Wanda and Luther's train pulled into Chichester station shortly before five o'clock. They boarded a bus for the five-mile journey to West Dean, which stopped outside the Selsey Arms on Midhurst Road. Having got their bearings, they noticed George Mundy's grocery and provisions shop. The shop door was open and they walked in.

'Good afternoon, sir and madam, I'm George Mundy, proprietor of this fine establishment, the best purveyor of finest provisions and groceries this side of London. Now what can I tempt you with? Maybe one of my legendary raised pork pies with a jar of my piccalilli to accompany it? Or how about some of my potted beef or potted ham, or maybe a slice of my rabbit pie, not to mention my renowned game pie?'

'Very kind, Mr Mundy, and I'm sure your culinary offerings are indeed legendary,' said Wanda. 'But all we require are directions as we've never been here before.'

'I always remember a face and I didn't recognise either of yours. Tell me where you need to get to, and I'll point you in the right direction.'

'We're here to visit Mr Walderne Smithers.'

'Are you indeed. Then you'll be wanting Wren Cottage. If you turn around, across the street that's Church Lane; follow the lane to the end, and Wren Cottage is opposite Saint Andrew's church. A five-minute stroll.'

'Thank you, Mr Mundy, you've been exceedingly helpful.'

'It's a pleasure. Have you ever met Walderne?'

'No, we haven't.'

'Well in that case, a word to the wise, if you will permit, madam.'

'But of course.'

'He's an odd 'un.'

'Really? In what way?'

'Keeps himself to himself and keeps odd hours, always disappearing with that battered suitcase of his and returning days later. No one knows where he goes.'

'I see. Well, thank you for the directions.'

As they left the shop, Wanda said, 'Luther, at some point we will need food this evening, so let's avail ourselves of some of Mr Mundy's food to see how legendary it is.'

'That's just what I was thinking.'

'Of course you were.' She gave him an affectionate nudge.

Ten minutes later, they left Mr Mundy's emporium with a hamper.

*

It was a picturesque scene as they walked through the village of flint-faced houses and cottages with their neat and well-tended gardens, typical of the South Downs area. They got the impression nothing much had changed for centuries. They arrived at Saint Andrew's church and there, set back on the opposite side, they found Wren Cottage. It too had the local flint walls. The front garden was well maintained and stocked with an abundance of roses, and the air was fragrant with their scent. Wanda knocked on the front door. A few moments later a man answered it. He was tall, maybe over six foot, but his face looked gaunt and he had unnaturally black hair. He was dressed immaculately in cream trousers, an azure shirt, with a green paisley silk cravat. On his feet he wore white nubuck Oxfords.

'Mr Smithers.'

'Yes, and you are?'

He was on his guard immediately. 'I am Miss Wanda Cushway and this is Mr Luther Spaulding. We are investigating the disappearance of Miss Florence Eastoff.'

'Are you the police?'

'No, we are not. The detective agency we work for has been hired by Sir Chester Eastoff.'

'I know nothing whatsoever about her disappearance. The only things I know are what I've read about it in *The Times*.'

'Well in that case, you have nothing to fear. Can we come in, please, and ask you a few questions?'

He glanced anxiously at the neighbouring cottages to check that they weren't being observed. 'Well if you must, but I won't be able to help you.' He turned around and held the door open. 'Please go straight through to the parlour.'

The parlour was a snug room, with floor-to-ceiling bookshelves on every wall. The French windows were open, leading to a beautiful garden. The raised beds were bursting with colour and a pergola covered in wisteria ran down the middle towards a pond. In its centre was a statue of Apollo which was in fact a fountain, creating a wonderful sound of summer rain pitter-pattering on the water's surface.

'Gardening is a passion of mine, Mr Smithers, and yours is exceptional.'

'Thank you, Mr Spaulding, but I don't think you came here to discuss horticulture.'

'Quite, we didn't.' Wanda gave Luther the briefest of smiles. 'Sir Chester Eastoff isn't your favourite person, is he, Mr Smithers?'

'No, he's not. He ruined me. I had a very successful architectural practice in Chichester employing ten people. An inquiry found that the building company I contracted used substandard building materials. Why would they do that? I've worked with these builders on two projects before in the north-east and they were exemplary; that's why Sir Chester asked me to bid for the contract. In my opinion the wing collapsed due to an earthquake.'

'An earthquake?'

'Yes, the wing was built on a fault line.'

'Really, and how do you know that?'

'It stands to reason, doesn't it. How else would a sound structure collapse?'

'Maybe because substandard materials were used in its construction. But we digress. The fact that Sir Chester put your business into liquidation gives you a motive to seek revenge, does it not?'

Walderne didn't respond. He sat and stared across the garden and into the distance. A good minute passed.

'Mr Smithers, you have a motive, have you not?'

'Damn you, of course I have a motive. The bastard wrecked my business and the livelihoods of my wonderful employees. I loathe the man with a passion, and the world would be a better place without him. But I had nothing whatsoever to do with the disappearance of his daughter, and unless you have any evidence to the contrary I want you to leave my house now!'

Walderne spat the words out and was trembling with rage. 'Now get out!' he screamed.

Wanda and Luther stared at him until he seemed to calm down. 'Mr Smithers, you are not helping the situation, so please try and remain calm. Now can you tell us what is the nature of your relationship with a Mr Clement Featherstonehaugh?'

'Who?'

'Mr Clement Featherstonehaugh, of Xanadu Villa in Brighton.'

He shook his head. 'No, the name means nothing to me.'

'You surprise me, Mr Smithers. Can you therefore explain to us why an architectural drawing and sketch of his villa is hanging on his drawing room wall, ascribed to a certain Walderne Smithers, RIBA, Wren Cottage, West Dean?'

'No, I can't explain why a drawing purportedly by me is hanging on his wall.'

'Mr Smithers, you are not a very good liar. We've just travelled from Xanadu Villa, and unless there is another Walderne Smithers, RIBA, of Wren Cottage in West Dean, you are that person! So, I ask you again: why is an architectural drawing and sketch hanging in his drawing room?'

Walderne let out a long sigh and stood up. 'Let me check my client index.' He went over to a roll-top bureau, opened the bottom drawer and produced a leather-bound alphabetical journal. 'Featherstonehaugh, you say.' He put on a pair of glasses. 'Here we are: F.' He made a show of studying the journal and turning the pages slowly.

'Ah, my apologies, Miss Cushway, I am mistaken. A Mr Clement Featherstonehaugh commissioned me to produce a set of architectural drawings of his villa and a sketch of the property in March last year.'

'As an architect you are trained to observe minute detail, and yet you couldn't remember being commissioned by Mr Featherstonehaugh? I find that implausible. You are a deceitful person, Mr Smithers. What is your relationship with Mr Featherstonehaugh?'

'Purely professional.'

'I don't believe you, and furthermore, I believe you are involved with the disappearance of Miss Eastoff.'

'I can assure you I'm not and if you had any evidence to that effect, you would have come out with it from the outset of your wasted visit. Now get out of my house.'

'Far from it, Mr Smithers. We have had a very illuminating visit. We will go now, but rest assured we will find evidence of your involvement in her disappearance. So, shall we just say au revoir?'

*

They set off back towards Midhurst Road. 'Well, what do you make of our Walderne Smithers?'

'Wanda, any man who dyes his hair must be insecure.'

'"Don't run down dyed hair and painted faces. There is an extraordinary charm in them sometimes."'

'What?'

'Don't you know your Oscar Wilde?'

'Obviously not.'

'It's a quote from *The Picture of Dorian Gray*, but the operative word is "sometimes". I agree with you, he's insecure and shifty, and more to the point, I wouldn't trust him as far as I could throw him.'

'So, what do we do now?'

'We settle down and enjoy our picnic, Luther, whilst we observe Wren Cottage. I see that Church Lane returns to the main road past the church. We can do a loop and return unnoticed. I spotted a small copse adjacent to the church where we should be able to see the cottage without being seen.'

They came up behind the church and entered the copse. There were several gorse bushes on the edge of the copse which afforded a good view of the cottage. They settled down and found that indeed Mr Mundy's pork pie was exceptional, with plenty of savoury jelly, and the piccalilli was the perfect accompaniment along with his home-grown sweet tomatoes. Wanda checked her watch; it had just gone seven thirty and there had been no sign of movement from inside the cottage.

'Don't move.'

Luther froze. 'Why not?'

'You have a *Cicindela campestris* sitting on your left shoulder.'

'How marvellous. What is it?'

'A green tiger beetle.'

'Is it dangerous?'

'Exceedingly. Now sit still while I grab my sketchbook and coloured pencils.'

Within five minutes Wanda had produced a beautiful, exact drawing of the beetle.

'There, what do you think?'

'It's exquisite, just like you.'

'Thank you, now you're making me blush. Hold on.' She grabbed her bag and produced a magnifying glass, handing it to Luther. Carefully cupping her hand, she picked the beetle off his shoulder.

'Take a close look.'

He did so. 'The shiny green is so vivid and the creamy yellow spots on its back stand out. Wow, look at its jaws.'

'Yes, they are big. It uses them to catch small invertebrates. And do you know also that it's one of the fastest running insects in Britain, reaching speeds of up to five and a half miles an hour?'

'Speaking of running, turn around, Wanda.'

Walderne Smithers was making his way down his garden path, carrying a battered suitcase. He was dressed exactly as before with the addition of a raincoat draped over his arm. He turned left and disappeared from sight along Church Lane.

'Do we follow him?'

'No, Luther, we wait here until we are sure he's not going to return, then we go and search for the evidence we need.'

'As in breaking into his cottage?'

'In a word, yes.'

'The last time you roped me into that, we only just managed to escape without being caught.'

'It's one of the hazards of the job, I'm afraid. We'll be fine.'

An hour passed and there was no sign of Walderne. The sun had set and in its place twilight was slowly taking over. 'I don't think he will be returning here any time soon. Come on, Luther, let's see how security conscious our architect is, and remember to keep our voices to a whisper.'

First, they checked for any signs of life from the two neighbouring cottages. There were none. Walderne's cottage was set further back from his neighbours, so from the back they shouldn't be seen. They crossed the road, walked up the garden path and straight around to the back of the cottage.

The French windows were securely locked; likewise, all the downstairs windows. They surveyed the upper-floor windows and they too looked firmly secured. The roof was thatched and curved down the sides of each of the two upper-floor windows to the level of the ground-floor windows. In the centre of the roof above the first floor was a mansard window set into the thatch, which they assumed was an attic, and they both noticed that one of the windows had been shut by the insertion of a wooden wedge from the outside.

'Wanda, look, there's a drainpipe that runs into that large barrel over there. I can climb up on that and get up onto the thatched roof. All I need is something I can smash down into the thatch that I can use to haul myself up.'

'Let's see what we can find in his garden shed. He's obviously a keen gardener so I'm sure he must have some implement we can use. Come on.'

Wanda opened the shed door and they went inside. It was neat and tidy with a variety of garden tools hanging from the ceiling.

'There, that's what I want, that long-handled three-pronged cultivator.' Luther took it down. 'Now I need something to extract the wedge.' They found a wooden toolbox and helped themselves to a pair of pliers and pincers, which they put into a haversack that was conveniently hanging on the back of the shed door.

Luther managed to haul himself up onto the barrel where he could easily touch the thatched roof. Wanda handed him the cultivator and haversack and retreated to a safe distance. He gripped the cultivator with both hands behind his head and using as much force as he could muster, smashed it down into the thatch.

'Well done, you looked like Poseidon wielding his trident.'

'I've often wondered what it must be like to be a god, and now I know. Let's see if I can haul myself up.' With a great deal of effort, he managed hand over hand to pull himself up the long handle of the cultivator, until he was on the roof.

The wooden wedge in the mansard window was well and truly jammed and wouldn't budge. It took Luther a good five minutes to work it free and then he was in. A few moments later he appeared at the French windows and let Wanda in.

'Anything of note in the attic?'

'No, it's completely empty.'

'Right, it's getting pretty dark. When we were here earlier I noticed a couple of oil lamps on the dining table. I'm not concerned about the neighbours seeing lights on as they will think Walderne is at home. You take the upstairs, and remember to replace everything exactly where you found it.'

Luther completed his search fairly quickly and joined Wanda. They searched every nook and cranny and left nothing unturned, but after a good hour and a half had found nothing incriminating.

'Wouldn't a cottage like this have a cellar?'

'Possibly, Wanda, but we would have noticed a doorway leading down into one.'

'Yes, we would have, but there may be a trapdoor somewhere. Let's start in the dining room.' They checked every inch of the floor in the dining room, parlour, hall and toilet and drew a blank.

'Just the kitchen left. Maybe Walderne is telling the truth and he didn't have anything to do with Florence's disappearance.'

'My instincts tell me he did,' Wanda said. 'Come on.'

They studied the kitchen floor but there was no sign of a trapdoor. Wanda opened the pantry door and studied the floor – again, no sign. She walked in and stopped, then backed out again and stamped on the kitchen floor. Then she went back into the pantry and stamped on the floor there. It was different, a hollow timpani sound as opposed to a dead sound.

'Help me move these stoneware flagons off the floor.'

As they moved the flagons, the outline of a trapdoor was revealed. On the right-hand side was a heavy iron ring.

'Would you do the honours?'

'Of course.' Luther lifted the heavy ring and pulled the door up and rested it against the left-hand wall. They both stared at stone steps that led down into blackness.

'Let's see what secrets this cellar might reveal.'

They held their oil lamps and descended into a whitewashed room. It was neat and tidy, packed with shelves full to bursting of architectural drawings. On the wall opposite the stairs, a floor-to-ceiling wine rack was filled with bottles. At the rear was another roll-top bureau and a well-worn mahogany-and-leather desk chair.

Wanda sat down and tried to open the bureau, but it was locked. She opened her bag, had a rummage and produced a hairgrip, and within a matter of seconds had picked the lock.

'Crikey, Wanda, where on earth did you learn that skill?'

'I'm self-taught. I read a novel recently where the villain was constantly picking locks using a hairgrip, so I practised until I mastered the technique.'

'Have you read *Oliver Twist?*'

'I've read all the works of Dickens, and no, I won't be taking up pickpocketing. Now shall we see what this bureau can tell us about Walderne?' She pushed open the roller top.

Laid out in front of them in a neat line was a box of Brousses writing paper and envelopes, a magnifying glass, various scissors, a scalpel, a steel ruler, cutting board, a stack of ten cheap books, a pot of glue, a pair of cotton gloves and a leather-bound notebook. Wanda put on the cotton gloves and picked up one of the books. Various pages fell out onto the desk. They noticed that each page had neat, precise cuts where letters had been removed.

'We've found the author of the ransom notes. No wonder he's fled the nest.'

'Do you think he delivered them as well?'

'I imagine so, Luther. The least amount of people you have in an operation like this, the more chance you have of success. Having said that, he has somehow to deliver the final ransom note.' She glanced at her watch; it was nearly ten o'clock. 'I need to contact Tony so he can deploy some officers to watch the house in Lennox Gardens in case he is stupid enough to deliver the note in person. He can also arrange for a police photographer from the local constabulary to come out here and create a record of our findings.'

She picked up the notebook; it had hardly been used. On the first page was the Eastoffs' London address and telephone number. On the second and third page there were notes which she read out loud: '"Head of the Paris fashion house Élégance Féminine, Jean-Baptiste Laurent, is romantically linked to the wife of his bitter rival, Toussaint Bigot, of the fashion house Petit et Beau".' Listed below this statement were various dates and times when the two were seen at a number of Parisian restaurants and clubs.

'So it was Walderne who made the telephone call to Florence on the evening of the twenty-sixth of June.'

'It would appear so. Can you tell me why these fashion houses have such ludicrous names?'

'Might it be something to do with creating a brand?'

'I suppose so. There's no chance of us getting back to London tonight, but I noticed the Selsey Arms has rooms, so with any luck they may have a couple for us. We will need a very early start so that I can get a telegram to Wispy and Tony about our discoveries, and Tony can arrange for a watch on the Eastoffs' house.'

She found an envelope, inserted the notebook and placed it in her bag, replaced the gloves and closed the bureau. They shut the trapdoor, replaced the flagons and headed towards the French windows.

'Hold on a moment.'

Luther went over to an occasional table and picked up two books.

'I thought I might borrow these; they are a couple of books on garden architecture.'

'Borrow? It's not a lending library!'

'Yes, I know, but I was thinking of designing a new feature for the gardens at Pit Prop Lodge.'

'Really, Capability Brown, and you intend to return them?'

Luther raised his arms in mock surprise. 'But of course.'

They left through the French windows and walked arm in arm to the inn.

CHAPTER 24
WEDNESDAY, 16 AUGUST 1922
CALAIS

The two of us met for breakfast at eight o'clock, in plenty of time for being picked up by Chief Inspector Bombelles. Constanza had arrived yesterday afternoon with the films, and we wished her bon voyage on the early evening sailing back to Dover.

Last night's dinner was excellent; well, the food was. *Consommé Madrilène, moules marinière, filet de boeuf* with Béarnaise sauce, *pommes fondantes, fromage*, and *cômpote des fruits* with Chantilly meringue. The wine that accompanied our dinner was exquisite: a Château du Cléray and a Châteaux Haut-Brion Pessac-Léognan.

The company, on the other hand, was, although I'm sure very nice, rather trying. All we wanted was to have a quiet evening and to focus on the job in hand, and not have to make small talk with the mayor, councillors, stationmaster, various other dignitaries, and Uncle Tom Cobley and all.

As we were enjoying our breakfast, a bellboy approached and handed me a telegram. I slit it open: 'Walderne involved STOP Responsible for the notes STOP May deliver the final note STOP Suggest a watch on Lennox Gardens STOP Need to revisit Featherstonehaugh STOP On way back to London STOP Wanda'.

'Here, read this: Walderne's involved!'

Tony scanned its contents. 'Wanda is truly a loss to the Yard. Let me contact the commissioner and arrange for a round-the-clock watch to be put on the Eastoffs.' With that, he scuttled off.

He returned ten minutes later as the chief inspector bustled into the restaurant, shortly before nine o'clock. He had a completely different disguise on from yesterday, this time dressed as a car mechanic, complete with grease smears on his face. Our fellow diners looked at him in bemused astonishment. He joined us for coffee and reported that last night's dinner was a resounding triumph and he assured us that we had made a lasting impression on his guests. I took this to mean that his kudos amongst his peers had benefited from our presence and that his rather large ego had been suitably massaged. He agreed to our request to get the films developed.

He reported that it had been a quiet night at Maison Hugo with no one leaving, which he thought boded well for this morning's 'Operation to Rescue a Nightingale' as he had his prey right where he wanted them. As we headed out to Fréthun in the old, rusting Citroën, it was another beautiful sunny morning without a cloud in the sky. Arriving bang on ten o'clock, we entered the surveillance property that looked out onto the front of the hideout.

At ten forty-five the chief inspector asked his Morse code operator to send a signal to the other surveillance team's inspector to get his men into position. I was impressed with the speed the men took up their positions without making any noise whatsoever. Now we would see if their meticulous training was about to pay off.

The minutes to the hour passed slowly and we were all pretty tense by the time the church clock started to chime the hour. Our postman came cycling around the bend on the cart path, resplendent in his postman's uniform, whistling a ditty for all he was worth. He propped his bike against the fence and walked up the garden path, still whistling, rapped on the front door knocker three times and stood back. Nothing. He knocked again. Still nothing, not even a twitch of a curtain.

I looked at Tony and tension was etched on his face. The chief inspector looked distinctly uneasy and had lost his earlier confidence. Something was not as it should be.

The postman gave a series of military hand signals, dispatching one of his colleagues to the back of the cottage whilst the other two men drew their weapons and stood to the left side of the door. He waited until his colleague had returned and then slowly lifted the latch and tentatively opened the door ajar. One of the men peered in through the small gap and urgently signalled to the postman to shut the door, which he did very carefully.

The postman signalled again, and his colleague disappeared behind the cottage whilst the three of them slowly backed away from the front. A few moments later they joined us, and the postman entered into an urgent dialogue with the chief inspector.

'The front door appears to be booby-trapped. There is a fine wire attached near the bottom of the door that is linked to what we think is the firing pin of a Mills bomb which is held in place on the opposite door jamb. There is not much play in the wire so if he'd opened it any more, it would have armed the bomb and exploded.'

'Chief Inspector, if I may?'

'Of course, Sir William.'

'I'm very familiar with these devices as we used them on the western front all the time. They are fragmentation grenades and once detonated will release their lethal fragments, killing and maiming.'

'I'm assuming the back door of the house will be booby-trapped as well, and who knows where else in the building.'

'Agreed.'

'It should be relatively easy to render the device useless if we can get a pair of wire cutters through the gap in the front door and cut the wire. We can then proceed with caution into the house and check for other devices.'

'Very well, Sir William, as you are familiar with the grenade might I suggest you go along with Sergeant Lafontaine, our excellent postman, and do us the honour of defusing the device.'

Bloody hell, I didn't see that coming.

'Sergeant, how much of a gap was there?'

'I would say five centimetres.'

'Not much to work with, but two inches might be enough to get the wire cutters through and onto the wire. How is the Mills bomb secured to the door jamb?'

'It has been placed in a wooden box that has been screwed onto the jamb. The grenade is clearly visible and the wire is attached to the pin.'

'Fine. Have we any wire cutters?'

One of the gendarmes brought in a large toolbox which he opened up. I selected a pair of long-handled bolt cutters and a small pair of wire cutters and a torch.

'Chief Inspector, I'm sure our suspects are long gone and there won't be a soul in there, but in the interests of safety can you evacuate the surrounding houses?'

'Of course, Sir William, I should have thought of that. We don't want our citizens being blown up, do we?'

A fair point, but what about me?

The chief inspector barked out a series of orders and his officers scurried off, evacuating the surrounding area. After a bit of local resistance, the area was cleared in fifteen minutes. 'Right, Sir William, over to you and my sergeant.'

'Thank you, Chief Inspector, much appreciated. Right, Sergeant, please lead on.'

We went out of the front door of the cottage, crossed the cart path and walked up the garden path to the front door. We went around the whole property, walking slowly and looking for any signs of other booby traps, but there was nothing obvious. I checked my bearings once we were outside the front door again. The cottage was the last one in a line of five and to my left the cart track led into a cornfield.

I squatted down on the left side of the door. 'Sergeant, I want you to open the door to the exact position you did earlier and not a millimetre wider.'

'Yes, sir.'

I shone the torch inside and there it was. The wire stretched to the ring pull on the Mills bomb and it was pretty taut, so there was little margin for error. The grenade seemed to be sitting in its wooden box but unencumbered by any strapping. However, there was a spring attached to the other side of the ring pull, which in turn was attached to another wire. My guess was that the wire attached to the door and the wire attached to the spring were of equal tension. Then as soon as I released the tension on the wire attached to the door, the tension would increase on the other wire and the spring would pull the firing pin out. In other words, the booby trap was itself booby-trapped. We were dealing with someone who was exceptionally clever around explosives.

'Sergeant, we have a slight problem.' I explained the situation. 'What I'm not sure about is if this device is connected to any other devices in the building and could start a chain reaction. Now please close the door.'

I walked back with him and explained the situation to everyone. 'Sir William, might I have a word?'

'But of course.'

Tony led me out of earshot of the others and in a whisper said, 'Bloody hell, Wispy, do you know what in blue blazes you are doing?'

'Of course I do, I've been trained in the handling of munitions.'

Being trained is one thing, and that was a good six years ago. It was another thing entirely defusing the bloody thing.

'Well in that case I'll come with you; you might need an extra pair of hands.'

'No, Tony. Thank you, but it's best that I work alone.'

We turned back and faced the rest of the team who looked on expectantly. 'Now please let me get on with the job in hand.'

I stood in the middle of the cart path and watched them walk away, evacuating any residents who were at home, until they reached the furthest cottage. I then turned and walked towards the cottage. I paused at the gate and took off my jacket, hung it on the gatepost and placed my panama hat on top.

I unlatched the door then sank to my knees and opened it ajar with my right hand. With my left hand I inserted the wire cutters and held them just above the taut wire. Sweat had started to drip into my eyes, which stung them and blurred my vision. I blinked several times and my eyesight cleared.

Right, Wispy, old boy, here goes.

I cut the wire, and as I predicted, the tension on the other wire increased and the spring whipped out the firing pin.

For the love of God, Wispy, you need to move!

In one move I grabbed the Mills bomb and depressed the striker lever. Technically it should now not explode until I released the lever, but with old munitions one never knew what might happen.

I ran for all I was worth towards the cornfield and hurled the bomb as far as I could throw it. It helped that I opened the bowling for the first eleven at Gresham's and still had a reasonable bowling arm. I managed to launch it thirty-odd yards before it hit the deck. A few seconds later, there was an almighty explosion and clods of earth and ears of corn rained down on me. I rolled over onto my back and propped myself up on my elbows, staring at Maison Hugo, expecting it to explode at any second. But it didn't.

I got up and started to walk towards the cottage. All the others were running towards me, clapping and cheering.

'Sir William, on behalf of the citizens of Calais I salute you. You are indeed a very brave man.'

'Thank you, Chief Inspector. It was nothing.'

Who am I kidding? I'm still shaking and my ears are ringing. There was a more than fifty-fifty chance that it could have gone horribly wrong. Then what would Libby say? God, it doesn't bear thinking about.

'I need to enter the cottage and check for other booby traps, so gentlemen, if you wouldn't mind returning to your places?'

I cautiously went in and immediately noticed the back door was fitted with the same device. I checked all the downstairs windows and there were no further signs of any more booby traps. I knelt by the back door and again with a degree of apprehension cut the wire. The exact same sequence happened and the firing pin was whipped out.

I managed another corker of a ball, but my cream trousers and white shirt were beginning to suffer as more clods rained down on me. Monsieur Peyronnet's field now had two large craters in it, but I was sure that the chief inspector would be able to smooth things over with him.

The chief inspector stood down his undercover team with instructions to Sergeant Lafontaine to return with the police photographer. He and his inspector would help us search the cottage. I consulted my watch and time had marched on; it was nearly two thirty.

'Inspector D'Arras and I will take the ground floor, whilst you, Sir William, and Inspector Finkelstein can take the upstairs rooms.'

Why doesn't that surprise me? I doubt whether the chief inspector will even fit on the narrow stairs, let alone be able to climb them.

At the top of the stairs was a landing. On the left was a single door and on the right, two doors, all shut. We took the right-hand side doors first. The first one was a box room, which was completely empty bar a few boxes on the floor. We took a box each and methodically went through them. They contained nothing more than old paperwork belonging to the tenant farmers concerning the running of their smallholding.

The next-door room contained a dirty mattress with sheets and a couple of pillows on it which had obviously been slept on recently.

We turned our attention to the door on the left. Tony put his hand on the door handle and opened it. The smell that assailed our nostrils was overpowering. The stench of death greeted us, along with the frenetic buzzing of hundreds of blowflies that had invaded the room and that we had just disturbed. We both recoiled and shut the door.

'Heaven have mercy. Was that Florence?'

'Oy gevalt! I didn't look, but we're going to have to go back in there.'

'I know. Come on, let's get this over with.'

We re-entered the room. The blowflies were still mad. The temperature in the room was stifling, and the sickly sweet odour of death was cloying. I flung open both windows as wide as they would go, then turned and looked at the corpse with Tony. God have mercy, it was a male. He was propped up against the metal bedstead, and already the body had bloated and looked grotesque. Maggots were going about their business in the nostrils, eye sockets, mouth and ears. He had three bullet wounds in the middle of his temple, which the maggots were exploiting. But despite his distorted features, we both recognised him from the photograph taken at the Eastoff company annual procurement Christmas dinner. Jack Potts.

'My guess is that he has been dead for two days at the most. This warm weather will speed up decomposition,' said Tony. 'But where's the blood?'

'A good question. Maybe Boutroux cleaned it up.'

'Or he was shot post-mortem.'

'Why would he do that?'

'Because he's a sadistic bastard.'

A pang of anguish came over me as I thought of Mrs Potts and her two children back home in Magpie Cottage, alone and desperate for news of his whereabouts. He wouldn't be going home; his children had lost a father, and his wife, her 'kind and gentle man'.

So, Mr Potts, how on earth did you get yourself into this mess?

He was dressed as a farm labourer, wearing a chore jacket, denim trousers, a collarless shirt and boots. Tony went through his pockets and on the inside of his jacket he extracted an envelope which was addressed to 'My darling Olive, Daisy and Archie'.

'A dilemma, Wispy: do we replace this and leave it to the French authorities, or do we make sure it gets delivered safely into the hands of Mrs Potts?'

'The crime was committed on French soil, so technically it should be left where we found it. But morally I think we owe it to Olive Potts and her children to make sure it's delivered into her hands.'

'My thoughts entirely.'

I put the letter in my jacket pocket. 'At our first opportunity we must get it to her. Now let's focus on the room.'

I turned around and to the right of the door was a pair of manacles chained to the wall.

'Look, the inhuman bastards have had her manacled in here.'

'They have, but remember how resourceful Florence is.'

We both got down on our hands and knees and scoured the walls and floor for any signs of a clue as to her whereabouts.

'There.' I pointed. 'Look in the corner, scratched into the plaster.' We both peered at the three words: 'Caletum', 'navis', 'Anglia'.

'"Caletum" is the Latin for Calais, "navis" is a boat, and "Anglia" is Blighty. She's on her way to England!'

'God, she's one hell of an operator.'

'She is, and a bloody formidable opponent. Come on, I think it's time to get Chief Inspector Bombelles and Inspector D'Arras.'

We went out onto the landing and Tony shouted for them to come up. This was easier said than done. The chief inspector huffed and puffed and wheezed his way up the stairs, with D'Arras bringing up the rear in case he toppled backwards, which if he did, I would fear for the safety of the inspector. He finally made it to the top and was perspiring profusely. Tony explained in detail what we had discovered.

The chief inspector opened the door. '*Mon Dieu.*' He went in, followed by Inspector D'Arras. We left them to it and went downstairs to examine the three rooms. A good thirty minutes later they joined us.

'I agree with your estimated time of death, Inspector, so it would appear that Boutroux and Miss Eastoff left here at some point before we arrived on Monday evening. By now they will be in England, while we have been watching a cottage with a corpse in it. We've been made to look like fools. Blast, that bastard has stolen a march on us. If only we'd gone in sooner. Apologies, gentlemen.'

'No apologies necessary. We are where we are, Chief Inspector.'

'Thank you, Inspector, that is a comfort to me. Now, the photographer should be here soon. I will return to headquarters and arrange for the undertakers to get out here, and I want a post-mortem carried out as soon as possible; in any case, no later than this evening. I think we know the cause of death but you never know what secrets a body can hide.'

'Quite. I need to update the commissioner on today's developments, so can I suggest that we travel back with you and you can drop us off at the hotel? We can reconvene later after the post-mortem.'

Well done, Tony. I need to speak to Strangely urgently.

'Of course. Inspector D'Arras, I will see you back at headquarters once all the photographs have been taken and the body removed. I'll send you a couple of gendarmes to help secure the scene. Come, gentlemen.' We left the scene as the church clock struck the hour of five.

*

Strangely came on the line from Paris and I gave him a detailed account of our gruelling day.

'God, he's a cold-blooded good-for-nothing psychopath. I bet you he always had the intention of killing Potts once he was no longer of any use to him.'

'Yes, I think you're right. I actually have a tad of sympathy for him.'

'Bloody hell, Wispy. How can you say that? He's exactly the same as Boutroux. Contemptible!'

'Yes, you're right. I suppose I'm just feeling sorry for Mrs Potts.'

'Well Potts should have thought about his family before embarking on this inhuman venture.'

'Of course he should have, but...'

'Now put Mrs Potts to the back of your mind. By the way, I never had you down as a bomb-disposal expert.'

'I'm not. You had exactly the same amount of munitions training as I did, and that little knowledge is a dangerous thing!'

'But the main thing is that you pulled it off. You deserve a medal.'

'Don't be stupid. You'd have done the same if you were there.'

'Maybe. So, he's on his way to Blighty?'

'It would appear so, and time is starting to catch up with us. Any sightings of the Lacroixs?'

'Yes, they both ventured out a couple of times today, once for lunch in a nearby café and then a little while ago for groceries – nothing exciting.'

'Very well, don't let them out of your sight. If there are any further developments from this end, I will call you.'

Next I phoned Wanda and thanked her for her telegram about Smithers and Featherstonehaugh and took comfort that her sympathies too were with Mrs Potts and the children.

'Well at least we have broadened our knowledge of the pronunciation of English surnames in that Featherstonehaugh is pronounced Fanshawe. And also, thanks to Luther's knowledge of what a slug is, MacCabe's loathing of Sir Chester Eastoff has been laid bare.'

'We can't keep this from Alberta and Chester. I would normally do this, and I'm more than happy to call them from here. But, in my opinion it should be done in person.'

'There is no need to ask. I will call them now and go straight over.'

'Thank you, and call me if there are any further developments from your end.'

'Will do.'

*

I had a long-deserved soak in my bath and called Libby, leaving out my exploits with the two Mills bombs, then went to the bar to meet Tony for a pre-dinner aperitif or two. We had just made ourselves comfortable with a gin and French when the chief inspector bustled in, wearing what for once looked like a normal uniform. I offered him a drink but he declined and handed me a packet containing the photographs that Strangely had taken. Unfortunately, he informed us, the post-mortem had been put back until eight o'clock the following morning as the pathologist was still on his way back from Paris. He said that as soon as he had the results, we would have them.

We looked through the photographs with growing horror. The black-and-white images left us in no doubt that we were up against a psychopathic killer. That evening, dinner was a sober affair, and the two of us turned in early as we were both utterly exhausted.

CHAPTER 25
THURSDAY, 17 AUGUST 1922
CALAIS

I met Tony for breakfast at eight and we'd already packed in the vain hope of catching the ten o'clock sailing to Dover. The post-mortem should be just about getting underway and that would last at a guess three hours. The next sailing wasn't due until this evening, and heaven alone knows where the rendezvous was going to be with Boutroux.

It's looking more and more likely that our course is nearly run. Boutroux is a very clever operator and has in essence been in control all along. Failure is starting to loom large on the horizon, and my father is again gnawing away at my ability. Blast it, Wispy, for God's sake, pull yourself together! 'Our doubts are traitors, and make us lose the good we oft might win, by fearing to attempt'.

Breakfast restored my spirits, and Tony and I were deep in conversation about the security aspects of transporting the gold, when our waiter interrupted us and said there was a Miss Cushway on the telephone for me.

'Good morning, Wanda.'

'And a good morning to you. Chester and Alberta have received what I assume will be Boutroux's final ransom note. It was left on their doorstep at some point early this morning, with the daily papers, and discovered by Strutton at six o'clock. Chester rang me straight away at home and I dashed across to Lennox Gardens.'

'So, Smithers found a way of getting the note delivered.'

'Yes he did. Let me read it to you.'

'Hold on, let me go and grab my notebook.'

I dashed back into the restaurant, told Tony about the note and rushed back.

'Right, Wanda, fire away and speak slowly. I haven't your ability to listen and write quickly.'

Wanda took a deep breath.

"'My dearest Lady Alberta and Sir Chester,

"'Firstly, let me give you some context as to why we are where we are. I trust you know your scriptures. Exodus 21:23–27: 'An eye for an eye and a tooth for a tooth'. In my case an EYE!

"'Secondly, I am very excited at the prospect of finally meeting you. I always think when exchanging gifts, it is so important to do it face to face. It gives the occasion much more solemnity. I do hope you agree.

"'Now onto the practicalities. At three o'clock precisely, at the now disused Royal Flying Corps Station Southfields, Acklington, coordinates 55° 17' 46" North 1° 38' 04" West, we will exchange our gifts. The runway runs from east to west, and at the west end of the runway I want the four ammunition boxes placed in a line with their lids off, ready for inspection.

"'Once I'm satisfied that my gold is as it should be, I will escort Florence from my car to a shortened telegraph pole which I have had positioned at the side of the runway. I will then securely tie her to the pole.

"'Now here's the rub: I will have a sniper positioned somewhere on the airfield and if any attempt is made to apprehend me, Florence will be shot through the head.

"'Finally, it goes without saying that if the police are involved tomorrow, you will never see your daughter alive again.

"'Yours affectionally,

"'YOUR VERY WORST NIGHTMARE MAY SOON BE OVER.'"

Bloody hell, Wispy, the absolute bastard is expressing a possibility this may not happen. What if... no, stop right there. Oh God, where's Libby when I need her? Wispy, stop this NOW!

'Wispy, are you there?'

'Yes. Sorry, Wanda, just concentrating on making sure I've got it all down.'

'Shall I repeat it?'

'Yes, please.'

'Thanks, Wanda, I've got it word for word.'

'Excellent. Now the airfield is known to Chester; it's not far from their estate at Rothbury. The nearest town is Amble, on the coast.'

'Interesting. I wonder why he has chosen there for the exchange?'

'He must know the area well, but how on earth does he think he can get away? Scotland Yard, with the help of their Northumberland colleagues, will have every road, cart path and potential escape route blocked up tighter than a drum. He will have nowhere to go.'

'I'm sure he'd have thought of that. Now let me go and give Tony the news. He and the commissioner will have a lot to put in place.'

'Fine, I'm going straight back to Lennox Gardens and am meeting Luther there. We will not leave their sides. When all the arrangements are in place, we will travel with them and the gold.'

'Good. At the moment our plans are to catch this evening's ferry, but to be honest it will be touch and go as to whether we get there for the three o'clock rendezvous. This isn't exactly going the way I envisaged. After I've briefed Tony, I will call Strangely and find out what plans he has for the Lacroixs, so you may well be on your own at this rate.'

'Don't worry about this end, I will have it all covered.'

'Good. Now once I've spoken to Libby, she will contact you as I want her and Constanza to travel with you. I need them to deliver what I hope is a very important letter to Mrs Potts.'

'Fine, I'll expect her call.'

I returned to the restaurant with my equilibrium fully restored, ordered a pot of Earl Grey tea, and read Tony the ransom note.

'Feh! The man's insane, but Wanda is right; he doesn't have a cat in hell's chance of making an escape. The Northumberland constabulary will have that place locked up tighter than a prison. Now I need to get a call through to the commissioner.'

'Right, you do that and I'll call Strangely.'

I read Strangely the ransom note.

'That confirms it. The man is completely and utterly deranged.'

'He most certainly is. What plans do you have for the Lacroixs?'

'Fabrice and I hatched a plan last night and as soon as we finish, he will go to the post office and send them a telegram purportedly from Boutroux, asking them to return to England immediately. We've already got our train tickets to either Calais or Boulogne, so we will follow them as soon as they are on the move.'

'Don't let them out of your sight.'

'We won't. Now I might have a plan to solve your travelling arrangements. I'll call you back. Oh, and give me those coordinates again.'

I went back to the lounge and ordered another pot of Earl Grey, and Tony joined me half an hour later.

'We have a plan, Wispy. The commissioner is going to liaise with the chief constable of Northumberland, and they will come up with an operation to seal off the whole area around the airfield up to a distance of two miles, so as not to draw attention to themselves. The area will be locked down bang on three o'clock, so he can drive to the rendezvous but he won't be able to escape.'

'I don't understand. He must know he's walking into a cage.'

'Maybe he does and maybe he doesn't care. Who knows what his warped mind is thinking.'

I shrugged and shook my head. 'What about the gold?'

'At the moment he envisages organising a special train to transport Wanda, Luther, Libby, Constanza, the Eastoffs and the gold to Amble. They will be accompanied at all times by a hand-picked team of eight of the Yard's finest officers, led by a colleague of mine, Inspector Hindmarsh, who hails from Northumberland originally. They are used to surveillance and undercover work, and once at the airfield they will work with their local colleagues to finalise their plans. One of their number is a top marksman and sniper who will be travelling with his tools of the trade.

'The inspector hopes to have the exact plans in place by mid-afternoon, and he will call me here to confirm the schedule. Hopefully by then we might have some inkling if we are going to make it back.'

'On that point, Strangely thinks he might be able to solve our transport issues.'

'And how might he do that?'

'Who knows, but knowing Strangely it will be interesting.' I consulted my watch; it had just gone ten thirty, when the concierge appeared to say that a Mr Drye was on the telephone for me. I hurried off to the telephone booth in the hotel reception.

'I've put together your travel itinerary with the help of my new-found chum.' He proceeded to outline our travel arrangements and I listened in an amazed silence.

'Wispy, are you still there?'

'Yes, yes, I'm here and I'm totally awestruck by your plan. Bloody marvellous.'

'Should be fun, what?'

'Bloody right.'

'Can you get Tony to contact the commissioner to get the RAF's approval to land at Wittering?'

'Of course.'

'Wish I was coming with you, but after we finish our call, I will get Fabrice to pull the pin on "Operation Lacroix". So, I think we should be on the move ourselves in pretty short order.'

'Well, *bonne chasse.*'

'You too.'

I walked into the lounge and slapped Tony on the back. 'We will be going to the ball.'

'So, he's turning a pumpkin into a carriage, mice into horses, a rat into our—'

'Tony, I didn't know you had aspirations as a thespian. Strangely has just hatched a plan with his new-found friend, Count von Delmenhorst, and a certain Baron Waldemar von Scharmbeck, to fly us to the rendezvous. I've always wanted to take to the skies. As we speak, they are preparing to fly the count's two Albatros C.X biplanes to Saint-Inglevert Airfield, which is not far from here. After planning their route, and gaining permission to land at each of their chosen airfields en route to the Royal Flying Corps Station Southfields, they should be ready to depart from Schloss Delmenhorst at one o'clock. He calculates the flying time will be five hours, wind permitting, with a half-hour stop to refuel. Therefore, they should arrive at six thirty.'

'But, Wispy, I have a fear of heights!'

Ah, that might present a tad of a problem.

'Look, old boy, you'll be fine. Perhaps a snifter beforehand will help, and remember the chaps in the front of the plane are experts.'

'If you say so.'

'I do say so.' But he looked a bit crestfallen. 'Now after half an hour to refuel and for them to make their necessary ablutions, we should be ready to depart by seven o'clock. We will then fly to RAF Wittering, near Stamford. The count calculates that it should be about two and a half hours' flying time, so we should arrive there by eight thirty British time. Can you call the commissioner and ask him to have a word with the RAF boys to get their permission to land at Wittering?'

'I'm still not convinced by this, Wispy.'

'You'll be fine. Flying is a piece of cake!'

Now who was I kidding?

'I know a rather splendid hostelry nearby where we could hunker down for the night: the George at Stamford. I'll get Ernest to book four rooms and we can treat them to dinner.'

'I can't wait to get there – the positive will be that my feet are back on terra firma.'

'That's the spirit. You never know, flying lessons might be on the cards for you after this.'

'I don't think Mrs Finkelstein would sanction them.'

'Of course she will once she sees that photograph of you standing by your plane. Now, on Friday morning the count wants to leave at seven o'clock, and the flying time should be two and a half hours to Southfields airfield. So, we should be on the ground for nine thirty.'

'So, we will be able to go to the ball.'

'Yes, we will. Now let me call Ernest and get him to make a booking at the George. Then I must update Wanda and give Libby a call.'

'And I will call the commissioner to see if he can have a word with the RAF boys.'

*

'Libby, darling, it's me.'

'Hello, me.'

I'd ummed and ahhed about telling her about our forthcoming aeroplane flight, and decided the best policy was to come clean. To my surprise she was thrilled for me.

'Why don't you take up flying lessons?'

'Would you mind, darling?'

'Don't be silly. In actual fact, I think I will join you.'

'Really?'

'Yes, just think of the adventures we can have. I'll have a chat with Constanza. They are bound to have some spare land they can turn into an airstrip.'

'Really!'

'Yes, really. Now tell me where you are on the case.'

I updated her on everything and asked her to telephone Wanda and make arrangements for her and Constanza to join the party travelling to Amble. I explained I needed them to deliver what I hoped would be a rather important letter to Mrs Potts.

'Of course, darling. I'm glad to be involved and I know Constanza will be too. I'll call Wanda straight away and then walk over to Constanza's.'

'Thank you, darling, I don't know where I would be without you.'

'Neither do I.'

'Oh, I'm cut to the quick.'

'Of course you are. Now enjoy taking to the skies.'

'I will, and I'm looking forward to seeing you tomorrow.'

'Me too, and I miss you.'

'And I love you.'

CHAPTER 26
THURSDAY, 17 AUGUST 1922
NORTHUMBERLAND

Florence had lost all track of time and was drifting in and out of consciousness. She had a temperature and her left hand had started to swell and throb. Her instincts told her she needed to get urgent medical help.

She was in the back of a van and thought they must have been travelling for two to three days. Her captor gave her bread and water but she had constant hunger pangs. She was filthy, bedraggled and smelt but she didn't care. When she slept she had a recurring nightmare of the van driver smothering Napoleon and the battle he put up to avoid death. But her captor was too strong for him and he lost. What she found even more grotesque and horrific was that when her captor returned to her room a few hours later, he shot Napoleon three times in the head, before unshackling her and taking her with him to Calais.

Her captor seemed to be enjoying the perceived power he had over her and was never far away from an explosion of his savage temper, but she refused to fear him. Her mental strength was very apparent to him, which only increased the verbal abuse and threat of more violence. Despite all this, her overriding determination to capture every detail for her articles never diminished. When she closed her eyes she could visualise her words on the printed page of the newspaper.

She knew that her journey was nearing its end, and although she was not particularly religious her thoughts were focusing on her own mortality. She was frightened but knew, whatever the outcome, she had the fortitude and resilience to face what was to come.

CHAPTER 27
THURSDAY, 17 AUGUST 1922
PARIS

Strangely returned to the room and Fabrice headed off to the post office to send a telegram to the Lacroixs which read: 'Not safe where you are STOP Go to rendezvous site STOP We shall leave together from there FB'.

He returned ten minutes later and settled the hotel bill. Their suitcases were being forwarded as they were going to be travelling light with one overnight bag each. They made themselves comfortable in a nearby café which afforded an excellent view of the lobby to the Lacroixs' flat on the second floor. They ordered coffee, and now it was just a matter of time to see whether they had taken the bait.

They were both dressed in light linen two-piece suits – Strangely in eau de Nil and Fabrice in taupe – white silk shirts, bold striped ties, boaters and sunglasses on top, and white nubuck Oxfords on their feet. A pair of gentlemen about to venture off on holiday.

Strangely consulted his watch; it was nearly eleven thirty, and they spotted a telegraph boy pedalling furiously along Rue de la Bastille. He leant his bicycle against the wall and disappeared into the lobby. A few moments later he reappeared and sped off.

Thirty minutes later the Lacroixs appeared. Gone was the earlier confidence; there was a tenseness about them, and they looked haggard and drawn. They peered anxiously about and set off in the direction of Brégret-Sabin metro station.

Fabrice threw a few francs on the table and they followed them at a discreet distance.

'They're travelling light; not a single item of luggage between them,' observed Fabrice.

'My guess is that we've spooked them, and their clarity of thinking may be somewhat compromised.'

They arrived at the metro station and followed them down to the platforms.

'Something's wrong,' said Fabrice. 'They are on the wrong platform for Gare du Nord.'

'Crikey, so they are not going to Calais?'

'It would appear so – or they are taking a very circuitous route to get there. But we won't have long to find out.'

The arrival of the train was apparent before they saw it, the metal wheels protesting against the metal rails of a curve, which produced a loud screeching as it appeared through the tunnel. They sat down in a second-class carriage adjacent to the Lacroixs, and travelled on Line 5 as far as it went, checking at every stop to make sure they weren't disembarking. They changed at Place d'Italie onto Line 6. Seven stops later, the Lacroixs got off at Montparnasse.

'I have a fair inkling of where they might be going.'

'So do I,' replied Fabrice.

After a five-minute walk they followed them onto the concourse of Gare Montparnasse. The station was busy despite it being midday, and the usual smells and sounds greeted them. A steam engine announced its departure by blowing its whistle and slowly pulling away, snorting out smoke in huge chugs and releasing steam from the pistons. As it gradually gained momentum, a more rhythmic pattern took over and it disappeared out of the station, leaving the aroma of coal smoke hanging in the air.

The Lacroixs joined the small queue for tickets.

'Wait here a moment,' said Fabrice. He walked to the side of the ticket office window and started to intently study a timetable, peering at it as though he was short-sighted. Once the Lacroixs had bought their tickets, he returned. 'Our inklings were correct; they have bought singles to Carcassonne via Bordeaux Saint-Jean, which departs at four o'clock this afternoon.'

'So they're on the run and their instincts are driving them home. Right, Fabrice, can you find a post office and send a telegram to Wispy at Hôtel Meurice?'

He took out his notebook and scribbled: 'Lacroixs heading to Carcassonne STOP We're en route STOP Leaving at 4pm STOP Basing ourselves at Hôtel de la Cité.' He tore out the page and passed it to him.

Fabrice returned fifteen minutes later. 'All done.'

'Good. Look over there, they're sitting in the waiting room. I suggest we use our time productively and have a *plat du jour* in the station bistro, and we can keep an eye on them while fortifying ourselves for the tedious journey ahead.'

'Good. How do you English say? I'm quite peakish, and I could eat a donkey.'

'Peckish, and I could eat a horse. Come on!'

CHAPTER 28
THURSDAY, 17 AUGUST 1922
CALAIS

Just before midday Chief Inspector Monsieur Raphael Bombelles bustled into the lounge, wearing again what could only be described as normal police attire. He had obviously been overexerting himself as it took him a few moments to get his breath back and to mop his fevered brow.

'Gentlemen, the bullet wounds to Mr Potts's temple were not the cause of death; that was inflicted post-mortem. He was suffocated, I assume with a pillow.'

'Good Lord, that would have taken a huge amount of physical strength, and highlights – if even more evidence were needed – that Boutroux is a bloody psychopath. Why would you shoot a dead body?' I enquired.

'Because he's not wired like us. He might actually enjoy inflicting pain, albeit on an already dead person, and my guess is he was extremely angry, maybe with Mr Potts, or maybe he's just consumed with such hate that Potts was just collateral damage. Either way, Florence is in mortal danger.'

'I agree, Tony. Chief Inspector, our work here is done and we will be departing for England at six o'clock this evening.' I relayed our travel arrangements to him.

'I'm sorry that you did not have a satisfactory outcome to your visit, but at least you only have to contend with one kidnapper now, albeit an extremely violent one. I will make the necessary arrangements to have the body of Mr Potts interred in a pauper's grave.'

'I don't think that is a good idea, Chief Inspector. I believe that Mrs Potts, despite what he has done, will want to say farewell to her husband and to give him a Christian burial.'

'Well in which case I will arrange for the body to be kept in the mortuary until notified of the arrangements. Now, if you will excuse me, I have a few pressing issues to attend to, but rest assured I will pick you up at six o'clock and take you to the airfield, where I can wish you bon voyage!'

I was afraid of that.

'Splendid, Chief Inspector, we will be most delighted to see you later.'

On the way out, I passed the concierge who approached me with a silver tray.'A telegram for you, Sir William.'

'Thank you, much obliged.' I read its contents and passed it over to Tony.

'So, the Lacroixs are returning to Carcassonne. They think they are running away from danger, but quite the opposite with Strangely and Fabrice on their tail.'

*

Strangely and Fabrice enjoyed a leisurely light lunch of *bouchées à la reine*, which Fabrice informed Strangely literally meant 'queen's morsel', named after the Queen of France, Marie Leszczynska, wife of Louis XV. When the dish arrived, Strangely smiled to himself; it was a humble vol-au-vent with a delicious filling of sweetbreads, chicken quenelles and button mushrooms in a supreme sauce, followed by a *salade Lyonnaise* and a selection of cheeses from the cheese trolley to finish – they chose a Bleu d'Auvergne and an Ossau-Iraty. The meal was accompanied by a perfectly chilled bottle of Alsace Riesling. All the while they kept a beady eye on Odette and Jean-Pascal, who far from enjoying a leisurely lunch looked increasingly more nervous as the hour of their departure came near.

At three forty-five they followed them onto the platform and watched as they entered a standard-class carriage. They then boarded their adjacent first-class carriage. They had agreed that at every stop they would take it in turns to lean out of the carriage-door window to make sure the Lacroixs weren't getting off. At exactly four o'clock, the train pulled away.

CHAPTER 29
THURSDAY, 17 AUGUST 1922
CHELSEA

Strutton knocked and entered the drawing room. 'Excuse me, Sir Chester, the commissioner of Scotland Yard is on the telephone for Miss Cushway.'

'Thank you, Strutton. Wanda, please take the call in my study.'

She went with Strutton, consulting her watch on the way; it had just turned midday. Twenty minutes later, she returned.

'We have a plan. At exactly four o'clock this afternoon, an Inspector Hindmarsh will arrive at your bank, Coutts on Lombard Street, accompanied by seven hand-picked plain-clothes officers, two of whom will be driving an armoured Rolls-Royce whilst the rest will be in two police cars. It goes without saying that these officers will be armed to the teeth. They will collect the gold and transport it to Temple Mills marshalling yard, near Stratford.

'The commissioner has organised a special train consisting of a first-class carriage and two guards' vans to transport us to Amble. It will leave at six o'clock this evening and will travel non-stop, arriving, he thinks, at about one o'clock in the morning. The commissioner will meet us at Temple Mills to see us off.

'The train will be met by the chief constable and an Inspector Muckle and his men. We will then be taken to St Cuthbert's vicarage where the Reverend Tulip and his wife have kindly agreed to put us up for the night.'

'Ah, the Reverend Tulip, a good solid man. We've met him a

few times; Alberta and I have been guests of honour at the Amble summer fête on many occasions.'

'Really? It's a small world. At dawn the Scotland Yard officers, along with their Northumberland colleagues, will go to the airfield and deploy their teams, ready for action. Wispy and Inspector Finkelstein should fly in at nine thirty so we will head out shortly before then. Any questions?'

'No questions, it's just good to be doing something constructive. I will ask Strutton to have the car ready for four thirty.'

'And I will ask cook to prepare food hampers for the journey,' said Alberta.

*

Shortly before four thirty, all the staff ventured out onto the pavement. The yellow Rolls-Royce Silver Ghost was parked outside, and two hampers were loaded into the car. Strutton cleared his throat. 'Sir Chester, Lady Alberta, Miss Cushway, Mr Spaulding, on behalf of all the staff we wish you Godspeed. Please bring Miss Florence home safely.'

Sir Chester nodded his appreciation. 'Strutton, your kind words and thoughts mean a great deal to us. Thank you.'

An hour later they turned into the main entrance of the Temple Mills marshalling yard and were ushered straight in, following a car that took them through a myriad of sidings. Steam engines were puffing and snorting as they busied themselves shunting wagons around, which to the untrained eye looked like organised chaos. They were led to a quiet siding where a huge, powerful Pacific-class steam engine called the Great Northern was slowly hissing. It was coupled to a gleaming teak first-class carriage and two large guards' vans.

The armoured Rolls-Royce and two police cars were already parked. The commissioner's chauffeur-driven Rolls-Royce was parked alongside them, and he was engrossed in conversation with Libby and Constanza, who had arrived in a London cab ten minutes earlier. As they came to a stop, the commissioner greeted them.

'Please allow me to introduce myself: I'm Sir Redvers Preece, Police Commissioner for Scotland Yard.' He shook hands with everyone.

'I will leave you in the capable hands of Inspector Hindmarsh, who will keep me posted of all events, until Inspector Finkelstein arrives. I have spoken to my counterpart, the chief constable of Northumberland, and he is happy with the progress his officers are making and is very much looking forward to the collaboration between our two forces on this heinous crime committed against your daughter and both of you. I pray for a speedy and successful conclusion to this by tomorrow afternoon.'

'Thank you, Sir Redvers, we really appreciate your involvement, and I now realise it was a mistake not to involve you as soon as we realised Florence had been kidnapped. If it wasn't for the foresight of Sir William, we wouldn't be in the advanced position we now find ourselves in.'

'I agree with you, Sir Chester. Sir William and his agency are certainly the exception that breaks the rule. Now your train awaits. The Great Northern Railway Company have been extremely cooperative and are giving your train priority over every other train on the line. I wish you Godspeed.'

The hampers were being loaded on and Sir Chester was helping Alberta to board.

'Miss Cushway, might I trouble you for a word before you embark?'

'Of course, Sir Redvers.'

'I hear from Inspector Finkelstein that he greatly admires your work. If you ever feel inclined to seek a commission at Scotland Yard, you would be pushing at an open door.'

'Thank you, I'm most flattered, but as I said to Inspector Finkelstein, I like it where I am.'

'I'm sure you do. Sir William runs a first-rate outfit. But if you ever fancy a change of air, you know where to come.' He took a silver card holder from his waistcoat pocket, extracted a card and wrote on the back of it. 'Here is my card; if you ever have a change of heart, please contact me. I've put my home number on the back. Now, you must be off. Good luck, Miss Cushway, although I'm sure you don't need it.' They shook hands, and she boarded the train.

Bang on six o'clock, the train pulled out of the siding and made its way over many points, until it was held at a stop signal prior to being allowed onto the main east coast line. The signal raised its assent, and the driver opened the regulator. The power of the engine was felt throughout the train. With a loud blast of its whistle, the magnificent train eased onto the main line and with impatient snorts and chugs, accelerated away towards the north-east of England.

CHAPTER 30
THURSDAY, 17 AUGUST 1922
CALAIS

The clock in the hotel lobby had just started to strike the hour of six o'clock when Chief Inspector Bombelles bustled in. My heart sank.

Just what I didn't want; gone was the normal police attire and once again he was in full dress uniform. All I wanted was to get back to Blighty with the minimum of faff.

'Most gracious of you to pick us up. I trust we haven't put you to too much trouble?'

'It is never too much trouble to pick up a knight of the realm and an esteemed officer from one of the world's most venerated police forces. Now, gentlemen, your carriage awaits.'

It was a short drive to Saint-Inglevert Airfield and as we drove onto the field, I realised we weren't going to get away with the minimum of faff. The police band were assembled at the end of the runway along with a police guard of honour, and in the middle a stage had been erected with a canopy, with the Union Jack fluttering gently in the sea breeze on one side and the Tricolore fluttering on the other. I recognised the mayor and other councillors sitting in two neat rows on the stage.

We heard them before we saw them, and then they came into view. The two planes were camouflaged in a lozenge pattern with various shades of violet, grey-blues, browns and olive green. On the wings, fuselage and tail were the insignia of the German iron cross.

They looked magnificent as they flew straight over us and banked away to the right in a loop to fly back over us once again; this time, they did a canopy roll. It was an amazing sight; these boys knew how to fly. They banked to the left and came into land, pulling up side by side in front of the stage. I glanced at Tony who had turned a shade of green. As they climbed out of their aircraft, the chief inspector signalled for me and Tony to walk out and meet them. The three of us stood in a line, and at that point the band struck up 'Das Lied der Deutschen', their newly adopted national anthem.

They took off their leather fur-lined flying helmets and goggles and stood to attention during the playing of the anthem, in their black leather flying coats and moleskin trousers.

Good Lord, the mercurial chief inspector has surprised me yet again by his magnanimity, by playing the German national anthem. How incredibly moving.

'Please allow me to introduce myself. I'm Chief Inspector Bombelles, and a very warm welcome to our wonderful town of Calais.'

'A pleasure to meet you, Chief Inspector, and thank you for a most gracious welcome. We feel truly humbled. I'm Count von Delmenhorst and this is my very good friend Baron Waldemar von Scharmbeck.'

They shook hands. 'Now please, allow me to introduce Sir William Fescue, and Inspector Finkelstein of Scotland Yard.'

'Ah, Sir William, Inspector Finkelstein, an honour to meet you both. But I feel I know you already as Marjorie has told me all about you.'

'Nothing too bad, I trust.'

'Far from it, Sir William.'

'Good, and can I thank you for what you are both doing for us? It means a great deal.'

'It is nothing, Sir William. If we can help in a small way in reuniting a daughter with her mother and father, that is the only thanks we need.'

'Now, gentlemen, please allow me to introduce you to the mayor and our town councillors.' As we turned around, they had descended from the stage and lined up as if for a military inspection. The chief inspector took them down the line, introducing each and every one.

After the formalities were over, the count gave myself and Tony our flying paraphernalia. He and the baron then organised the refuelling of their aircraft. Just before seven o'clock we were ready to depart, and the dignitaries had reconvened on their stage. I got into the rear seat of the count's aircraft with my bag and briefcase, and Tony got into the baron's.

The count turned around and looked at me. 'Are you ready, Sir William?'

'Yes, Count, I am, and I'm very much looking forward to this.'

'*Sehr gut.* Me too, and it's Reinhardt.'

'Wispy.'

'Wispy, how so? Never mind you can explain later over dinner.'

He gave the engineer the thumbs up and rotated the propeller so the engine kicked into life. Together with the baron, he taxied to the end of the runway so they could take off into the light sea breeze. He turned again and looked at me, pulling his goggles over his eyes. I followed suit. He gave me the thumbs up, and I responded. He then opened the throttle and we started to accelerate down the runway.

Our wheels left the runway just before we went past the stage, and we waved a farewell to the chief inspector and the dignitaries. I caught a refrain of 'God Save the King' as we climbed into a near-perfect cloudless sky. We climbed to a height of sixteen thousand feet and the baron and Tony drew alongside us. There was a huge grin on Tony's face, and we waved at each other. In ten minutes, we were flying over the white cliffs. The views were spectacular.

*

We made good time as we had a tail wind, and landed at RAF Wittering just after eight o'clock. The commissioner as usual had pulled various strings, and the station commander was there to greet us. The two aircraft were taken into a nearby hangar by a team of engineers and a few moments later, our transport arrived to take us on the seven-mile journey into Stamford and the comfort of the George Hotel.

The journey to the hotel was very companiable, and Tony was now hooked on flying and expressed his wish to take up flying lessons. We arrived at the George and they were very accommodating, having kept the restaurant open for us, and after a freshen-up we sat down for dinner at nine thirty.

I ordered dinner and selected potted Morecambe Bay shrimps, with a bottle of crisp dry Chablis, followed by châteaubriand cooked rare, with roasted tarragon new potatoes, asparagus, grilled tomatoes and sauce Béarnaise, accompanied by a bottle of Châteauneuf-du-Pape.

'So, William, before we took off you asked to be called Wispy. What are the origins of this name?' enquired Reinhardt.

'It's my nickname.' And I explained how I came to be called Wispy by my close friends.

'I see. I like that very much. You'll be telling me next that Marjorie has a nickname too.'

'He didn't tell you?'

'No, what is it?'

'Strangely.'

'Really? Now that is indeed intriguing. How did he come by that?'

I explained the origin of his nickname.

'I see, but I don't think there's much wrong with the name Marjorie. Do you?'

I sputtered. 'Well, it's not actually very common to call a boy Marjorie.'

'All the more reason to be proud of it.'

'What about you, Tony? Do you have a nickname?' asked Waldemar.

'Not really, well not anymore. At school I was called Finks.'

'Finks. I like that a lot,' I said. 'Now, gentlemen, how about a spot of dessert?'

'Yes, that would hit the spot, something traditionally English. And I must say the beef was absolutely first class.'

'Traditionally English, Reinhardt? Let me have a look on the menu. Ah, here we go, Eton Mess.'

'As in Eton College?'

'Yes, it is believed to have originated there and was served at the annual cricket match against Harrow.'

'Really, you English and your love of cricket. Give me fencing any day of the week.'

I managed to attract the waiter's attention and ordered the Eton Mess and a small cheeseboard to finish off, Montgomery Cheddar and Colston Bassett Stilton, and a glass of Warre's vintage port.

The Eton Mess hit the spot, and over the cheeseboard we discussed their love of flying. By the end of the meal Waldemar was going to teach Tony to fly.

I arranged with reception to have an early breakfast at a quarter to six as we were being picked up at half past.

CHAPTER 31
FRIDAY, 18 AUGUST 1922
AMBLE

The Great Northern pulled into Amble station at twelve thirty in the morning. The driver and fireman had worked with an industrious determination to get their train to Amble as fast as was humanly possible. They did not know the nature of their mission, but by the tenseness on their passengers' faces and their send-off by the commissioner of Scotland Yard, they knew it was of a significant magnitude.

On the platform they were met by the chief constable, Inspector Muckle and the Reverend Tulip and his wife, and all the introductions were made. Chester and Wanda broke off from the party and walked up to the footplate of the engine to thank the driver and the fireman personally for all their efforts.

The Great Northern then pulled into a siding where a small contingent of local police officers were on guard duty to protect her precious cargo, which allowed the Yard's officers to take advantage of the first-class carriage and get some well-earned rest before first light.

The party was then driven in several police cars to St Cuthbert's vicarage where Mrs Tulip, with the help of an overzealous Reverend Tulip, made sure that her guests were made comfortable in their rooms with reassuring cups of cocoa.

CHAPTER 32
FRIDAY, 18 AUGUST 1922
CARCASSONNE

The train pulled into Carcassonne at seven thirty and Strangely and Fabrice disembarked, waiting a discreet distance from the Lacroixs' carriage. But they didn't emerge. They approached the carriage, but the couple were nowhere to be seen.

'Where the bloody hell are they? We checked at every stop and they didn't get off.'

'They might have spotted us, Strangely. Let's search their carriage in case they are hiding.'

They walked the length of the carriage checking under every seat, and as they reached the end they noticed that the door opposite the platform was ajar. The door on the adjacent carriage was wide open.

'Heavens below, how on earth did we let them make their escape?'

'It's heavens above, Fabrice. There's no point in beating ourselves up. They've gone, but where?'

'They wouldn't be stupid enough to return to Montlaur?'

'Who knows, but it's as good a starting point as any. Come on, let's see if we can borrow Bastien's Torpedo.'

Fabrice drove as fast as the roads would allow and they arrived at the Lacroixs' farm as the church clock struck the hour of nine o'clock. The farm was completely deserted, the livestock having been removed, and the doors to the house were locked. Nevertheless, they forced a window open and thoroughly checked each room. It was as they had left it last Monday; nothing had been moved.

Next, they drove to the top barn and walked down to the chapel. There was now a substantial padlock on the chapel's wrought-iron gates.

'Fabrice, if you were the Lacroixs, where would you go?'

'I would be heading across the Pyrenees, into the Basque region, and disappearing.'

'I agree with you, but before we go over the mountains, I have a hunch they might be a bit closer to home. Do you remember Jean-Pascal telling us about the caves where they place their cheeses whilst they mature? I would like to explore them.'

'But we don't know where they are.'

'I think Baron Pierre-Édouard Gascoigne will know. Come on, let's pay him a visit.'

*

The butler showed them into the drawing room and the baron and baroness stood up to greet them.

'Back so soon, Marjorie? Have you found that Boutroux fellow?'

'We are closing in on him, but at the moment we are after the Lacroixs.' Strangely related how they tracked them down in Paris and followed them here, then lost them.'

'I see, and how can we help?'

'I have a hunch that they might be hiding out in some caves where they leave their cheeses to mature. Do you happen to know where they are?'

'As a matter of fact, we do. The caves are near the top of Montagne d'Alaric, which is our nearest mountain, at a height of six hundred metres. It's about five kilometres from here, and we're particularly proud of her. We'll take you there. Are you up for a spot of mountaineering, darling?'

'Of course, wouldn't miss it. Are these Lacroixs dangerous?'

'I think they are desperate, Your Ladyship, and desperate people will do dangerous things.'

'Now, Pierre, darling, I suggest we change into something more suitable. Can you get Allard to get the car ready? I think the four of us should travel together.'

'Of course, darling. Can I enquire, Marjorie, what you are going to do if we find them?'

'Ideally I would want to escort them to the local gendarmerie and have them arrested.'

'Arrested, on what charge?'

'I see no reason not to tell you now. They would be arrested on a charge of kidnapping.'

'Kidnapping! God have mercy. And who have they kidnapped?'

'They are complicit in the abduction of a Miss Florence Eastoff.'

'What? As in Chester and Alberta Eastoff's daughter?'

'Yes, the very same.'

Maria gasped. 'They were here last summer. The poor girl must be terrified. I'll contact Alberta immediately.'

'I wouldn't advise that at the moment. We are at a very delicate stage in trying to secure her release. How do you know them?'

'Before the war, I invested in the Eastoff Shipbuilding Company, and we became friends. And to think we've been doing business with the Lacroixs for more years than I care to mention. Darling, we'll need to take the Purdeys with us. I'll get Allard to put them in the car with a couple of boxes of cartridges. Do you need a shotgun, Marjorie?'

'No, thank you, I've got my service revolver, but Fabrice could use one.'

'I'll arrange it. Now we must change.'

Ten minutes later, they reappeared, both wearing tweed shooting suits with breeks and heavy brogues on their feet. 'I've been thinking it would be far easier to take a gendarme with us to arrest the Lacroixs on the mountain.'

'An excellent idea, Pierre.'

'Good, then we'll pick up Honoré Camusat on the way and he can follow us on his motorbike.'

They set off to Montlaur in the Gascoignes' Rolls-Royce

Silver Ghost, and ten minutes later drew to a halt outside the gendarmerie.

'Good, Honoré's bike is here, so he can't be far away; although I fear he won't want to be torn away from his mid-morning snack.'

Pierre got out of the car and entered the gendarmerie, and ten minutes later appeared with Honoré, who was clutching the remnants of a baguette. He was of medium height but very rotund.

'Is Honoré going to be capable of climbing a six-hundred-metre mountain?' enquired Fabrice.

'You'll be surprised. He was awarded the Croix de Guerre with a bronze palm, and despite his rotundness he's as fit as a flea.'

Pierre got back in the car and explained they were going to climb up towards the caves from the northern side of the mountain, starting off through the lower vineyards. The caves were on the southern side, approximately one hundred metres from the summit. Once they were level with them, they would make their way around to the cave entrances.

*

Honoré Camusat lived up to his billing. He didn't lag behind, far from it; he led at a pace from the front with the agility of a mountain goat. He brought the party to a halt as the sound of the Montlaur church bell carried the news that the hour was two o'clock.

'The cave system is literally on the other side. We will need to traverse along this ridge very carefully.' Pierre pointed out the route to their left. 'It should take us about fifteen minutes to reach the caves, and just below them there is a wooded area where we can monitor the scene without being observed.'

Honoré addressed them and Strangely got the gist of his conversation: that Jean-Pascal was an excellent shot as he hunted wild boar in the surrounding hills for his charcuterie and was bloody good at hitting a moving target, and Odette was one of the fastest loaders he knew. This information was coupled with the fact that they would be at a disadvantage in trying to attack an uphill target.

So, if they were there, he proposed a waiting game for the Lacroixs to come to them. There was a freshwater spring just below the wood, and when either one of them went to the spring we would tackle them there. Then the other person would come looking when they realised they weren't returning. Lastly, he made a firm point that sign language was only to be used once they neared the woods.

Fabrice filled in the detail of the plan for Strangely, and with the thought that they faced a formidable couple firmly planted in their minds, Honoré led them along the ridge. The scenery was stunning but Strangely hardly noticed it. He had the same feeling in the pit of his stomach that he'd had ahead of the whistle sounding before he was due to go over the top.

They entered the wood and made their way to its upper edge and found a vantage point behind a thicket. They could see one large cave entrance and on either side two smaller ones. Honoré signalled for Strangely and Fabrice to cross the path that led through the woods and take up a similar position on the other side, out of sight of the path.

Strangely trained his binoculars on the caves. There was absolutely no sign of life. The church bell announced the passing of more time; it was now three o'clock.

They all froze. Some way off below them, the distinctive sound of two barrels of a shotgun being fired rang out. Birds took flight, and then silence once again descended. Their senses were straining to pick up any sound or movement from below them, and all their guns were in hand. Time seemed to stand still. A twig cracking broke the silence, and they lowered themselves into prone positions against the woodland floor and trained their guns towards the path. A few seconds later, Jean-Pascal appeared with a shotgun tucked under one arm and a couple of rabbits in the other. He passed by and headed up towards the larger cave. As he neared the entrance, he gave a barely audible short whistle, which passed for a very acceptable swallow. A moment later, Odette appeared.

Strangely looked at Fabrice and mouthed the words *We've got them trapped. Now we wait.*

They disappeared into the cave, then reappeared a few moments later. Jean-Pascal set about lighting a fire whilst Odette started skinning the rabbits. Having got the fire going, Jean-Pascal went into the cave and emerged carrying his shotgun and a pail, and purposely strode towards the path. Honoré lowered his hand and they all took up the prone position again. Jean-Pascal marched past, and when he had disappeared around a bend, Honoré gave the signal to advance. The party moved with the stealth of trained soldiers and hunters, halting at the bottom edge of the wood.

Jean-Pascal had laid his shotgun down and was filling his pail at the spring. Honoré gave the signal to take aim, then with the agility of a cheetah ran towards Jean-Pascal, who turned in utter surprise. But he wasn't quick enough and Honoré kicked his shotgun away whilst training his pistol at Jean-Pascal's chest.

'One move, Jean-Pascal, and you're dead. Put your hands on your head.' Jean-Pascal looked flabbergasted as he did what was requested.

'Good, you have just saved your life, for the present. Now allow me to introduce some friends of mine.' The hunting party emerged from the wood and Jean-Pascal's demeanour turned to utter dejection.

'You have already had the pleasure of meeting Monsieur Drye and Monsieur Barsalou. Now turn around.' As he did so, Honoré brought Jean-Pascal's arms down behind his back and handcuffed him. 'I'm arresting you for kidnap—'

A shot rang out somewhere off to the left, followed by another. Honoré clutched his left arm.

'Quick, Fabrice, Pierre, grab Lacroix and get him into the woods,' commanded Strangely. 'Maria, help me with Honoré.'

They just made it before two more shots kicked up dirt behind them. 'Right, Pierre, stick to me like glue. Maria, tend to Honoré. Fabrice, train your gun on Lacroix – if he moves, kill him.'

Strangely sprinted as best as he could, followed by Pierre, back up the path and out into the open. They followed the treeline to the edge of the wood, all the while hearing shotgun blasts. Strangely pointed to the telltail sign of smoke as another two cartridges were fired off.

'She's down there on the left, in that outcrop of rocks. When she fires again, we'll return fire and dash across the open space, then we should be able to sneak up behind that rock formation and see where she is.'

They waited for what must have been ten seconds. When two more shots rang out, they returned fire at the smoke then sprinted down the slope, hurling themselves to the ground behind the outcrop. Strangely edged around the side. Another blast rang out, and he managed to take a glance as Odette emptied the second barrel.

'She's standing in a trench that is part of the rock formation. Wait here.' Strangely disappeared around the other side of the outcrop. Two blasts later he was back.

'Good, as I thought. I want you to edge your way around to the other side, where you can drop into the trench. I'll wait here, and when she fires her next two shots we move into position at each side. When she fires her second shot, we both drop into the trench. I want you to distract her, whilst I disarm her before she has a chance of reloading. Are you good with that?'

'Yes. Well, sort of. How do I distract her?'

'You'll think of something.' Two more shots rang out and they got into position. Seconds passed and nothing happened. 'Come on, come on. Damn you, woman. Fire, for God's sake,' Strangely said to himself.

An explosive sound ripped through the air and on instinct Strangely dropped into the trench as the deafening explosion of the second barrel was discharged. Pierre dropped milliseconds later and as Odette turned to look at him, Strangely ripped the shotgun from her hand and threw it out of reach. Odette glanced at both of them then made to escape by climbing out of the front of the trench, but Strangely and Pierre hauled her back and held her firmly by the arms.

'Madame Lacroix, it is futile to struggle. We have Jean-Pascal, so the most sensible thing you can do is to cooperate and come with us. As you can see, your game is well and truly run.' She looked at Strangely in abject defiance and spat at him.

'Come, Pierre, help Madame Lacroix out of this trench.'

They struggled to get her out of the trench, but eventually she realised that any more resistance was a complete waste of her energy, and with head bowed, she acquiesced and they rejoined the others at the spring.

Maria had tended to Honoré, who had sustained flesh wounds to his left arm. She had made him a sling from material she had torn from the lining of her tweed jacket.

'Gentlemen, good to see you back safe and sound. Odette, I have charged and arrested your husband with kidnapping, and all that now remains is for me to charge and arrest you for the same offence, plus one for attempted murder, of me. Might I add that if you fully cooperate with the judiciary, you just might escape an appointment with Madame la Guillotine.'

*

It was well past seven o'clock by the time they got back to Montlaur, but despite Honoré's injuries they were a happy band. Strangely thanked Honoré for his heroic efforts, which he batted away, but they shook hands and saluted each other. Gascoigne's chauffeur drove them back to the château and both Pierre and Maria insisted they stay for the night.

'But we haven't brought our black tie!'

'Marjorie, I'm sure that we can dig you out something suitable. I'll get Solé on to it. Now let me ring for him and he will take you to your rooms, where he can run you a couple of well-deserved baths.'

'Before we do that, can I ask you one question?'

'But of course, fire away.'

'What did you say to Madame Lacroix when you jumped into the trench?'

'Marjorie, I said, "Madame Lacroix, I have a complaint to make about the quality of your latest *saucisson* order"!'

CHAPTER 33
FRIDAY, 18 AUGUST 1922
WITTERING

There was a knock on my door at five o'clock. 'Come in.'
'Your morning Earl Grey, Sir William.'
'Thank you, please put it over there.'
'Certainly, and shall I open the curtains?'
'Most kind.'

Gone was the beautiful pre-dawn light of the past week, and I was greeted by a heavy and lead-laden threatening sky.

'Looks like there's a storm brewing, sir.'
'I sincerely hope not.'
'Mark my words, sir, it's coming.'

I met the others for breakfast, which was excellent, especially the Lincolnshire sausages with the lovely taste of sage, parsley and thyme complimenting the chunky minced pork.

Bang on the dot of six thirty our RAF driver arrived, and as we went out into the courtyard, we all looked heavenwards and the skies had turned blacker. As we drove through the gates of RAF Wittering, a huge flash of lightning illuminated the sky, followed by an enormous deafening crack of thunder, and seconds later the heavens opened.

'I'm sorry, Wispy, we can't fly in this weather. Our aircraft would act as lightning rods.'

'But Reinhardt, we must get to RAF Southfields.'

'We all want to get there, but if you want to get there alive, we must wait for the storm to pass.'

'Of course, I totally understand, and the lovely Mrs Finkelstein would never forgive me if Tony wasn't there to enjoy her cooking.'

'How very thoughtful of you, Wispy, most grateful.'

We were shown into the wing commander's office to wait until the storm had passed, buoyed by a constant supply of tea – to my surprise they actually had Earl Grey. I kept pacing around the office, constantly consulting my watch.

'Wispy, will you sit down? You're making me nervous.'

'Sorry, Tony,' I said, glancing again at my watch. It had just gone ten past ten.

'Yes, Wispy, sit down and have another cup of tea,' suggested Reinhardt. 'Incidentally, why do you British drink so much tea?'

'A good question, Reinhardt. Gladstone once remarked, "If you are cold, tea will warm you; if you are too heated, it will cool you; if you are excited, it will calm you". So, in answer to your question, it keeps us calm in situations like these.'

'Really, well to soothe your nerves, might I suggest you turn around and look out of the window?'

I did, and to my relief it had stopped raining and was looking a bit brighter.

'Come, gentlemen, action stations.' Reinhardt picked up his goggles, gloves and flying helmet and marched out of the office. The ground crew swung into action and our aircraft were pulled out of their hangar and fuelled. We took off simultaneously just before eleven o'clock and climbed into the breaking grey sky. By the time we reached the North Yorkshire Moors, the sun was out with just a few light cumulus clouds scattered here and there.

We'd been flying into a headwind, and Reinhardt estimated our time of arrival at just after two o'clock. I checked my watch: fifteen minutes to go.

'There, look, the Royal Flying Corps, Southfields airfield,' Reinhardt shouted and pointed off to his right, and there in the distance I saw an airfield with a few outbuildings and a hangar. We circled twice before the count and the baron landed side by side. We taxied towards the hangar and as we neared, four policemen appeared from behind it and slowly pulled the doors back, and we entered. The noise from the engines was deafening in such a confined space, but silence was soon restored when the engines were cut.

From the back of the hangar our welcoming party came forward to greet us. I made the necessary introductions, and Reinhardt was pleased to see Constanza again. It was lovely to see Libby, and I needed her strength and reassurance.

'Don't you look dashing in your flying gear. Now give me a hug.'

As I did so, I noticed Sir Chester and Count von Delmenhorst walking over to the hangar doors, deep in a conversation which ended in a very warm handshake and a salute from Reinhardt.

The time was now two thirty; we had thirty minutes to go. Inspector Hindmarsh and Inspector Muckle brought us all together and ran through the plan one final time. 'Right, it's time to take your positions.'

Two policemen dressed as farm labourers appeared, pulling a handcart with the four ammunition boxes containing the bullion. I noticed they had a revolver each, tucked into the back of their trousers. The welcoming party, at Chester's express wishes, consisted of myself, Wanda, Tony and the count. We too tucked our revolvers into the back of our trousers, and Wanda checked hers and replaced it in her shoulder bag. The rest of the group were going to watch from an outbuilding next to the hangar.

At two fifty exactly, the hangar doors were pulled open and we made our way to the west end of the runway, where there was indeed a cut-down telegraph pole, which I estimated to be six foot in height. A gentle breeze was blowing at our backs, but other than that, the airfield was silent apart from birdsong. I kept checking my watch, and away in the distance, a church clock struck the hour of three. Five past three came and went, ten past three came and went – nothing. Then from far away we picked up the faint muffled sound of an aeroplane, which slowly grew louder. 'Look!' Wanda shouted, pointing to the east.

And there in the distance we made out a tiny speck, which as it drew nearer we could make out as a biplane, flying in a very erratic manner. So, this was how Boutroux planned to make his escape, assuming he could land the damn thing. He was flying pretty low and was closing fast towards the eastern end of the airfield.

'He's coming in too fast; he'll never land her,' Reinhardt shouted.

The aircraft was lurching from side to side and was yawing into the breeze. The noise of the engine was deafening as Reinhardt shouted at Boutroux to cut the throttle back, to no avail. He did manage to get the wheels to touch the runway, but because of the plane's speed it just bounced back into the air. Boutroux pulled back on the stick and climbed back into the sky, working his way around until he was lined up for his second attempt. This time he seemed to have more control and on his approach you could hear that the engine had been throttled back. He still managed to bounce her on landing but somehow stopped about one hundred yards from us. He got out, leaving the engine running, and with a great deal of difficulty managed to extract Florence from the rear seat.

He carried her in his arms. Her head lolled from side to side, and her arms hung loose. It was obvious she was unconscious. He walked the fifty yards to the telegraph pole and laid her on the ground next to it; there was no need to tie her to it as it was blatantly clear she wasn't going to go anywhere. Then, from a small knapsack he had slung over his shoulder, he produced a pineapple and placed it on top of the telegraph pole. The plane was idling noisily behind him, but we could just make out what he shouted.

'Sir Chester, nice to finally meet you in person. I never had the pleasure when I worked for you. Now I'm sure you are all armed, and despite my request you will have the airfield surrounded with police, against my specific instructions. So, I just want to show you an illustration of what will happen to your lovely darling daughter if any harm befalls me.'

He raised his right arm in the air, and then held the flat of his palm out and gestured towards the pineapple. A second later, the pineapple exploded into pieces.

'You see, Sir Chester, I too have my sniper in place, and if I receive the slightest scratch, that will be Florence's head exploding next.'

He started to walk towards us and stopped ten yards short. He looked different from the picture taken at the procurement Christmas dinner; he hadn't shaved for weeks and his clothes were bedraggled. I noticed his opaque left eye, and his right eye had sunken into its socket. He had a look of utter insanity, yet he stood tall and radiated defiance. He was indeed completely mad.

I glanced at Chester and tears were running down his face, but he cleared his throat and pushed his shoulders back. 'You are a vile piece of human detritus...' He paused, searching for the right words. 'No, "human" gives you far too much worth; you are not human, because normal humans have feelings.' His voice was strong, firm and confident. 'You don't have feelings; you are devoid of even a crumb of morality. You are the most base creature I have ever come across. You are carrion, fit for nothing but the attention of crows, for in time they will devour you!'

A grin spread across Boutroux's face and he slowly started to applaud. He abruptly stopped and raised both his arms in the air, then held the flats of his palms out and, like Moses parting the Red Sea, spread his arms out wide, turned to face Florence, and bowed. A shot exploded into the telegraph pole just above Florence's head and sent splinters of wood flying everywhere.

'Your words can't hurt me; your sticks and stones can't even hurt me; nothing can ever hurt me again! Now get those two large oafs to load my gold onto my aircraft.'

He turned back towards the aircraft, blowing a kiss to Florence as he walked past her lifeless, pitiful form, never looking back. He climbed into the cockpit and waited for the two policemen to load the bullion onto the vacated passenger's seat.

He pulled the throttle, and slowly his aircraft started moving in a wide arc. He was now facing east, and with the deafening sound of the engine, he started to accelerate and climbed into the afternoon sky.

At the same time his wheels left the airstrip, we jumped at the sound of an explosive blast away to our left that reverberated all around us. A few seconds later, away to our right, we saw Boutroux's sniper fall from a tree. We watched as he seemed to fall to the earth in slow motion. When his body hit the ground, it was our cue and we all sprinted to Florence. On the other side of the airfield, the outhouse door was flung open and everyone sprinted towards us.

*

Alberta knelt down beside her daughter, felt her pulse, put her hand on her forehead and listened to her breathing. 'She's barely alive. Her heartbeat is slow, her breathing is erratic and she's burning up. Get Treadway here now. We need to get her to Wingrove Hospital. Oh, and bring water.'

Luther set off at a lick back towards the hangar, and moments later Treadway pulled the Rolls up next to us. Chester picked up his daughter and carried her to the car, placed her on the back seat and covered her in a blanket. Alberta sat next to her and cradled her head in her lap, and started to try and get her to sip some water. Chester rejoined us.

'Wispy, if it's the last thing you do, get the bastard.'

'Oh, I intend to. Now Godspeed!'

'Call Groves for anything you need.'

Treadway gunned the Rolls and we watched until the car disappeared from view.

*

'Right, everyone, gather around, we have jobs to do. Reinhardt, Waldemar, get your aircraft ready to go here.' I handed Reinhardt a piece of paper with our destination written on it. 'Inspector Muckle has arranged to have you refuelled.'

'Jawohl,' they said in unison and started to jog off towards the hangar.

'Tony, can you brief Inspector Hindmarsh on our plans?'

'Certainly, Sir William.'

'Wanda, we need to find Clement Featherstonehaugh and Walderne Smithers.'

'Of course. It will be a pleasure to reacquaint ourselves, and to highlight their perilous positions whilst persuading them of their very limited options.'

'Excellent, I'm sure they will be absolutely delighted to see you again.'

'Inspector Muckle?'

'Yes, Sir William.'

'Can you take Miss Cushway and Mr Spaulding to Amble Station?'

'Of course. Please.' He gestured towards the hangar and off they went. 'Oh, and Inspector, when you return can you kindly take Lady Fescue and Mrs Drye to Eastoff House?'

'Yes, it will be my pleasure.'

'Much appreciated, Inspector.'

Tony rejoined our diminishing group as Inspector Hindmarsh and his men also headed off back towards the hangar.

'I've briefed them, Wispy, and they're on their way back to the Great Northern.'

'Then you had better go and get your flying gear on.'

'On my way.'

'Darling, now I need you and Constanza to deliver the news that Mrs Potts will be dreading and to hand her Mr Potts's letter. It's in my briefcase back at the hangar. Stay the night at Eastoff House, and Groves can arrange a car to take you there tomorrow morning.'

The three of us walked slowly back towards the hangar and Libby slipped her hand into mine. I retrieved the letter and handed it to her.

'Here you are. I very much hope she will be willing to share its contents with you.'

'And if she doesn't?'

'Depending on its contents, I suppose Tony could claim the letter as vital evidence, but let us hope it doesn't come to that.'

Inspector Muckle had returned.

'Ah, here is your transport, darling.'

'Wispy, you know what I'm going to say.'

'Yes, darling.'

'But I'm going to say it anyway. No heroics.'

'No heroics; of course not, you know me.'

'That's what I'm afraid of.'

'I'll be fine. Now goodbye. Constanza, I was hoping we would have heard from Strangely by now.'

'Me too, but no news is good news. I'm sure he and Fabrice as we speak are improving Anglo-French relations.'

I checked my watch; it was nearly five. 'It's nearly six o'clock where they are so I imagine they are enjoying an aperitif before settling down to some fine French gastronomy.'

'I'm sure they are.' Constanza got in the car.

'Now you remember what I said.'

'Yes, darling, I do. Now come here, you.' I gave her a huge hug and a kiss, and waved them both off.

*

Reinhardt and Waldemar had four Ordnance Survey maps spread out on a workbench and were studying them intently with Tony. I went over and joined them.

'So what's the plan, Reinhardt?'

'The plan, Wispy, is we fly from here to RAF Montrose. We've lost the headwind now so it should take us roughly two and a half hours. The problem we may have is they're not expecting us, so quite what they will make of two German aircraft landing on their airstrip, who knows. But we'll cross that road when we come to it.'

'Bridge!'

'What bridge?'

'We'll cross that bridge when we come to it.'

'I think as the British say, you're splitting hairs.'

'Point taken.'

'We'll spend the night there. Now Alladale Lodge is here, near Ardgay, and you can see from the contours it's in a very hilly and rugged area, so we won't be able to land. I think we might be able to land here.' He tapped the map. 'Royal Dornoch. We can set off at first light tomorrow morning.'

'A splendid plan, Reinhardt, but I don't think the members of the Royal Dornoch Golf Club will take too kindly to you using their links as an airfield.'

'Well, there's nowhere else.'

'Fine, then Royal Dornoch it is. Now, Reinhardt, do you know anything about our final destination?'

'Other than where it is, no.'

'Well you'll be pleased to know it's the country estate of a certain Mr Mungan MacCabe.'

'Really! Well I can't wait to renew my acquaintance with him.'

'I'm sure you can't. Now when we get to Montrose, Tony, can you contact the commissioner and see if he can arrange for someone to meet us at Royal Dornoch and transport to get us up to the Alladale estate?'

'Of course, and I must telephone Mrs Finkelstein and placate her as I thought I'd be home by now.'

'Good man. Well, gentlemen, Bonny Scotland beckons.'

*

It was a gorgeous evening and great flying weather. We flew over the Southern Uplands, across the Firth of Forth, over St Andrews and Carnoustie. Reinhardt turned around and pointed off to his right; RAF Montrose was in our sights. I waved at Tony and I swear that a grin had never left his face from the moment we took off. He waved back.

The boys flew twice around the airfield, waving their wings a few times in an attempt to say hello. We landed in unison and taxied to the wooden control tower. A rather portly gentleman wearing a wing commander's uniform emerged from what I assume was the officer's mess because he had a pint of beer in one hand and a pipe in the other. He supported the most amazing handlebar moustache.

The engines died and we all climbed out. 'What in blue blazes are you doing on my airfield, gentlemen? Could you kindly remove yourselves and aeroplanes at once!'

'Tony, over to you.'

'Might I have a quiet word, Wing Commander?' Tony led him off by the elbow and a few moments later they were back.

'Sir William, Count von Delmenhorst and Baron von Scharmbeck, and of course Inspector Finkelstein of the Yard, who has just confided in me your mission, it's an honour to welcome you at RAF Montrose, and the least we can do is to put the mess at your disposal. I should think you're bloody hungry, what? I'll get the chef to rustle something up for you and I will ask my batman to sort out accommodation. Your aircraft will be taken to a hangar overnight. Come, gentlemen, my fellow officers will be delighted to meet you.'

Tony got through to the commissioner who was going to organise the local police officer to meet us at Dornoch. He also confirmed with Tony that the Great Northern was now en route to Dornoch with Inspector Hindmarsh and his men on board.

*

'Eastoff House, Groves speaking.'

'Groves, it's Sir William. Might I speak to my wife?'

'But of course, Sir William, I will go and get her right away.'

A few moments later she was on the line.

'Are you taking the low road or the high road, Wispy, darling?'

'The high road, of course.' I explained where we were.

'You be careful with those RAF chaps; you will need a clear head in the morning.'

'I know, darling, we're going to turn in shortly. Is all well at Eastoff House?'

'As well as it can be under the circumstances. Treadway returned a little while ago. Florence is in a bad way. She's still unconscious, and the doctors and nurses are trying to hydrate her and bring her temperature down. Alberta and Chester are staying at her bedside.'

'God, if only I had acted sooner in Fréthun, we could have got her then.'

'Wispy, you did exactly what was required. You had no way of knowing that Boutroux wasn't in the cottage and he had already moved her.'

'I know, Libby, but I missed the main chance.'

'No, you didn't. The main chance is now, in the present; not in the past, not in the future, but now.'

'As ever, you're right. I couldn't do this without you.'

'Thank you. Now, the vicarage at Amble have just sent over a telegram addressed to you. Shall I open it?'

'Well, what do you think!'

'Wispy!'

'Sorry, darling.'

'Right, it's from Strangely.'

'Brilliant, what does it say?'

'If you'd stop interrupting, I might be able to read it to you.'

'Sorry.'

'Lacroixs arrested, charged with kidnapping STOP Odette charged with attempted murder STOP Dining at Château Domneuve STOP On way back tomorrow.'

'Bloody, bloody marvellous. Good old Strangely.'

'It's fantastic. Constanza will be relieved, she's been fretting a bit.'

'She must be. You must show her immediately.'

'I will, darling, but Wispy…'

'What?'

'You've now seen him in action. He is unpredictable and dangerous, and I want you back in one piece.'

'That makes two of us.'

CHAPTER 34
SATURDAY, 19 AUGUST 1922
ROTHBURY

Treadway parked the Silver Ghost outside Magpie Cottage. Libby and Constanza noticed the curtains twitch. As Treadway opened the car door, Mrs Potts was already standing on her doorstep, with her two children clutching at her apron and her arms pulling them tight to her.

'Mrs Potts, please allow me to introduce myself. I'm Lady Elizabeth Fescue, and this is Mrs Constanza Drye. You've already met my husband, a week ago.'

'Yes, I did, and he promised to do whatever he could to find my Jack. Has he found him?'

'Please, might we come in?'

She led them through to the kitchen and persuaded the children to go out and play in the garden.

'So, has Sir William found him?'

'I'm sorry, Mrs Potts. Your husband is dead.'

She didn't react. Instead she pulled out a chair and sat down at the kitchen table, clasped her hands and stared into space. Libby and Constanza sat down with her. Five minutes must have passed and she hadn't moved an inch. Constanza place a hand over hers. 'Do you understand, Mrs Potts? Your husband is dead.'

'I know, Lady Elizabeth just told me. Now if you will excuse me, this is no place for our children at the moment, so I will take them up the road to their aunt's house where they can play with her children.'

She opened the back door and called them. They came running in, and in a bright, clear voice she explained that she had to spend a little while with her two guests on grown-up talk, so she was taking them to play with their cousins. They seemed excited at the prospect as she led them out of the house. She returned some ten minutes later.

'She knows, you know.'

'Who knows, Mrs Potts?'

'Mavis. I can see it her eyes; she knows her brother is dead. Now let me put the kettle on.'

She went over to the sink and started to fill the kettle, but she didn't move. The kettle started overflowing, but she still didn't move. Libby got up and with some difficulty managed to prise the kettle out of her left hand.

'Come and sit down, Mrs Potts.' She led her back to the table and helped her back into a chair.

In the faintest of whispers, she said, 'I knew I would never see him again. That day he never came home from the Boathouse, I knew then I would never see him again. He was my rock. He loved me, and I him, and what brought us joy and happiness above all else was our wonderful children and our love for them. He took such happiness and pride in them, and he's never going to see them...'

She started crying, tears streaming down her face. The crying turned to sobs, which grew deeper, until she was struggling to take a breath. Libby and Constanza engulfed her in a tight hug until the sobbing abated.

Libby broke off, retrieved the kettle from the sink and put it on the stove. She found the teapot and tea caddy and soon had a pot of tea, milk, sugar, strainer and cups on a tray. Mrs Potts slowly took a few tentative sips.

'How did he die, and where?'

'We don't know how, Mrs Potts, but we do know that he died near Calais.'

'Calais? What was he doing there?'

'We don't know, but what we do know is that his body is being looked after.'

'Thank you. He deserves a Christian burial here at the church of St Michael and All Angels, near his mother and father. Would that be possible?'

'I don't know the answer to that, but I hope so.'

'But where has he been all this time?'

'Mrs Potts, sorry, we don't know, but I have a letter here from him addressed to you.'

Libby opened her bag and placed the letter in front of her. She picked it up and pressed it to her chest.

'Would you like us to leave you in peace so you can read his letter?'

'No, please stay here. I will excuse myself if I may and read it in the parlour.'

She stood up and walked out. A good thirty minutes passed before she returned, and she seemed more detached than before. She sat down and pushed the letter across the table to Libby.

'It is a sad, emotional and difficult letter to read, and I'm still not sure I can fully absorb its contents, but I would like you to read it.'

'Are you sure?'

'Yes, Lady Elizabeth, I am.'

Libby read the contents and then reread them with growing unease and astonishment. 'Mrs Potts, would you mind Mrs Drye reading the letter?'

'No, of course not.'

Constanza read the letter and exchanged a fleeting glance with Libby. She refolded the letter, replaced it in the envelope, and put it back on the table in front of Mrs Potts, who was now quietly sobbing. Constanza put her arm around her and offered her a handkerchief.

'Mrs Potts, unfortunately this letter will not bring back your husband, but his words may help bring to justice an evil, violent and depraved being. Would you mind if we kept hold of the letter for a while longer?'

'My Jack was not an evil person, he was a loving husband and a doting father. If his last words on this earth can help in any way, please keep the letter for as long as you need it.'

'Thank you, Mrs Potts. I too believe that Mr Potts was not an evil person. Can I also request that we take the two tender documents with us? I can assure you they will bring no harm to you.'

'Of course you can. You'll find them in the potting shed. If you go out into the garden, it's at the far end. Gardening was his love, and he was never happier than when he was pottering around in his garden.'

CHAPTER 35
SATURDAY, 19 AUGUST 1922
CLAPHAM

After a trying journey back from Amble, arriving back in London in the small hours of the morning and after very little sleep, Wanda and Luther arrived at Clapham Junction station at seven o'clock. They boarded a train to Brighton and breakfasted on the way down.

Wanda rang the doorbell to Villa Xanadu and moments later it was answered by the housekeeper. 'Good morning, Dorothy, we are here to see Mr Clement Featherstonehaugh.'

'Good morning, you were here last Tuesday?'

'Yes, we were. We weren't formally introduced. I'm Miss Wanda Cushway and this is my colleague Mr Luther Spaulding. Now, might we see Mr Featherstonehaugh?'

'I'm afraid you can't. Mr Featherstonehaugh went away last Wednesday, for an indefinite period.'

'I see. Might we come in for a few moments? There is something of extreme importance, concerning Mr Featherstonehaugh, and it is imperative we find him.'

'Gosh, well you had better come in.' She led them into the drawing room. 'I don't really see how I can help.'

'Dorothy, when we were here last Tuesday, we came to warn Mr Featherstonehaugh of a potential danger to him. That danger is now turning into a reality and it's vital we find him. Have you any idea where he might have gone?'

'Oh dear, I'm coming over all unnecessary. Do you mind if I sit down? I'm feeling quite faint.'

'Not at all. What you need is a nice cup of sweet tea. Luther, would you kindly make Dorothy a cup of tea whilst I sit here and comfort her?'

'Of course.'

'Oh, and a cold compress for her forehead.'

'Thank you, both of you. You're too kind.'

'Nonsense, now you just sit still and take a few deep breaths.'

Luther went off in search of the kitchen. Five minutes later, he returned with a wet flannel and gave it to Wanda.

'Here we go, Dorothy, let's put this on.'

'Right, I'm off to make your tea.'

Ten minutes later he was back. 'Sorry for the delay, I couldn't find the sugar.' Luther placed the tea tray on a coffee table and poured a cup of tea, adding milk and two sugars. 'There you are, Dorothy. This should perk you up.'

They looked on as she slowly sipped her tea. 'Is that hitting the spot?' enquired Wanda.

'It's working a treat, but I could manage another, if I may.'

'But of course, let me pour you another one.' Luther handed her another cup of tea.

Again after a few moments, Wanda enquired how she was feeling. 'Much better.'

'Good,' Luther said, 'I'll leave you two together whilst I go and do the washing-up.'

'No please, leave the tray. I'll do the washing-up later.'

'I won't hear of it.' He picked up her cup, placed it on the tray and left the room.

A further fifteen minutes elapsed before Luther returned. 'Sorry I took so long. I have a confession to make, Dorothy. Whilst washing up, your cup slipped out of my grasp and I'm sorry to report I broke it. It took me ages to find the bin, but I've cleaned up the breakage. Can you let me know the cost to replace the cup?'

'Don't be silly, Mr Spaulding. If the truth be known, I've been breaking a few myself; far too chintzy for my taste. It's about time we got another tea service.'

'Whilst you were out breaking crockery, Dorothy felt restored enough to continue our conversation on the whereabouts of Mr Featherstonehaugh. Despite the considerable shock of knowing he is in danger, she hasn't a clue as to his whereabouts. Well, Dorothy, we must be on our way.'

'I'm terribly sorry you've had a wasted journey and I haven't been able to assist your good selves, especially as you have Mr Featherstonehaugh's best interests at heart.'

'Indeed we do. Now we must be off. No, don't get up, we will see ourselves out.'

*

Wanda slipped her arm through Luther's as they walked to the seafront. 'By my calculations you took thirty minutes to produce a cold compress, a pot of tea, and washing up and breaking a piece of Clement's fine bone china. So where is Mr Clement Featherstonehaugh?'

'My best guess is that he's gone to Broadstairs.'

'Broadstairs?'

'Yes, Broadstairs. I don't have your finesse at lock-picking, so I forced open his bureau – before you say anything, you wouldn't know it's been forced.'

'You're learning.'

'Thank you. I found the details of a property, on Foreland Heights, Broadstairs. It was number ten, but across the top of the page "Monet Lodge" had been written. I checked various other documents and notes and the handwriting is exactly the same.'

'Aptly named: no doubt purchased from selling fake paintings. Right, onwards to Broadstairs.'

*

They took a train from Brighton and changed at Canterbury onto a train to Broadstairs. It was a tedious journey and they arrived just after two o'clock. They sought directions to Foreland Heights from a newsagent in the station. It was a short walk, and they stopped on a right-hand bend outside number four.

'Look, further up on the right is number ten,' observed Wanda. It was a large Victorian detached house. 'Luther, there's a side gate. Can you make your way around to the back of the house and block Clement's escape route, wherever the back door is located? I will give you two minutes then I'll knock on the door.'

They slowly walked up to the house, and Luther shot off through the side gate. After a few minutes, Wanda approached the large front door and extracted her revolver from her shoulder bag and held it in her right hand behind her back. There was a large, polished brass door knocker in the shape of a lion's head. As she reached for it, it somehow reminded Wanda of the brass knocker described in *A Christmas Carol* and she had a vison of Jacob Marley appearing. She knocked with three firm raps and stood back.

After about half a minute she heard footsteps on the hall floor, and the door was opened. 'Clement, lovely to—'

He went to slam the door but Wanda had put her foot in the way. Clement turned and fled into the house, with Wanda after him. He was joined from a side room by a panic-stricken Walderne Smithers. The two of them reached the back door. Clement threw it open and they both ran into Luther. He stood his ground, but the pair were flailing wildly at him with their fists, like a couple of schoolboys in a playground fight.

Wanda raised her revolver and fired two rounds into both doorjambs above their heads. The sound was deafening in the confines of the kitchen, and wooden splinters rained down on Clement and Walderne as they cowered on the floor.

'As I was saying before you rudely ran away, it's lovely to see you, Clement, and what a surprise, Walderne Smithers! Two birds with one stone. Unfortunately, I don't have any handcuffs to hand. Luther, would you see what you can find to restrain our two partners in crime? Now, both of you, into the drawing room, and don't think for one second I won't use my revolver.'

Luther returned with a rope washing line which he had cut into two, and tied their hands together behind their backs, then sat them both together on the settee. There was a loud knock on the front door. 'I'll go.'

Luther returned. 'It was your neighbour wondering what those two large bangs were. I told him I was here repairing your radio and two balloon valves exploded. That seemed to satisfy him.'

'Well done,' Wanda said. 'Now, where to begin… ah, I know. In a concept put forward by Thomas à Kempis in his work *Imitation of Christ* in the early fourteen hundreds, I quote: "Of two evils, the lesser is always chosen". And that happens to be you, Clement.

'Firstly, you will face trial for fraud, in that you've admitted selling fake works of art; and secondly, you will face trial for fraudulently trying to sell a ball bearing factory that you knew was going to be stripped of its assets. These are serious offences that will result in a long jail term. If you cooperate with Scotland Yard, they just may take that into account.

'Now Walderne, you are a particularly pernicious person. Firstly, you telephoned Miss Florence Eastoff on the evening of the twenty-sixth of June, telling her of a scandal in a Paris fashion house, which lured her into the hands of her kidnappers.

'Secondly, you were the conduit for the production of the letters and final ransom note, and you delivered them to the Eastoffs. We even watched you leaving your cottage on Tuesday evening at just gone seven thirty, carrying that battered case of yours, heading towards Midhurst Road. No doubt in it you carried the final ransom note, that you then found a way of delivering early on Thursday morning to Lennox Gardens. How much did you pay the paperboy to deliver it?'

Walderne stared at Wanda and said nothing.

'Walderne, you will face trial for the kidnapping of Miss Florence Eastoff, and if found guilty, as we know you are, you will face a minimum of life in prison.'

'I didn't do any of these things. I'm totally innocent.'

'Really? I'm astonished. Can you explain to Mr Spaulding and myself why in your concealed cellar we found the following items: one, a box of Brousses writing paper and envelopes; two, a stack of cheap books with holes where letters had been cut out; three, a notebook containing the Eastoffs' London address and telephone number; four, in the same notebook, a script about a scandal in a Paris fashion house; and five, the various pieces of equipment and paraphernalia which enabled you to produce the ransom notes?'

'No, I can't explain why they were concealed in a cellar in my house. I didn't even know it had a cellar.'

She opened her bag, took out a pair of cotton gloves and lifted the notebook out of its envelope. 'This is your notebook, is it not? We've compared your handwriting with some of your other architectural notebooks and it's identical.'

Wanda stood and stared at Walderne for a good two minutes.

'I'm still awaiting your answer.'

He sat there in silence.

'Your silence speaks volumes, Mr Smithers. Now, Clement, one further question – and think of the consequences before answering. Were you aware of your friend's involvement in this despicable act of kidnapping?'

He looked at the floor and mumbled.

'Sorry, I didn't catch that. Speak up.'

He cleared his throat. 'Yes, I was aware.'

'Thank you. Now I need to use your telephone. Where is it?'

'It's in my study.'

'Luther, here is my revolver. I don't think they are capable of doing anything daft, but you never know.'

Wanda found the study and asked the operator for the number on the card she had taken from her purse. After a few moments it was answered. 'Sir Redvers' residence. Who's calling, please?'

'This is Miss Wanda Cushway. May I speak to Sir Redvers?'

'Miss Cushway, you do realise that it's Saturday afternoon and Sir Redvers is relaxing.'

'And you do realise that crime is not a Monday-to-Friday operation and I need to speak to the commissioner now!'

After a minute he came on the line. 'Miss Cushway, what a pleasant surprise. Have you changed your mind about coming to work at the Yard?'

'No, Sir Redvers, I haven't, but I've got some very important news to impart.'

Wanda explained every detail of their day. 'Good Lord, Miss Cushway, Sir William's agency is very lucky to have one of the best detectives I know. You stay put and I'll contact my counterpart in Kent to get some officers to you PDQ, so they can arrest these perpetrators and get them brought to London.'

'Thank you, Sir Redvers.'

'No, it's Scotland Yard that should thank you.'

Wanda returned to the drawing room. 'Thank you for letting me use your telephone. You'll no doubt be anxious to hear what is going to happen next, so I shall enlighten you. I've just spoken to Sir Redvers Preece, Commissioner of Police at Scotland Yard, and as I speak, police officers are on their way here to arrest you and take you both directly to London.'

Twenty minutes later, four policemen turned up, and the Featherstonehaugh and Smithers alliance took a turn for the worse. Clement decided to take the moral high ground and was most compliant with the officers. He was certainly looking after his own skin and extolling the virtues of the importance and the duty of a British subject to comply with the local constabulary. However, Walderne went berserk, screaming at the top of his voice that Sir Chester was the devil incarnate and that divine retribution would be wreaked on him and his family. It took all of the four officers' strength to overpower and handcuff him, but that failed to silence him, and for some bizarre reason he started to sing 'My old man said follow the van and don't dilly dally on the way' as the officers led them away, much to the astonishment of a small crowd of neighbours who had gathered outside to see what all the commotion was about.

It was past five when Wanda and Luther arrived back at Broadstairs station, where they boarded a train for London, and both agreed that a well-earned dinner was called for.

CHAPTER 36
SATURDAY, 19 AUGUST 1922
MONTROSE

'Good morning, sir, and a very pleasant one it is too. I'll just pop your cup of tea here. The wing commander requests you join him for breakfast in the mess at seven o'clock.'

'Thank you, I'm looking forward to a hearty breakfast.'

'Indeed, sir. You can't fly on an empty stomach.'

I joined the others in the mess and breakfast was delicious; other than fried eggs, mushrooms and tomatoes, we had the gastronomic delights of tattie scones, fried haggis, and Polony, which the wing commander described as a large cured pork sausage with various seasonings.

'Right, gentlemen, your aircraft are fully fuelled and await your presence. Please follow me.'

We walked out of the mess, and to our amazement the whole squadron had turned out.

'Just thought we'd like to give you boys an RAF send-off, what? Now please forgive me, Count von Delmenhorst and Baron von Scharmbeck, but the chaps wanted to send you on your way with a little token of your visit. Please.'

We walked across the apron to the aircraft and stood in front of Reinhardt's plane. The wing commander tapped the fuselage with his swagger stick. 'There, what do you make of that?'

We all stared at a small RAF roundel which had been painted just below Reinhardt's cockpit.

Well, this should be interesting; it could go one of two ways!

Both Reinhardt and Waldemar walked up to their aircraft and took a closer look at the new additions to their planes. They walked back towards the wing commander, who was twiddling with his moustache. 'During the war we looked up into the skies and watched in awe the skills demonstrated by our brave pilots from either side, and it is a considerable honour to carry your insignia alongside our German cross.'

'Thank you, and we hope it brings you luck. Now, gentlemen, the weather is set fair, so I wish you Godspeed.'

'Thank you for your hospitality, Wing Commander.'

'It's a pleasure, Sir William.'

As the mechanics rotated the propellers, the engines fired into life. The wing commander brought his squadron to attention. We took off and flew around the airfield and back towards the squadron, and as we approached them, Reinhardt and Waldemar did a canopy roll and then climbed into the sky. It was a beautiful day for flying, with cirrus clouds high above us. The scenery was spectacular as we flew over the Cairngorms, Nairn and the Moray Firth, and after two hours we had Dornoch in our sights. They circled over the golf course and Reinhardt identified the flattest fairway to land on; happily, on the plus side I noticed there was not a single bunker on it. He signalled to Waldemar and gave the thumbs up.

Now we just had the delicate matter of disturbing the local golfers. There was a group of four players standing on the tee, a group of four spread out across the middle of the fairway waiting to play their second shots, and a group of four putting out on the green. The planes banked off to the right and then approached really low towards the tee. The members saw them coming and hit the deck. We landed one after the other and the golfers on the fairway sprinted off to the left and right. Reinhardt and Waldemar managed to bring their planes to a halt just shy of the green.

As we got out, the four golfers on the green came to meet us. 'What in blazes are you chaps up to? You've just made me miss my birdie putt. Most outrageous behaviour!'

'I can only apologise for intruding on your game, gentlemen. I'm sure your fellow golfers will give you your birdie putt.'

We were now joined by the other four golfers from the middle of the fairway, who were demanding to know what the hell was going on. Tony and I were doing our best to placate them when we heard the honking of a car horn, and we all turned around to see two open-top Model T Fords driven by two policemen madly waving and coming towards us.

They parked next to the green and came across to join the ever-growing party as we had just been joined by four more golfers from an opposite fairway.

The sergeant managed to eventually quieten the affronted golfers. 'Now which one of you aviators is Inspector Finkelstein from Scotland Yard?'

This seemed to have the magical effect of silencing the mutterings of the disgruntled golfers.

'Sergeant, please allow me to introduce myself. I'm Inspector Finkelstein.' The sergeant saluted. 'And may I introduce my colleagues: this is Sir William Fescue, and our pilots, Count von Delmenhorst and Baron von Scharmbeck.'

'Welcome to Dornoch, gentlemen. I'm Sergeant Limond, and this is Constable Mar. Now in order not to interrupt the Saturday morning four-balls any more than necessary, can we move your aircraft off this fourteenth fairway and park them somewhere safe? For future reference, if you are tempted to land here again, this hole goes by the name of Foxy.'

Reinhardt took over now and organised the golfers into two teams of six, and they happily helped push the two aircraft so they were parked out of harm's way, beside the next tee box.

*

The sergeant and his fellow officer drove us the fourteen miles to the village of Ardgay, which we reached by midday. We then continued the nine miles to Amat Lodge, at the edge of the Amat Forest.

The sergeant pointed out the track that went through the forest to Alladale Lodge. He then set off back to Dornoch to meet the Great Northern, which was due in at three o'clock that afternoon, and bring Inspector Hindmarsh and his men here.

We spread out our Ordnance Survey map and saw that the track followed the course of the River Carron. It was just over three miles to the lodge, and it was nearly one thirty when we set off. We heard the waterfall before we saw it, and when we reached it, it was stunning. We went down to a pool below the falls and took a cool and refreshing drink.

On we pressed for another mile, then stopped to take in the breathtaking views. For a moment I was transfixed by the beauty and was only brought back to reality when Tony tapped me on the shoulder.

'Look, Wispy, over there.' He pointed to a track that went into the forest on our left. 'It's the fuselage of an aircraft.'

'Bloody hell, you're right. Come on, let's take a look.'

We set off up the track, which was about four yards wide, with revolvers in our hands. The fuselage was about five hundred yards up the track. As we neared it, to our amazement it was practically intact, although the propeller was missing, as were the wings.

'So, our hunch was right, Tony. Boutroux came here, but did he survive the crash?'

We examined the fuselage, and there were no signs of blood in the cockpit. The ammunition boxes had gone too.

Reinhardt and Waldemar attracted our attention from the top of the path. We walked up to join them and looked out onto a slope covered in heather.

'He must have flown over that ridge up there,' said Waldemar in a stage whisper. 'He tried to land on the downslope of heather, but more than likely was travelling too fast, similar to his landing at Southfields. If you look up there, you will see the remains of the aircraft wheels. He was fortunate and extremely lucky that his aircraft hurtled straight onto the track. If you look to the left and right you will see the wings that were ripped off as he entered the forest. The remaining fuselage must have glided along the track, coming to a halt where we found it.'

'So, we assume he's up at the lodge?' Tony said.

'Yes, we do, so we'll proceed with extra caution. We will keep off the track now and make our way to the lodge through the woods.'

*

We arrived at the edge of the woods, and I consulted my watch; it was coming up to three o'clock. The inspector and his team should be pulling into Dornoch about now.

Keeping out of view behind some gorse bushes, we stared up a steep slope of well-manicured lawns to the granite Victorian façade of Alladale Lodge. We must have been no more than fifty yards from the entrance. To the right-hand side of the front door was parked a Rolls-Royce and next to it, a Bentley similar to mine. To the left-hand side was a delivery van, from MacDuff's of Dornoch, established in 1832, purveyors of the finest meats and game and Mrs MacDuff's award-winning haggis and mutton pies. I trained my binoculars on the building and couldn't detect any movement from within.

'Right, we need to check for escape routes. The forest appears to border the whole lodge so we should be able to move unseen. Tony, Waldemar, you circle the lodge anticlockwise, and we'll go clockwise and we'll meet at the back. Let's go.'

Reinhardt and I had gone a hundred yards or so when we came upon the track that we were on earlier. It was on the apex of a bend, so if we crossed at this point we might be seen from the lodge. We moved to our left until we were out of sight and sprinted the short distance across the track. Moving on, we followed the track from the safety of the forest, meeting Tony and Waldemar at the back of the lodge. The good news from our surveillance was that there was only one track capable of supporting a motor vehicle.

'Tony, what are you thinking?'

'I doubt very much they will try and walk out, because trying to go east, west or north will eventually lead them into a wilderness. Look at the map: you see the track continues for a while until it reaches a ford, near the River Alladale, and then peters out into a footpath? To drive that short distance will be futile. They don't know we are here, so let's make our way back to the front and keep watch until Inspector Hindmarsh gets here, and then we can make our move.'

'Good, we have a plan.'

We crossed the track, out of sight of the lodge, and as we headed into the forest, I noticed a small group of outbuildings about fifty yards down to our right.

'Look, down there,' I said pointing them out.

We spread out and approached cautiously. We didn't detect any movement, and what we discovered was a stable block adjacent to the track. It was no longer used as a stable but as a gamekeeper's lodge and an estate office. We split into twos and carefully opened each door – not a sign of life. The last building we came to was an equipment store for the estate's gardeners and foresters.

Arriving back at our earlier vantage point, we made ourselves as comfortable as we could and kept watch. It had gone four o'clock and Inspector Hindmarsh should now be well on his way.

Ten minutes later we spotted the front door opening, and he appeared: Florian Boutroux. We watched transfixed. I trained my binoculars on him, and gone were the bedraggled clothes. His right sunken eye was now bright and alert, and gone too was the look of utter insanity. What I saw before me was a clean-shaven butcher, wearing a white shirt, dark trousers, grey waistcoat, a red striped apron, and a straw boater on his head.

Tony too was observing through his binoculars and whispered, 'It's apt, don't you think, that he's dressed as a butcher?'

'The irony hasn't escaped me, Tony,' I said.

Reinhardt and Waldemar were watching the scene through their binoculars too as Boutroux opened the back of the van and then went back into the lodge. A few moments later he reappeared carrying one of the ammunition boxes and placed it in the van.

'We've got to stop him leaving. Tony, you stay here. If he finishes loading and moves off, run hell for leather down to the track outside the stable block. Right, come on, you two, we've got some heavy work to do in pretty short order.'

We ran down to the equipment store. I flung the door open and rushed in, grabbing two large felling axes and a coil of thick rope. We ran the short distance to the track edge. I quickly scanned the trees on the edge of the track.

'Here, this conifer is perfect.' I'd selected a tree with a trunk that was approximately four feet in circumference at its base. 'Now cut a V here for all your worth.'

I started to shin up the trunk with the rope over my shoulder and managed to grab a branch and haul myself up. God, I hadn't climbed a tree in years and my arm and leg muscles were burning. I got nearly to the top and secured the rope around the main trunk, and then descended as fast as I could, dropping the last five feet to the ground with the rope.

'Keep it up, chaps, you're nearly there.' They couldn't respond on account that they were trying to breathe and sweat was pouring into their eyes. 'I'm going to the other side of the track and I'm going to put as much tension on the rope as I can to start pulling the tree towards me.'

At first it wouldn't budge, but then I felt a bit of give, and with an almighty crack, the rope went slack and the blasted thing was hurtling towards me. The main trunk missed me, but the upper branches felled me. I think I must have momentarily lost consciousness, but I came to with Reinhardt and Waldemar pulling me out and helping me to my feet. I'd taken a bit of a blow to the left side of my face, and as I touched my cheek, my hand came away covered in blood.

We looked at our handiwork and the track was well and truly blocked; there was no way around it. Boutroux was comprehensively snookered. Moments later, Tony came sprinting through the forest. He was panting hard but managed to get the following sentence out whilst he had both hands on his knees trying to get his breath back. 'He's talking to the chauffeur, but he's got some ignition keys in his hand, so I assume he will be leaving shortly.'

241

He stood up. 'Oy vey iz mir, what the hell happened to your face?'

'This tree fell on me.'

'Bloody hell, you're going to need stiches in that. How on earth did you manage—'

'I'll explain later. Now, Tony, Waldemar, you take the right side, we'll take the left. As soon as he comes around the bend, he'll nearly be on the tree and he'll brake hard. As soon as he hits the brakes, we're in the van and on him. We don't give him time to react, let alone put the van into reverse. Surprise is our friend. Are we clear?'

'Yes,' they said in unison.

'Good. Now, positions.'

Up in the distance we heard the van start and a gear crunch. The engine revs increased and by the sound it was making, he was accelerating fast, which was to our advantage. The van shot around the corner and he hit the brakes. Before it had come to a stop, we had the doors open. I piled in and had him in a stranglehold. Reinhardt went in low and wrestled with his feet. Tony secured his left arm which was flailing about, whilst Waldemar somehow managed to grab his right arm which he was using to punch my face. He was bloody strong, but he eventually gave up resisting.

After much untangling of limbs, we eventually extracted him from the van. Tony handcuffed his hands behind his back, whilst Reinhardt and Waldemar had reclaimed the rope, cut a piece off the length and trussed his feet together.

After we all had our breath back, Tony stood in front of him. 'Florian Boutroux, I am Inspector Finkelstein of Scotland Yard and I am arresting you for the kidnap of Miss Florence Eastoff and her attempted murder. Also, for the murder of Mr Jack Potts, and for obtaining money – or in your case, gold bullion – with menaces. You will be taken from here for questioning at Scotland Yard.

'Incidentally, your mother, Madame Odette Lacroix, and your stepfather, Monsieur Jean-Pascal Lacroix, have been arrested in Montlaur, also for the kidnapping of Miss Florence Eastoff. And your mother has also been arrested for the attempted murder of a police officer.

'We have also arrested a Mr Walderne Smithers for his part in the kidnapping of Miss Florence Eastoff, and a certain Mr Clement Featherstonehaugh, who you may not have had the pleasure of meeting. Is there anything you would like to say?'

A strange smile spread across his face. 'Yes, actually, I would. I would just like to say how much I have enjoyed the past eight weeks, and the planning time, which started in February. These things just don't come together on their own volition, you know. I do have a few regrets, namely I should have instructed my sniper to blow Florence's head off once I had taken off. And secondly, I should have dispatched that lump of lard Potts earlier.'

'You're one hell of a sick individual, Boutroux.'

'Really, Inspector, I wouldn't have it any other way, and I take pride in my accomplishments. More importantly, I will be remembered and exalted long after I'm dead, unlike you, who will not even be a footnote in history.'

CHAPTER 37
SATURDAY, 19 AUGUST 1922
ALLADALE ESTATE

'Reinhardt, Waldemar, you guard Boutroux. Come on, Tony, up to the lodge.'

We ran through the forest and took up our earlier vantage point. 'Bloody hell, the Bentley's gone. I thought we agreed there was no other route off the estate for motor vehicles?'

'There isn't.'

We sprinted up the slope to the lodge and burst in through the front door. We stopped and listened, and in the distance we heard a muffled conversation. Following the noise, we moved slowly to the back of the house with our revolvers drawn and located the conversation to the kitchen.

'On three: one, two, three.' We dived into the kitchen. Tony flung himself behind a butcher's block, and I ended up lying prone behind a preparation table, whilst knocking a butter churner over in the process, resulting in a rather painful knock to my left leg.

The two people having the conversation were the butler and chauffeur, who looked totally bewildered as we stood and pointed our revolvers at them. They slowly raised their hands above their heads, whilst dropping their teacups and saucers to the floor with a resulting crash.

'Where is he, Breathnach?' I enquired.

The butler took a gulp of air and managed in a faltering voice to say, 'Where is who, sir?'

'Don't play games with me. Where is he?'

'Do you mean Mr Mungan MacCabe, sir?'

'Who else would I bloody well mean?'

'I'm not sure, sir, but if you want Mr MacCabe, he's gone for a drive.'

'Drive? I thought there was only one car track in and out of the estate.'

'That is correct, sir.'

'Well in blue blazes, where the hell has he gone?'

'I think he set off down the track to the River Alladale, sir, in my opinion an unwise thing to do.'

'Quite!'

'Come on, Tony, we haven't a moment to lose.'

*

We belted through the back door and hurtled down the track back into the forest. We were coming to the edge of the forest and could hear the river flowing swiftly below us to our left. We stopped at the edge and looked down to the River Alladale, and there in the ford was MacCabe's Bentley, and in the distance, a small figure running with difficulty. I trained my binoculars on the figure.

'That's MacCabe. He's got a shotgun with him and a knapsack slung over his shoulder, so I assume he's got plenty of cartridges. He seems to be struggling to run very fast; I guess he is not very fit.'

'That makes three of us, Wispy!'

'Tony, we are a damned sight fitter than he is. Come on.'

We set off at a steady jog and although he was a good half a mile away, we were slowly reeling him in. Off to the right ahead of us was Carn Alladale, which according to our map rose to a height of two thousand and seventy-eight feet. MacCabe turned off the path and started to climb, and disappeared into a small wood on the side of the mountain. We stopped and both trained our binoculars on the wood and its surroundings. There was another, smaller, wooded area to the right of the wood that concealed MacCabe.

'Tony, climb up to your right here and when you're level with the first wood, disappear in there, and when you arrive at the far side, fire off a few rounds. It's a reasonably short distance, so your shots should reach. I hope they will distract him enough so I can make my way further down the path and then up through the wood to his position. How much ammunition have you got?'

'Three boxes.'

'Plenty, so you can keep him occupied for a while?'

'Yes, and you take care. That's a nasty gash on the left side of your face – in my opinion it will need to be sutured – and your left eye is nearly closed.'

'All the better for taking aim. Now off you go, and once you start firing, I'll run like the clappers down the path and climb up the slope into MacCabe's wood.'

'Good luck.'

'You too, Tony.'

There was a small hollow to my right and as Tony set off, I settled there and watched MacCabe's wood like a hawk through my binoculars. Ten minutes later, I heard the tell-tale sound of Tony's pistol being fired. He let off a few rounds every fifteen seconds. Then I heard the unmistakable sound of a twelve-bore being fired, but more importantly I saw the smoke discharge from the gun. MacCabe was firing from the right edge of the middle section of his wood.

Got you, you bastard!

I sprinted the hundred and fifty yards along the path and then climbed the slope and entered the wood. I stood stock still and listened. Tony let off another two rounds, and MacCabe returned fire with two barrels from his shotgun. He was about fifty yards away up to the right at about forty-five degrees.

I closed my eyes and cast my mind back to my time in the Norfolks. Bittersweet memories. Then, with my army training firmly to the fore, I slowly moved towards my target. His shotgun exploded again and I ran as fast as I could until the sound of the second explosion dissipated. I crouched down behind a tree, and slowly looked up ahead of me. There he was, kneeling down, reloading his gun. He was twenty yards from me.

I removed my knapsack, checked my revolver, and moved without a sound away from the protection of the tree. I dug the ball of my left foot into the ground until I felt I had enough purchase to spring forward. My breathing slowed, and I waited.

Two revolver shots rang out. I anticipated the first explosion from MacCabe's shotgun, and I was out of my block, starting to accelerate to my target, when it went off. I was nearly on him and when the second explosion went off, I was running flat out. With two yards to go I launched myself at him and flattened him to the ground. The force of the impact took the wind right out him. His shotgun flew out of his hand, and I managed to put my revolver to the back of his head whilst kneeling on the small of his back.

'Not bad for a stuck-up prig and an amateur sleuth, but I suppose an amateur wouldn't be good enough for you, so it's high time you met a professional detective.' In an instant I fired my revolver into the dirt next to MacCabe's right ear. It had the desired effect and completely dazed and disorientated him. At the same time, I shouted at the top of my voice, 'Tony, over here. I need the help of a proper detective!'

I watched Tony run towards me.

'Sir William, you requested a proper detective, so here I am.'

MacCabe was slowly regaining his senses. 'Mr MacCabe, allow me to introduce Inspector Finkelstein from Scotland Yard. Please, Inspector, would you do the honours?'

'But of course, Sir William. Mr Mungan MacCabe, I'm arresting you for the kidnapping of Miss Florence Eastoff, for fraud in relation to the sale of a ball bearing factory, industrial espionage against the Eastoff Shipbuilding Company, and for obtaining money – or in your case, gold bullion – by menaces. You will be taken from here for questioning at Scotland Yard.'

'Thank you, Inspector. Will you handcuff him where he lies, or shall we stand him up?'

'Sir William, I have a slight problem in that department because I used my only pair on Boutroux.'

'Ah, so you did. Give me a moment.' I wandered back into the wood and retrieved my knapsack.

'I had the foresight to chop a length of rope from the one we used to fell the tree. Let me do the honours.' I tied his hands securely behind his back and then we managed to get him upright.

I picked up his shotgun and we supported him slowly down to the footpath as he hadn't completely come to his senses. He was rambling on about how he intended to take over the Eastoff Shipbuilding Company. We eventually made it to the ford. 'Give me a moment, Inspector, let's see if I can start MacCabe's car.' I waded into the shallow water of the ford, cranked the car, and she fired into life at my second attempt. I got in and with a satisfying roar of the engine, I drove it out of the ford, turned her around and picked up Tony and MacCabe.

We drove up the track and past the lodge, and around the bend we were greeted by the sight of Inspector Hindmarsh and his men removing the remnants of the tree we felled earlier from the track. As I brought MacCabe's Bentley to a stop, I turned around and looked at him. 'MacCabe, I asked you a question once and you didn't answer it, so I'll try again. Do you know what they say about bullies?'

MacCabe just stared at me, his eyes unseeing.

'They say, MacCabe, that bullies are cowards!'

*

We looked quite a sight on the drive back to Dornoch in our eclectic range of motor vehicles, consisting of a Bentley, two police cars, a butcher's van, and two flatbed lorries commandeered by Sergeant Limond to transport Inspector Hindmarsh and his men from Dornoch station. Word had obviously spread about the 'goings-on at the Alladale estate', and most of the village at Ardgay had turned out to watch us drive through, with their attention firmly focused on the laird.

On arrival at Dornoch station, the sun was starting to set and the time had just gone nine o'clock. The Great Northern was sitting in a siding, gently hissing, almost anxious to get going. Tony, Inspector Hindmarsh and his men escorted Mungan MacCabe and Florian Boutroux into the first-class carriage. After ten minutes or so Tony disembarked and joined myself, Reinhardt, Waldemar, Sergeant Limond and Constable Mar, and we walked back to the platform.

'I see our callous cowards are travelling back to London first class, Tony!'

'It's the last bit of comfort they will experience in a long, long time. But I get the sense they will not even notice their surroundings.'

I nodded my head in agreement.

The Great Northern signalled her intent with a blast from the whistle. The driver opened the regulator and huge snorts of smoke thumped into the evening air, and she started to move slowly from the sidings onto the main line. The engine drew alongside us, and the driver leant out of the cab and shouted at the top of his voice, 'Job well done!' Then he fully opened the regulator and the Great Northern wheels spun until she gained traction, and with ever-increasing snorts, she sped further away until the red light of the lamp on the guard's van disappeared from view.

*

Sergeant Limond had arranged accommodation in Dornoch Castle, a hunting lodge, and on Tony's earlier insistence he had arranged for the local doctor to be there to meet me. He cleaned my face and as Tony predicted, it needed suturing; a total of ten stitches were required. He checked my left eye and although it was shut, he was satisfied that the actual eye was not damaged.

It was late by the time the doctor went, but I needed a long soak to sooth my aching body. After which, I managed to get a call through to Libby at Eastoff House although it was nearly eleven o'clock.

'Wispy, I've been worried sick. Are you all right?'

'Absolutely fine, just shattered.'

'What do you mean by shattered?'

'I'm just very tired, with a few minor cuts and bruises.'

'At least you're alive. Tell me, what happened?'

I gave her a sanitised overview of the day and felt her scepticism flowing down the telephone line; she knew me too well, but I would cross that bridge tomorrow.

'And how was your trip to see Mrs Potts?'

I listened in silence, completely absorbed in what she was telling me.

'The poor, poor woman. What future there is for her and her family, heaven only knows. What a complete mess. Why had Mr Potts got himself so far into this mire? I suppose he was trapped?'

'I agree, darling, but we can't bring him back. Now get some nourishment and rest.'

'I will, but one last question: how's Florence?'

'Better, she's regained consciousness and is taking on fluids. The fever is under control and her temperature is dropping.'

'Thank goodness.'

'She's not out of the woods yet; they will need to operate on her hand, then a period of convalescence.'

'But she will live.'

'Yes, now go and get some supper and rest.'

'I intend to, and I'll call you in the morning with our approximate time of arrival at Southfields. One last thing, darling.'

'What?'

'I love you.'

'I know you do, and I love you. Goodnight, Wispy.'

'Night night, Libby.'

God, I needed to unwind; we all did – what a couple of days. The others kindly waited for me. The butler and cook were most accommodating and despite the lateness of the hour treated us to a simple but delicious supper of a chilled vichyssoise soup, followed by a glazed aspic salmon with hollandaise sauce, accompanied by a rice and artichoke salad with a sharp vinaigrette dressing, and cranachan for dessert. We drank, which was a first for all of us, several glasses of Highland cordial.

CHAPTER 38
SUNDAY, 20 AUGUST 1922
DORNOCH

Word too had reached the town of Dornoch, and as we walked the short distance to the golf club, we were attracting a good deal of interest. As we approached the clubhouse, the captain and committee were there to greet us. The captain said a few words about what an honour it was for the club to be able, in some small part, to have helped facilitate the capture of such evil people.

We all walked to the fifteenth tee, where there was quite a crowd of golfers who had given up their morning foursomes to see us off. But on approaching the group I noticed various people wearing their chains of office. Sergeant Limond strode out to meet us, and then introduced us to the mayor, councillors and other local dignitaries.

A photographer was on hand to record the occasion, and after much toing and froing, managed to get us all in the order he wanted. He was just about to take the picture when we heard the honk-honk of a car hooter coming down the fairway. We all turned and looked, to be greeted by the sight of the MacDuffs' butcher's van being driven at speed. It drew up and out came, I assume, Mr and Mrs MacDuff dressed in their Sunday best. They apologised most profusely for being late, and joined the rest of us for the group photograph. Once the photographer had regained some sort of order he finally took the picture.

As we were breaking ranks, the couple who had driven the butcher's van approached the four of us to introduce themselves and indeed they were the MacDuffs. They thanked us for rescuing their pride and joy, and presented us with a hamper each for our journey home.

Finally, Reinhardt and Waldemar, with the help of the greenkeepers, who had earlier managed to get them refuelled, had their aircraft ready for take-off. With instructions from Reinhardt two of the greenkeepers rotated the propellers, and the engines roared into life. We took off and flew over the clubhouse, banked to our left and came back around, and as we flew towards the crowd standing around the fourteenth green, Reinhardt and Waldemar executed a barrel roll. The cheers from the assembled throng reached us in our cockpits, and then we climbed into a beautiful August sky and headed south.

*

We saw Southfields airfield in the distance and as we drew nearer, I could make out a small reception party. Reinhardt and Waldemar flew in side by side and we landed together, taxiing to a stop in front of Chester, Libby, Constanza, and to my delight, Strangely, Wanda and Luther as well. They cut the engines and we sat in silence for a few moments, taking in the scene.

God, it is hard to believe we started this quest fourteen days ago, and I had serious doubts as to my abilities to see it through. But we did it, we bloody well did it! Libby, my rock, was at my shoulder when my little enemies of self-doubt and self-belief sat on the same shoulder and questioned my abilities, but she knocked them off. I thought of my father doubting my ability and recalled the words of my darling Libby: 'Well, I've got news for you, Sir William. You are miles better than him!' Now, to face reality.

I dropped to the ground and started to walk towards Libby, and she broke into a run towards me. We embraced and hugged each other, not wanting to let go. After a few moments, we stood back and looked at each other. I still had my flying helmet and goggles on, and my flying jacket was zipped up over my nose.

252

'Come on, darling, let's get these off.'

She took my helmet and goggles off, undid my jacket then stared in disbelief and horror. I know I looked a sight, because I'd looked at myself in the mirror before leaving Dornoch Castle. My left eye was still closed and coloured a purplish black, my left cheek was severely bruised, and the stitches looked angry. My right eye was still recovering from Chester's haymaker and was a yellowy-green colour, and on top of that I hadn't been able to shave for a couple of days. To my enormous surprise, she didn't berate me. She drew me closer and whispered in my ear, 'I love you, more than you will ever know.' She stood back. 'When we get back to Eastoff House, I'll bathe your wounds and we'll get Chester's physician to come over and have a look at you. But now, there's someone waiting to speak to you.'

I turned around. Chester was some five yards away with a huge smile across his face. He walked towards us, and Libby rejoined the others.

'Wispy, words are futile at moments like this, but I'll give it a go. On the twenty-sixth of June, our daughter was kidnapped. Fourteen days ago, I asked you to find her, and you and your team – and I include the police in that – have brought her home. Alberta and I owe you…'

At which point he couldn't go on, and I drew him to me and held him until his tension started to drift away.

'Thank you, Wispy. There will be time in the coming weeks when we as a family can say our proper thanks, but for now, I repeat, thank you. Now if you'll excuse me, I must have a word with the count.'

I rejoined Libby and the others, and we all started talking at once, across each other, exhilarated, exhausted, but it didn't matter; what mattered was that we had managed somehow to get Florence back.

Just after six o'clock, we said our goodbyes to Reinhardt and Waldemar and waved them off on their long journey back to Bremen, but not before they executed two barrel and slow rolls as a final farewell.

CHAPTER 39
SUNDAY, 20 AUGUST 1922
ROTHBURY

Libby and I sat on our bed. I'd been seen by the Eastoffs' physician, and he was impressed by the suturing and thought over time any scar would slowly fade. Libby ran me a bath and after I had a long soak, she had a close look at my wounds. 'I concur with Chester's doctor; you'll live.'

'Thank you, darling, I feel much more reassured that your medical knowledge has confirmed the prognosis of Chester's physician.'

'Wispy!'

'Sorry, darling. Apologies.'

'Accepted. But how are you feeling?'

'Very tired, sore all over, but contented.'

'Strong enough to read Mr Potts's letter?'

'Good Lord, sorry, I'd put that to the back of my mind. Yes, I'll read it.' She hopped off the bed and delved into her shoulder bag and handed me the letter.

'Dearest Olive, Daisy and Archie,

'The sad fact you are reading this means I am dead. There is no way I can dress this up, but I have transgressed. Let me lay the facts out before you, so you can understand my situation.

'In late 1919, the company decided to tender for a contract to build ships for the British India Steam Navigation Company. I was the principal clerk assigned to manage the preparation of the first tender, which I did. I then passed the completed tender to my senior,

Mr Boutroux, to sign it off before he presented it to the general manager, Mr Babbage.

'Several days later, Mr Boutroux called me into his office and informed me that Mr Babbage insisted we needed to make a better margin, and to uplift all our margins by two and a half per cent. I knew that the tender was priced keenly and if we inflated these, we would price ourselves out of the tender. We never won the tender; it was awarded to MacCabe Shipbuilders.

'Several months later, Mr Boutroux suggested we should meet and have a pint or two, as he thought as we worked so closely together, it would be of benefit to get to know each other better. We had a convivial evening and at the end he gave me an envelope. On the bus home I opened the envelope, and it contained twenty pounds.

'The next morning, I challenged him on why he had given me such a large amount of money, and I tried to return the money, but he wouldn't accept it. He sat me down in his office and told me that Mr Babbage and he had been rewarded by the board of directors, and that both he and Mr Babbage felt that I too should share part of this reward. I felt very uneasy about this, but had nowhere to go and question it. My darling, I feared for my job.

'I opened a new bank account at our branch and put the money there. I haven't dared to touch the money, as it feels like a millstone around my neck. I knew at some point this terrible act I was part of would be bound to be exposed, and I don't know why but I took a copy of the first tender document and the one that I revised. I thought somehow I might be able to use them in my defence, but in all honesty why would they be useful? The copies are in my potting shed, under the workbench at the back, wrapped up in an oilskin. I suggest you burn them for your own protection.

'During the next few years, I received two more payments of twenty pounds, and they too are sitting in my bank account. Then in early February this year, Boutroux met me again for a beer and told me he had got wind that an internal inquiry was going to be launched as to why we failed to win any of the early tenders for the British India Steam Navigation Company. He told me that I had unwittingly priced Eastoff Shipbuilding Company out of the market, and that as I was a willing participant in inflating Eastoff's tender prices, I, as well as he, was liable for the fraud.

'Darling, I was ruined. I pathetically let myself be suckered in, without having the backbone to go to the board as I should have done as soon as I was given the first twenty pounds. I was frightened, a coward, and was about to bring shame upon my family. I had nowhere to turn. I felt utterly wretched. I didn't even have the strength to take the coward's way out.

'Boutroux then told me the truth: that he was in the employ of Mr MacCabe, the owner of MacCabe Shipbuilders, and that's where the money came from. He told me he had one last job to do for Mr MacCabe, and by the time you hopefully receive this letter you will know the extent to which I have fallen.

'From the outset of the kidnapping of Miss Florence Eastoff, I knew that I was going to die. I had never known evil in my life until the point when Boutroux wove me into his most brutal web. My own morsel of comfort was that when I could, I tried to show kindness to Florence.

'My darling Olive, I love you more than words can say. Please tell Daisy and Archie that they are the most precious children in the world and I will always love them. And I know it is unfair of me to ask, but if there is a way, can you shield them from my shame, and when they are old enough, can you explain what I did and allow them to read this letter?

'Lastly, my love, if you can find forgiveness, that would be a blessing to me. Remember me, but go and live your life to the full and raise our children to believe in themselves.

'Your loving husband and father,

'Jack.'

I reread it twice, put it back in its envelope, and gathered Libby to me and hugged her tight.

'Darling, I know it's an understatement, but he didn't deserve this. And his poor family... how are they going to cope? The stigma of this will always be with them. I need to show this letter to Chester.'

'I know you do, but above all you need rest. I have arranged with Groves to have supper here in our room. Then after a good night's sleep, you can show Chester the letter after breakfast tomorrow.'

'No, darling, *we* can show Chester.'

'Thank you.'

CHAPTER 40
MONDAY, 21 AUGUST 1922
ROTHBURY

Libby and I surfaced early, and after a cup of Earl Grey we went for a long walk through the various gardens down towards the dam that held Tumbleton Lake. It was a beautiful morning, and despite my aches and pains I felt somewhat restored after a good night's sleep. We got back to the house at eight o'clock and joined the others for breakfast, during which Groves informed me there was an Ernest White on the telephone. I took the call in Sir Chester's study.

'Morning, Ernest, how's things in Chelsea?'

'All good, Sir William. Sorry I've taken so long, but I've got some information on Mr Eamonn Babbage. I think you'll find it's pretty interesting.'

'Hold on, let me grab a bit of paper and a pen. Right, fire away, Ernest, and speak slowly.'

Ernest patiently relayed his findings.

'How on earth did you find all this out?'

'By making lots of phone calls and pretending to be many different people.'

'Ernest, I take my hat off to you.'

'Thank you, Sir William.'

I rejoined the others for breakfast, mulling over what I'd learnt from Ernest. After breakfast, I managed to grab a few moments with Strangely, Wanda and Tony, which I hadn't been able to do the day before. We found some solitude in the billiard room, and I showed them the letter from Mr Potts. Their reaction was much the same as mine. I then shared the information on Babbage.

Libby and I found Chester in his study. 'Come in, come in, sit down. I've just been talking to Alberta. Florence had the operation on her hand first thing this morning, and it was a success!'

'That's fantastic news, Chester,' said Libby.

'It is, and we hope she will be home by the weekend for a period of convalescence, which I somehow know she won't have the slightest intention of sticking to.'

'Well, from what we know about her, you are right. And hopefully soon we will all have the occasion to meet her.'

'I know she will be incredibly anxious to meet you all too, at the first opportunity, and I know she will make that happen sooner rather than later.'

'Excellent, that is indeed something to look forward to,' I said. 'Now, Chester, do you know a Mr Potts, a senior clerk in your procurement department?'

'Not personally. I've heard Babbage mention him a few times. Why do you ask?'

I apologised that we hadn't been keeping him informed on all the aspects of the investigation because of the speed at which the case unfolded. I explained about Wanda's and my trip to meet Mrs Potts, and that Tony found the letter on Mr Potts's body. Then, that on Saturday Elizabeth and Constanza had delivered this letter to her, and she was happy for it to be used in evidence.

I passed him the envelope and he took it. 'There's no need whatsoever to apologise for any of your actions. The fact you didn't share everything with us was a blessing.'

He took the letter out of its envelope and read. After he'd finished it, he got up and walked to the large window behind his desk and looked out over the gardens. He turned around again, picking up the letter, and reread it. He pressed the servant's bell and sat down.

He let out a long sigh. 'This terrible crime has spread its tentacles far and wide.'

'You are right about tentacles.' I passed him my notes from Ernest.

There was a knock at the door. 'Wait!'

He finished my notes and with a shake of his head he handed them back. 'Come in!' he barked. 'Ah, Groves, can you please ask Treadway to bring the car around? Sir William, Lady Elizabeth and I need to get to Newburn as quickly as possible. After which I need to visit the shipyard.'

'Yes, Sir Chester, I'll get him to bring it around right away.'

I managed to find Tony before we departed and asked him to meet me at the Eastoff Shipbuilding Company with his counterpart from the Newcastle constabulary. He thought that Inspector Muckle would fit the bill perfectly. I couldn't give him an exact time of arrival but suggested one thirty.

*

It had gone midday by the time we pulled up outside Magpie Cottage. I knocked on the door and Mrs Potts answered.

'Might we please come in?'

'I'll show you into the parlour. It's wash day today so the kitchen is a bit of a mess, and the children are at Mavis's.Can I offer you a cup of tea?'

'Maybe in a moment, Mrs Potts, but firstly, can I introduce you to Sir Chester Eastoff?'

Mrs Potts didn't quite know what to do. She sat and looked at her feet, and when she looked up, tears were rolling down her face. In a broken voice she said, 'My Jack didn't mean to do what...'

Chester stood up, went over to her and knelt down in front of her. 'I know he didn't, Mrs Potts, or may I call you Olive?'

She couldn't reply. 'Well, Olive, I think we could all use that cup of tea, and Sir William and I are going to make it. You sit with Lady Elizabeth, and we'll be back in a jiffy.'

Ten minutes later, we entered with a tea tray. Libby had worked her magic, and she seemed to have regained her composure.

Chester sat down in a chair next to her. 'Olive, are you feeling strong enough to have a little chat about your husband?'

'Yes, I think so.'

'Good. Now I know you expressed a wish to have a Christian burial for your husband, and therefore I am making arrangements to have your husband's body repatriated from Calais to here. I will let you know when the final arrangements are put in place.'

'Thank you, Sir Chester,' Mrs Potts said in a firmer voice.

'I've had the privilege of reading your husband's letter. He was just as much a victim in this whole horrible saga as any of us have been, and unfortunately he paid with his life. He has taught me that there are some fundamental things wrong with the way Eastoff Shipping is managed and run, and I intend to change them.

'Olive, I'm pleased to inform you that your husband is entitled to a company pension which will be paid to you monthly. Also, in recognition of his valued service to the Eastoff Shipbuilding Company, the company will pay off his mortgage. As for the money that was such a moral burden to him, and he did not touch, that too will be yours.

'These arrangements are between you and me as a representative of the company, and no one will ever need to know.'

'Thank you. I don't know what to say.'

'You don't have to say anything. I noted your husband's comments about shame, and the stigma that can attach to totally innocent persons. To that end, it is my intention that when the trial of these four people is concluded, I will publish a letter in all the local newspapers saying that your husband was an unwitting victim in this terrible event; likewise, I will write to *The Times*. This, I hope, should stop any gossip or malicious individuals in their tracks; if it doesn't, please be kind enough to let me know.

'Lastly, Olive, your husband's wish that your two children, Daisy and Archie, believe in themselves is a very laudable aim on their journey into adulthood. If I can be of any assistance in this aim, I will be only too pleased to help.'

'Sir Chester, I don't know what to say. I loved my husband and he won't be able to see—' She broke down again, and Libby took her in her arms until her sobs abated.

'If I might be bold for a moment, I know Jack will not see your children grow up, but take comfort that he is helping immeasurably in the shaping of their future, and you can be truly proud of him.

'Jack was a good man.'

'I know he was.'

*

Treadway drove to Wallsend and through the shipyard gates and drew up under the grand Gothic *porte cochère* of the Eastoffs' empire. Treadway opened Libby's door and a receptionist scuttled down the steps to meet Sir Chester.

Chester's office was on the top floor and as we entered the room, it was bathed in sunlight, which flooded in through a window at the opposite side of the room. It ran the length of the outside wall and afforded views over his domain and a beautiful panoramic sweep of the River Tyne, glinting in the sun. His office was large, as was his desk. Bookshelves lined the length of one wall, whilst the other two were covered in paintings, not of previous boats they had manufactured but family portraits. I recognised several of Alberta and Florence. Intermixed with the portraits were several framed copies of Florence's weekly newspapers.

'Now, you must be hungry. How about some sandwiches and tea? Elizabeth?'

'Perfect. I am a little peckish.'

'Wispy? Although I don't need to ask...' A warm smile spread across his face.

'Chester, I'm hurt. Of course, sandwiches will hit the spot.'

Chester pushed a button on his desk and a few moments later, an elegant woman entered the office.

'Welcome back, Sir Chester, and can I say how delighted we all are that Florence is home. Might I ask how she is today?'

'You can, Mrs Quintrell, but first, can I introduce you to two people who were instrumental in finding her and bringing her home, and for the arrest of the culprits responsible for this heinous crime.'

Chester made the introductions, and Mrs Quintrell was particularly interested in how I came by my injuries. The sandwiches were excellent, and after the butler had cleared away, we stood and looked out over the vast shipyard and Chester indicated the various large ships that were in varying degrees of construction. He took great delight in the vessel that was already looming large for the British India Steam Navigation Company. Looking beyond the shipyard, he pointed out various landmarks along the Tyne.

Chester pushed the bell on his desk and Mrs Quintrell reappeared. 'Can you ask Mr Babbage to come up, and ask him to bring the first tender documents he did for the British India Steam Navigation Company?'

'Of course, Sir Chester. Oh, and there's an Inspector Finkelstein and an Inspector Muckle here to see Sir William. I've put them in the boardroom.'

'Excellent, I will buzz you when we need them. Now I suggest you and Elizabeth sit there on the sofa, and I'll sit behind my desk.' Libby and I made ourselves comfortable, and a few minutes later there was a knock on the door.

'Come!'

In came Mr Babbage, crossing the room in that rather self-assured manner of his. Then he noticed me and his manner slightly changed, a flicker of apprehension crossing his face.

'Mr Babbage, I know you've had the pleasure of meeting Sir William, but can I introduce you to Lady Fescue, Sir William's wife? Please, take a seat.' Chester pointed to a leather armchair that was slightly to the left of the front of his desk.

'Mr Babbage, please pass me those documents.' Chester, with a practised eye, found the one he wanted and leafed through the pages quickly, and then turned the document and pushed it across the desk so that it was in front of Babbage.

'That is your signature next to the final total for the tender?'

'It is, Sir Chester. Might I enquire—'

'Not at the moment, Babbage. Were you one hundred per cent happy with the tender before you signed it?'

'Perfectly happy, Sir Chester, I remember it well. Mr Boutroux gave me the completed tender on a Friday afternoon. I worked here all weekend, double-checking the figures – I have to say much to the annoyance of Mrs Babbage as we were meant to be at a choral recital in our local church that Sunday afternoon.'

'Really, Babbage, most commendable of you. And were the figures to your satisfaction?'

'Totally, Sir Chester. I knew how keen you were to break the monopoly MacCabe Shipbuilders have with British India. The margins were tight but doable in that we were making just above our minimum profit margin.'

'Did you send the tender document off?'

'Not personally, as normally I left that to Mr Boutroux, who would have sent it out recorded delivery.'

'Now, Babbage, please cast your eye over the final figure on this tender document.' Chester slid the document across his desk.

Babbage leant forward, picked up the document and compared the two final figures. A frown spread across his face. He then flicked through both documents checking various figures against each other.

'This document has been doctored, and the original figures have been uplifted by two and a half per cent. How the hell has this happened?'

'How the hell indeed, Babbage? The revised copy of the tender that you have in front of you was sent by Boutroux to British India.'

'I'm at a loss to exp—'

'I bet you bloody well are. Now read this letter.' He stood up and handed him Mr Potts's letter.

As Mr Babbage read the letter, his facial expressions changed from surprise to swallowing hard, and beads of sweat started to appear on his top lip and forehead.

'Sir Chester, you will have my resignation in writing immediately.'

'How kind of you, Babbage, but that won't be necessary. When you concluded your inquiry, you said you found not one jot of evidence that our tendering process had been compromised.'

'Yes, I did, Sir Chester. I run a tight—'

'Shut up, Babbage. Of course you didn't find one bit of bloody evidence, because there was nothing to find! However, you endeared yourself so much to Sir William and Miss Wanda Cushway when they met you last Saturday, they decided to do a bit of digging into your personal affairs.'

'I must protest, sir—'

'Save your breath, Babbage. You're quite the little landlord, I understand. How many properties does Mr Babbage own and rent out in the Newcastle area, Sir William?'

'According to our research, twenty-five.'

'I see. I know I pay you reasonably well, Babbage, but not that well. And Sir William, where does Babbage reside?'

'He lives in the village of Milbourne, in the manor house, which he had renovated four years ago.'

'A manor house? It won't be long before it's Sir Eamonn bloody Babbage at this rate.'

'Sir Chester, I swear I had nothing whatsoever to do with your daughter's kidnapping.'

'Babbage, I know you didn't. Why would you? The whole kidnapping business has been most unfortunate for you; if it hadn't happened, your little world of corruption would not have been exposed. So, just how long have you been negotiating loyalty payments with our suppliers?'

Babbage just sat there, staring beyond Chester out of the window.

'Babbage!' He shouted and smashed his fists onto his desk.

Libby and I jumped out of our skins, and Babbage nearly hit the ceiling.

And I thought he was getting soft.

'How long, Babbage?'

He mumbled something into his chest.

'Babbage, I can't bloody hear you!'

'Since you promoted me to General Manager.'

'So that's eleven years. My, it's going to be interesting talking to our suppliers. I'm sure they will all be queuing up to make perfect witnesses at your forthcoming trial. Babbage, I will personally make sure that you are ruined. Sir William, would you kindly ask Inspector Finkelstein and Inspector Muckle to step in, so I can introduce them to my ex-general manager?'

CHAPTER 41
SATURDAY, 16 SEPTEMBER 1922
CHELSEA

L ibby and I came down for breakfast. We had just returned from Scotland and were feeling totally refreshed after ten days' salmon fishing on the River Naver, on the Syre Estate in the Highlands. The fishing was excellent, and the long walks without encountering a soul fully rejuvenated us. Libby had filled two sketchbooks, which promised some exquisite paintings to come. I poured Libby a glass of freshly squeezed orange juice and made myself a spicy Virgin Mary. We helped ourselves to Alice's wonderful breakfast spread and sat down. Eleanor came in with our Earl Grey tea and my ironed copy of *The Times*, which she placed next to me. I picked it up and was drawn immediately to the headline.

'Wispy, please can you take your head out of the paper and talk to me?'

'Sorry, darling, just bear with me a few moments. I need to read this article.'

'Really, you know I don't like you reading at the breakfast table. You've got plenty of time to digest the news when you go to your study.'

'Hmmm... sorry, darling, what did you say?'

'I said... oh, never mind.'

I hadn't touched my breakfast when I put down the paper with a satisfied chuckle. 'Well I'll be jiggered, Libby, read this.' I passed her the paper. I had just read the leading article on the front page, entitled

'MacCabe Shipbuilders to be sold'. The article informed me that Sir Chester Eastoff and Count von Delmenhorst's companies had just agreed in principle to the purchase of the disgraced Mr Mungan MacCabe's shipbuilding company in a joint venture.

It also went on to mention Boutroux's and MacCabe's forthcoming trial, which was set for early in the new year. We had already received some good press for our growing scrapbook, but with the trial date set I was anticipating some more positive publicity for my agency, especially as Tony had informed me that Mr Clement Featherstonehaugh and Mr Walderne Smithers would be appearing for the prosecution and were singing like canaries.

Libby put the paper down and smiled at me. 'Well, darling, I'll make an exception for this. There's a certain poetic justice in this, don't you think?'

'I do, darling. It couldn't have happened to a nicer man.'

'Agreed.' She folded the paper and placed it next to her. There was a knock at the door and Eleanor entered.

'Lady Elizabeth, Sir William, someone is here to see you.'

'Really?' I consulted my watch. 'Nine fifteen on a Saturday morning? Who is it?'

'Miss Florence Eastoff. She wondered if you could spare her a few minutes.'

'Spare her a few minutes? Eleanor, show her into the drawing room immediately.'

'I already have, sir.'

*

As we entered the room, she had her back to us and was looking out over Chelsea Reach. She turned around immediately. I was instantly reminded of the picture of her by Henri Matisse. She was like Alberta: tall, beautifully elegant, with high cheekbones. Her auburn hair shone in the sunlight and her piercing blue-grey eyes smiled at us.

God, how different she looked when I first clapped eyes on her at Southfields airfield. I thought she wouldn't make it, and here she was, standing radiantly before us, with a beaming smile. Instinctively my eyes were drawn to her left hand and I quickly averted my gaze.

'I see your eyes were drawn to my hand.'

You bloody idiot, Wispy, she's noticed!

She held it out. 'I think you will agree the surgeons have done a pretty good job. I still need some reconstructive surgery, but it shouldn't be too noticeable once that is done.'

'Please, my apologies. I didn't mean to stare.'

'No apologies necessary.'

'Thank you, Miss Eastoff. Welcome to our house.'

'Florence, please. Forgive me for calling in unannounced, but after everything you've done for me and my family, I was desperate to meet you, and this is my first opportunity before this evening's dinner party. Can I call you Wispy?'

'It would be an honour.'

'Thank you. My mother and father have told me all about how you and your agency played an absolute corker. Also, for risking your own lives to save mine. I'm in awe of your efforts. You have somehow become an integral part of my journey over the past twelve weeks without me knowing who you are, and yet without you I wouldn't be here. I have an overriding feeling that I want to share what I went through, and my emotions during that traumatic period, with you, and that somehow it will be cathartic for me.'

'If you feel up to it, it will be a privilege to listen.'

We listened transfixed as she told her story. The highs and lows of her captivity left us both exhausted, and once she had finished I was at a complete loss as to how to respond. Florence immediately came to our rescue.

'I have told the police in minute detail everything that has happened to me, which I did in a very matter-of-fact way. I've told my parents, which was a raw experience, but now, in telling you, it has somehow started to release me. *Dum vita est, spes est* – while there is life, there is hope.'

Libby knew exactly what to do, and went over to her, sat down and held her tight. Florence started to cry quietly into the nape of

Libby's neck, then wept huge sobs whilst trying to catch her breath. They slowly subsided and she sat there spent for several minutes before releasing Libby.

'Gosh, I feel so much better. Thank you, I needed that.' Our mantel clock struck the hour of midday.

'Good Lord, is that the time? I must be off. I promised Mother that we would go shopping for a couple of new dresses to wear this evening. It's been absolutely marvellous to meet you both, and thanks once again for everything you've done. I'm looking forward to seeing you both later for what promises to be an extremely exciting evening.'

We saw Florence out to her car and we decided a long walk along the river was called for.

'Libby, darling, I'm intrigued by what she meant by "an extremely exciting evening".'

'So am I. It sounds like we might be in for some fun.'

'Let's hope so, because as the bard said, "Unquiet meals make ill digestions"! Come on, you, best foot forward.' I held out my hand, which she took, and we set off.

CHAPTER 42
SATURDAY, 16 SEPTEMBER 1922
FLEET STREET

Libby and I arrived at the *Daily Clarion* with Constanza and Strangely and a rather nervous Ernest in tow, in a dinner suit I had lent him and had altered to fit him by my tailor. It was shortly before seven o'clock and Strutton greeted us warmly, complimenting us on our success. He showed us upstairs into the boardroom, where we accepted a glass of champagne before we were warmly greeted by Florence, Alberta and Chester. We were followed in fairly short order by Wanda and Luther, who looked exceptionally happy.

Next to arrive was Inspector Finkelstein, Mrs Finkelstein, and Fabrice and Florence Barsalou who had travelled over from Boulogne, shortly followed by Count and Countess von Delmenhorst, and Baron and Baroness von Scharmbeck. The count and baron looked resplendent in their dress uniforms. They were followed by Baron Pierre-Édouard Gascoigne and Baroness Maria-Françoise Gascoigne.

Last to arrive was the woman's editor of the *Daily Chronicle*, Miss Eunice Wade, who strode into the room like a whirling dervish, her curly red hair still slightly out of control. She was wearing a creation that was marginally out of vogue, I thought, but nonetheless very bright, although with my limited experience in these matters some of the colours seemed to clash – but maybe they were meant to.

A selection of delicious canapés had been produced by the Eastoffs' cook to match the vintage champagne we were drinking.

I was particularly impressed that their cook had produced two favourites of mine, anchovy toast and angels on horseback.

Dinner was served bang on eight and the menu was a gastronomic marvel. To start we had consommé brunoise, followed by fillet of sole bonne femme, both accompanied by a dry white burgundy from the Domaine Leflaive Montrachet. Our main course was beef Wellington, perfectly matched with a Gevrey-Chambertin. Dessert was Grand Marnier soufflé, which Chester had chosen to partner an exquisite Sauternes from Château d'Yquem, which when I tasted it had wonderful notes of crème brûlée. Alberta must have done her research because the cheeseboard consisted of a Montgomery Cheddar and a Colston Bassett Stilton, with a nod to our French and German cousins with the inclusion of a Roquefort and a Limburger. I was delighted that Chester broke with tradition and continued to serve the Château d'Yquem with the cheese. Chester tapped his glass with a knife and stood up.

'Ladies and gentlemen, friends, on behalf of Alberta, Florence and myself, thank you all for coming this evening. All of you have played a part in the safe return of our wonderful daughter. I'm not going to dwell on the barbaric treatment she received, but suffice to say that the might of our judicial system will deal with them.

'Tonight is a celebration and a thank you to all of you for your part in her safe return.

'To Wispy, Strangely, Wanda, Libby, Constanza, Ernest, Luther, Fabrice, Eunice, Reinhardt, Waldemar, and all your other colleagues, friends and acquaintances, a huge thank you.

'To Inspector Finkelstein, and the lovely Mrs Finkelstein for supporting your husband. To your colleagues at Scotland Yard, your colleagues in Northumberland, your colleagues in the Highlands, and your colleagues in Calais and the Aude, I give you all a huge thank you.

'To all your police colleagues I will be writing a personal note of thanks and providing them with the means to have a celebratory party on us.

'Now I would like to propose a toast. You gave us our life back, you gave us our daughter back, so please, raise your glasses. To Florence.'

'To Florence.' We burst into a round of applause. Eventually, he managed to quieten us down.

'Now I have two very exciting announcements to make.'

A general murmur swept through the room. Chester waited for silence.

'Thank you. Firstly, you might be aware that Reinhardt and my company have formed a joint venture and are in the process of purchasing MacCabe Shipbuilders. This is nearly complete, and the new company will be known as Delmenhorst and Eastoff Shipbuilders, or DES for short.'

Again, we broke into applause. 'Thank you. The new company will support the Eastoff Housing Trust and Florence will now sit on the board of the trust.'

Again, more applause, and Chester waited patiently for us to come to order. 'Secondly, I have taken a controlling interest in the *Daily Clarion.*' Murmurs broke out across the room.

Libby and I exchanged glances and she mouthed to me, 'So this is why we are here!'

This is going to be interesting; I can't quite see Chester fitting into the mould of a newspaper baron.

'This paper has been losing circulation numbers for some time and it has lost its direction. I know it has great potential and needs a new, enlightened board and a different direction of travel. It's about time that Fleet Street was dragged kicking and screaming into the twentieth century, and I am absolutely committed to achieving this.'

Well if anyone can, he can.

'My new board members have approved, with immediate effect, a new appointment to the board, and that is the paper's new editor-in-chief. This person has the talent, tenacity and personality to achieve what is the board's vision to create a paper that reflects the changing views and opinions of our modern post-war society. Ladies and gentlemen, I give you your new editor, Miss Eunice Wade!'

It took a moment to absorb what Chester had just announced and he was greeted with a stunned silence until the penny finally dropped. We all arose to our feet and gave her a standing ovation, which she eventually managed to quell.

'Thank you, Sir Chester. Ladies and gentlemen, what an honour it has been for me to accept the post of Editor of this great Fleet Street institution. Not only an honour for me but for all the women who have fought so hard and are still fighting for women's suffrage. We will not rest until we can cast our vote alongside our men at the age of twenty-one. And I will use my editorial column where appropriate to further this cause.'

This was greeted with a sustained round of applause and it took Eunice a few moments to quieten the room. 'I take up my position this coming Monday, but my first duty has been to appoint a new deputy investigations editor, and it is with a great deal of pride that Florence Eastoff has agreed to take on the role and come with me on this journey. She is unquestionably ready for this step up, and I have no doubt she will expose wrongdoing, scrutinise power, and, with me, hold to account those who govern and run our country. Florence, the floor is yours!'

We arose as one and applauded her to the rafters. She stood before us and her radiant smile lit up the room. 'Firstly, let me endorse the thanks to each and every one of you made by my father. And can I thank Wanda for deciphering my rather difficult conundrum, which set in motion a race against time to find me.'

We all banged the table.

'Secondly, can I thank Eunice for the faith she has in me, and my father, who has invested in the *Daily Clarion*. When he makes business decisions, they are not made with the heart but with the head, and this paper now has a bright future. *Verba volant, scripta manent* – spoken words fly away, written words remain.

'Whilst I was in captivity, I wasn't idle, and I used my time to write a series of articles about the moment I left our house on that fateful evening of the twenty-sixth of June, up to my discharge from hospital. And just to reassure you all, I haven't pulled my punches.

However, due to legal constraints they cannot be published until after the trial of my kidnappers, but the day after my captors and accessories have faced justice at the Old Bailey, they will hit the headlines in the *Daily Clarion*!

'On a lighter note, it's amazing what the mind can turn to when being held captive. I have invented a character by the name of Miss Edwina Whybrow, a local second-hand bookshop owner in the city of York and an amateur sleuth. I have planned out a novel of her first adventure, and with Eunice's help I have two publishers who are interested in the novel. So, I have started to write, and if it wouldn't be too much trouble, I'll be asking the Fescue's Detective Agency for a few tips en route. And if permitted, I might even ask Inspector Finkelstein.'

Tony gave an approving nod.

'My dear friends, I thank you from the bottom of my heart for saving my life. As Shakespeare so aptly put it in *Henry VI*:

'"Thy friendship makes us fresh.

'"And doth beget new courage in our breasts."'

She clapped her hands. 'Right, everyone, the evening is young, so I suggest we recharge our glasses. And if I might be so bold, I will venture to play some gramophone records and we can dance the night away!'

CHAPTER 43
WEDNESDAY, 27 DECEMBER 1922
BLAKENEY

Libby and I were sitting in our drawing room in front of a roaring log fire which Mildred had set earlier. The burning apple logs created a delicate fruity aroma. We got up and wandered over to the French windows and arm in arm stared out across our gardens. It had snowed on and off since Christmas Eve and our gardens had been transformed under a carpet of beautiful pristine snow. The marshes beyond looked eerie in the watery afternoon sun as the dark tidal inlets snaked their way inland through the small islands that were blanketed under a good two feet of snow. It looked like an intricate mosaic. Beyond was a vast Norfolk sky that met the North Sea out on the distant horizon. The sky was devoid of clouds, which meant for a frosty star and moonlit night.

Our contented silence was broken by a knock on the door and Mildred entered with our afternoon tea of potted beef and Melba toast, accompanied with my pickled shallots and piccalilli. I poured Libby a cup of Earl Grey and handed it to her.

'Thank you, darling, I do love the winter landscape, but do you think Strangely and Constanza will make it over for dinner later?'

'Of course they will. He won't let a bit of snow get in his way; coupled with the fact Thelma is preparing jugged hare for dinner, wild horses couldn't stop them! I would imagine that all the farmers have been out clearing the lanes and if they haven't, and speaking of horses, they can ride over.'

'Isn't it a bit cold for horse riding?'

'Nonsense, darling, horses love a bit of snow and the cold doesn't bother them. It's going to be a clear night so the moon will give them plenty of light to guide them on their way.'

'Gosh, Wispy, it sounds rather fun. Maybe I should take up riding again.'

'You and me both. Maybe we should make it a new year's resolution. We've got the stable block, after all.'

'What a cracking idea. We'll discuss it with Strangely and Constanza and they can advise on what horses to buy.'

'Excellent. I'll call Strangely in a while, and if they intend to ride over, I'll let Wilbur know and he can stable them when they get here. More tea?'

'Yes, please.'

As I was pouring, Mildred knocked on the door and entered. 'Excuse me, Sir William, there's a telephone call for you.'

'Who on earth is calling? Don't they know it's Christmas? We're on holiday.'

'I tried to explain that, but she was most persistent.'

'Who was most persistent?'

'Lady Beatrice Bonsor.'

'Who?'

'Oh, come on, darling, you must have heard of her. She's a prominent supporter of women's suffrage, and very outspoken too. She was constantly a thorn in the side of our last prime minister, Lloyd George. Her husband is the renowned professor of archaeology at Christ's College, Cambridge, Sir Ulysses Bonsor, and she too is a distinguished archaeologist. They are known for their work on Anglo-Saxons.'

'Really, as I live and breathe, I've never heard of them; and as for Anglo-Saxon archaeology, I wouldn't know where to begin!'

'Wispy, sometimes I despair. How can you not have heard of them? They've been on the wireless and in the papers recently, being interviewed about their friend, Howard Carter. You'll be telling me next that you have never heard of Tutankhamun!'

'Of course I've heard of Tutankhamun; it was only a month ago that Howard Carter opened his tomb. But what would Lady Beatrice Bonsor want with me?'

'Wispy, for goodness' sake, I doubt she will be telephoning to discuss what we had for Christmas dinner, or what we are planning to eat on New Year's Eve. And as neither of us, to the best of my knowledge, is psychic, you'd better go and take her call and find out.'

'But how did she get our numb—'

'Wispy! Go!'

I went into my study and picked up the receiver. 'Lady Beatrice, Sir William Fescue here. How may—'

'Call me Beatrice.'

'Yes, right, sorry. How can I be of assistance, Beatrice?'

'My husband was murdered two weeks ago today, on the thirteenth of December.'

'Really? Gosh, how appalling! Please accept my condolences. But how do you know he was murdered?'

'Look, Sir William.'

'William, please.'

'Right, yes, William. Let me be perfectly clear. We had a break-in three weeks ago, and several diaries detailing every aspect of our current archaeological dig, including descriptions of our wonderful finds, were stolen. Ulysses was totally distraught, and as a result, he had a fatal heart attack a week later.'

'What was the cause of death on Ulysses's death certificate?'

'Cardiac arrest.'

'I see, and who signed the death certificate?'

'Doctor Quitch. He's our local doctor.'

'And you question his abilities as a doctor?'

'I do.'

'On what grounds?'

'Because he doesn't know what he's talking about. My husband was perfectly healthy and was murdered. It was made to look like a fatal heart attack.'

'Really, and how do you know that it was made to look like a fatal heart attack?'

'Women's intuition.'

Good Lord, this is going to be interesting!

'I see. And have you been to the police with your theory?'

'I have.'

'And what did the police say?'

'They concurred with Doctor Quitch.'

Why doesn't that surprise me!

'In that case, Beatrice, you are just going to have to accept the sad fact that Ulysses died of heart failure.'

'Well, I don't. And what if I tell you I have just received a death threat?'

'Ah, that might just add a degree of complexity to the situation. And what form did this death threat take?'

'It was a letter stating that unless I divulged the location and details of our significant archaeological find, and was prepared to hand over one very specific artefact, I too would meet the same fate as my husband. They have given me two weeks to cooperate from today, which takes me until the ninth of January – if not, I will be killed. They warned me that if I went to the authorities, I would meet my maker sooner!'

'So this is why you haven't shared this letter with the police.'

'Exactly, and that's why I have very little choice and few options and have turned to you.'

I puffed out my chest, and a smile broke out across my face. My detective agency was at last establishing a reputation.

Well, Father, who would have thought it: a distinguished archaeologist beating a path to my door. I trust you're not doubting my abilities now?

'Tell me, why is this site so important?'

'Because the site is of such significance to our nation! What we've discovered will change the way we think about Anglo-Saxons and our history. It will, I believe, show that they did not live in the Dark Ages. No, these finds will show that this title was an unwarranted myth, and that the period should be described as the First Age of

Enlightenment! These people who murdered my husband will stop at nothing to get their hands on our finds. In particular, the one artefact that they are determined will not see the light of day.'

'What exactly have you unearthed, and in particular, what is this artefact that they are so desperate to get their hands on? And where is this archaeological site?'

'I am not prepared to divulge that information. However, suffice to say that once this priceless artefact is in the public domain, it is of such significance it could have the potential to change the way we view one of our most sainted saints, pardon the pun, St Cuthbert. It's already cost my husband his life, and I'm particularly keen on preserving my own.

'I totally understand. Who was this letter from?'

'The Acolytes of St Cuthbert.'

Of course it was!

'The Acolytes of St Cuthbert? Who and what the hell are they? Some sort of ecclesiastical overzealous religious order that has gone off the rails?'

'Don't be flippant, William. From the letter I received, yes, they appear to be fanatics, and deadly serious ones – as that has demonstrated!'

Great! Just what I didn't want for Christmas – deadly serious religious fanatics!

ACKNOWLEDGEMENTS

Thanks to my editor, Nicky Taylor, whose help, guidance and support has been invaluable.